WHAT COMRADE OLDIE KNEW

H. A. Willis

WHAT COMRADE OLDIE KNEW

First published in Australia (Private Edition *MMXV*) by H.A. Willis 2015 ©

This edition published in Australia by H.A. Willis 2021
Copyright © H.A. Willis 2021
All Rights Reserved

 A catalogue record for this
book is available from the
National Library of Australia

ISBN: 978-0-6451884-0-0 (pbk)
ISBN: 978-0-6451884-1-7 (ebk)

Typesetting and design by Publicious Book Publishing
Published in collaboration with Publicious Book Publishing
www.publicious.com.au

All persons, living and dead, are purely coincidental,
and should not be construed.
— Kurt Vonnegut

For Erica

There will be everything in this country in time
except plenty of water and honest men.
— George Thomas William Blamey Boyes,
1824, in a letter from Sydney.

I

As the old have been telling the young since we climbed down out of the trees, some things can really only be known and understood from experience. Such wisdom, it is said (repeatedly), is especially pertinent when it comes to sudden changes of fortune. You may think you can empathetically understand particular events by observing what others do and say in those moments, by reading books or watching dramas depicting such events, but when the time comes for you, yourself, to experience the thing — the sudden death of a loved one, say, or winning the lottery — you discover it is not, after all, what you had imagined it to be. Divine revelation or the Platonic forms may be useful (perhaps even essential) in framing an explanation of experience, but nothing quite prepares you for that moment when the knife goes in, when the ground beneath your feet suddenly, violently shifts.

What it comes down to is this: some stories are owned, they cannot be told by others and it is a foolish presumption to think otherwise.

So when, on that rainy night all those years ago, his father told him to get back in the car it was the seed in his child's understanding that, when he did come to speak of that woman dead in the gutter, it would not be in the telling of her story, but of his own.

He awoke in a fizzing. The words "spill the beans" effervesced and then dissipated with an evaporating dream.

He became aware of Max moving away from the side of the bed.

"Little bastard," he mumbled, without rancor.

Max flicked his tail in curt acknowledgement as he left the bedroom and turned into the dark passage, heading for the back door to wait for Oldie to let him out into the night.

"Spill the beans," the Old Man muttered, and heaved his bulk off the bed. He steadied, upright — always an achievement. Modern beds are too damned low. The Girl stirred in her sleep and he stood still a spell to get his bearings and for her to settle.

Well, first of all, although you don't necessarily have to know how many beans make five before you spill them, you do have to know where the little fuckers are kept. The water-tight logic of his reasoning impressed him.

Somewhere down the passage, impatient to be out, Max meowed. The poor old bugger's prostate apparently gave him as much grief as Oldie took from his own.

He navigated through the house by touch and the LED lights of assorted appliances.

All the same, if he put his mind to it, he sort of knew where there were a couple of pots of beans he could spill. Or attempt to spill. Trouble was, such spills could have messy consequences. Cats out of bags, as the Old People used to say.

He unlatched the fly-screen door, pushed it open and Max shot out into the darkness of the garden, a silence on a shadow.

He waited, listening to the night. He could hear the sea — just. He could hear it breathing. At something past three in the morning there was not even the sound of a distant car on the main road at the bottom of the hill.

Stepping outside, he crossed the patio and then the lawn in order to piss on the herbaceous border. Legs spread so as not to splash his feet. No breeze. The moon already feathered down. Scorpio rising. Cloudless night, but not cold.

A backyard to piss in on a balmy night, a place to savor the reassuring pungency of your own warm urine — the Australian dream. In the long dry spell he had to be careful about pissing in the same place too often. When the Girl said something, he blamed Max and casually watered over the offending spot for a bit longer.

The backyard was a convenience in more ways than one. He had come to an age when taking a leak was sometimes a protracted affair, something that required a relaxing atmosphere. During the day, in the house, with his memory so shot and the time it now took him to piss, he often forgot to do up his fly after he had finally shaken off the last amber drop. There'd been a few odd moments when people came to the door. Like the little blonde honey tits trying to sell him a new phone plan, reflective house numbers or some such crap. He'd been unbuttoned that day, as he discovered next time he needed another piss. That kid must have noticed, but it hadn't fazed her. She no doubt encountered weirder stuff doing that job.

Anyway, the question remained. Even supposing he had beans to spill and could actually remember all the details: Who would care? Irrelevant people like him were not listened to; they had no access to the public address system. At some stage the Old Man had understood the world was not good, that the cracks in the system had become just too damned numerous to be addressed. It was not going to get any better. Not by his efforts. The safest, most prudent course was to keep quiet and do

3

nothing. Then, with a bit of luck, he would not make matters worse. That's what he told himself.

He felt he had never quite lived the life he was supposed to. But if the world had refused him what he aspired to, then it had nevertheless also handed him gifts he could never have imagined he would cherish so. It was a mystery he never quite figured out. All he could be sure of was that things that once mattered now no longer did. That was the stone cold, hard truth of it and stiff shit to all those who didn't see it.

In the small hours the neighborhood was at last quiet.

He lived in a suburb populated by tradesmen, men addicted to power tools and ceaseless renovations. Power tools have replaced even the simplest implements — in Yoberia the garden rake is left in the shed while its work is done, ineffectively, by a buzzing blower. There is always, somewhere within earshot, a concrete pour, an extension, an "improvement", a pool installation, a tree being cut down and dismembered, a shed being erected. Tradies like an early start and Perth's tradies take it as a constitutional right to have a boombox thumping while they work, usually loud enough to be heard in the next street. The younger ones prefer something with a solid bass line, something to cut through the buzz or squeal of whatever machinery is in use.

And then, on the weekend (and often as not through the week) there are the parties. Then he really knew he was in enemy territory. His nearest neighbors knew he was a noise Nazi who would call in the cops, but they constantly pushed it to the limits. He knew, too, that it would be counter-productive to call the cops (always busy elsewhere) every time the din aggravated him — which was most nights and many days during the summer.

But now, in the small hours, the place was quiet. He could hear the sea.

The forty-year-old garden suburb he had moved into seven years earlier was changing, and he didn't like it. As water rates rose, the garden suburb became a paved suburb. When the Council's periodic green waste collections came around the ratepayers went into a competition (as fiercely driven as that over Christmas lights) to see who could get the biggest pile on the verge.

He didn't like the noisy boofheads moving in. Shirtless blokes pumped up on steroids thinking they were Tarzan and all their Janes embroidered with tatts no longer quite chic — overgrown babies sucking on their plastic drink bottles. And he didn't like their shoddy prefab industrial estate style of home improvement. To friends elsewhere he called his suburb Yoberia, a place where drunken children could be heard shouting in the streets at night and the roads glinted with smashed bottles in the morning sun. He had always been something of an outsider, but as he aged and the tide had run in directions he loathed, he came to see himself as a stranger in his own country, one of those unfortunate souls out of step with his times and ill at ease in the place where he had washed up.

He was not an easy man to live with. Even the Girl had to admit that.

The Old Man and the Girl held many of their defining stories in common. In a deep, private space they relied upon each other, and had long ago understood they would look after each other. In recent years, such closeness has come to be termed "co-dependency" and generally judged to be not quite an acceptable thing. But from the day they met, they had never had any problems with living in contradiction to fashionable wisdom. His mother put her finger on it when, within a day or so of meeting Anna, she pronounced her "loyal".

He was almost ready to get out of the shower when he heard her sing "Good Morning" as she left the bedroom and crossed the hall.

"*Dobro ootro,'* he responded, basso profundo.

"I was talking to Max," she trilled, entering the bathroom.

"Ha! Thrown over for a black cat!"

"Yep!"

Waiting for him to vacate the shower she asked whether he had sorted out what he was wearing to the funeral.

With his limited wardrobe, the choice of funeral clothes more or less came down to which shirt it was going to be. He couldn't recall the last time he wore a tie, or attended a function that would have been even likely to require one.

He stepped out and took the towel she offered.

"How'd you sleep?"

"OK," he said, truthfully enough, looking into her lovely grey eyes. "But You-Know-Who wanted *OouwT* at the wee-wee hour.

"The wind stirs him up," she said.

"What wind?"

"Well, the moon, then."

"The moon was down. When did you let him back in?" he asked.

"I didn't — you must've."

"Oh," he paused in the business of the toweling of his crutch, "then I slept better than I thought."

"So, what's green and likes to sing?"

He thought about it and ventured that it could be about half of Ireland.

"Wakey, wakey," she scoffed. "Elvis Parsley!"

The other word his mother had applied to the Girl, almost at first sight, was "wholesome".

He dropped Anna at her school so he could have the car for the day. An hour later he was dressed and driving little Black Betty down West Coast Highway. The sun was warm and the easterly still cool; agreeable weather for those who do not suffer hay fever — all that wheat ripening out there. A band of cirrus, mares' tails, ran across the northern sky, otherwise heaven was immaculate blue. Rottnest Island stood high and clear upon a pristine *ultramarinus* sea. The big rotating sprinklers twirled glittering diamond arcs across the immaculate green parks. The silhouette shadows of trees lay crisp and sharp on the luminous lawns. The roads were lined, walled, by bottlebrush, heavy with crimson display. The peppermint trees were already braiding their tresses with delicate ribbons of tiny white flowers. Pretty soon the Cape lilac trees would put on their show, and then the jacarandas would upstage everything. Bees were busy everywhere. Perth shone in the bright air and the Old Man made his way to attend Paulo's funeral.

Yet another funeral. Another cremation.

And what music would be played as the coffin sank out of sight?

Ah, these days, that is the question. One to ponder while stuck at the Scarborough lights. He reckoned it was only a matter of time before he heard Arvo Pärt's *Spiegel im Spiegel* at a funeral. Personally, he thought the chill of the *Silentium* more appropriate. Or one of Satie's *Gymnopedies*. Of course, for old time's sake, there was always Ludwig van.

"Christ all mighty," he said aloud as the traffic finally moved. Here he was, planning his own funeral, again.

He did not like the way funerals had become little shows — short grabs of popular music (entrance, reflection, exit) interspersed with the reading of a poe-hem and someone eulogizing and summing up the dead one's life in six or seven minutes: "Loved sport, family and had a terrific sense of humor". It was the sort of stuff that did service on internet dating sites. In seeking to discard the rituals of religion, people had embraced the set pieces of platitude. No matter how inadequate, how grossly inappropriate it was to play some trite old pop song at the lowering of the coffin — people persisted, hell bent on expanding the catalogue of trivialization. Of course, broadcasting such views would not make him any friends. People take their funerals seriously.

He thought about turning Betty around and going home. Or perhaps to Leederville to sit in the coffee place where he and Paulo used to meet for their talks.

But he didn't. That would be pointless.

Besides, it was a matter of being seen to have made the effort to show respect. Despite everything, making up the numbers remained important. He held to that duty, at least.

Passing through City Beach he glanced up at one of the mini-palaces and remembered the last church funeral he attended. Greek Orthodox. The cousin of the man whose house he was passing. That was four years back. It had been a matter of paying respect to a man who had taught him something, a man who had died gracefully. Not a trace of self-pity. No small feat.

It was only a couple of months after the old Greek's death that a blood test revealed the nature of his own mortality. "Five years," the specialist had said, four years ago.

In the meantime … Paulo, more than ten years his junior, had a melanoma that got away.

Everybody liked Paulo, a decent man who left a fifty-year-old widow with two adolescent boys to bring up. It would be a big funeral.

A quarter of an hour before start time he drove by Karrakatta's main gate. A few hundred people were standing around near the coffee shop, waiting for the hearse and funeral cars to arrive. Karrakatta is a big place, a whole suburb for the dead and buried. By the time he parked Betty under the trees half a kilometre along Railway Road and, joining a procession of other mourners, traipsed back up the dusty track to the entrance, the cortege had arrived and the crowd was marshalling for the amble down the avenue. He quickly jotted his name on an attendance card, took an Order of Service and slipped into the middle of the mob — reckoning it to be 300 to 350 strong. He saw a few vaguely familiar faces, but at first scan nobody he knew to speak to. Blokes in good suits; blokettes with ear studs. Paulo had moved in varied and wide circles. The dress code for funerals was obviously in flux, but what was that drongo over there doing wearing that dopey porkpie hat? He was glad Anna had his jacket dry-cleaned and insisted on ironing his shirt.

Inside the chapel he made his way around the side wall to stand close to the exit into the condolence room. Pole position. Been here before. Once the gig was over he could be away quickly, before anyone buttonholed him. But then ... there didn't seem to be anyone. Hundreds of people and not one he knew by name. That fellow over there. Ted something, a journo, some years ago he used to be on a local TV current affairs show. And, hey ... that was one very good looking woman with him. Tall, refined. Pity about the small tatt on her shoulder. A heart with a name on it? Hmm.

His attention drifted during the monotonous, halting eulogies, but the slide show — Paulo with hair — gathered him back in. And he used to play in a band — fancy that. The slim, dark-haired woman with the tatt quickly dabbed her eyes. A tear? Or had she taken a discreet swipe at a fly? All the doors at the back of the auditorium were open to allow the overflow to hear and see something of the goings-on and a crew of tiny flies were relentlessly working the warm throng. The less genteel souls were using the stiff, folded A5 Order of Service to deal with the little buggers. With his compound eyes, the last thing Louie the Fly (apple of his old mother's eye) would see was a thousand smiling Paulos coming at him.

The Death of a Flie ... ah, no, let's not go that way. Not today.

He glanced at the Order of Service ... pitiful. Whatever became of decent epitaphs?

Nick Cave was moaning and people were placing their flowers on the coffin. He'd have to let Anna know in no uncertain terms that there had better not be any damned Nick Cave at his funeral. The Girl knew he really did not care if there was no funeral for him, but he understood it was her call. There'd be family pressure and, as usual, it would be easier to just do what was expected. But, please, no Nick Cave. Fuck that.

The time for lowering the coffin was approaching. Sometimes the Commitment music was continued as the family led the way into the Condolence Room. Others preferred to play something different during the Exit. The best Exit music he'd heard was way back in the mid-nineties, in this very chapel. That was for an American academic who spilled the beans on some sordid shit at the University of Western Australia and was then drummed out of his job. After several bitter years of legal and administrative struggles, during which time he discovered who his real friends were, he had a heart attack. Dead at 49. David Rindos was gay and those who organized his funeral had Tammy Wynette's *Stand by your Man* played as the crowd moved out. Commitment — a nice, old-fashioned camp moment.

Here we go … *Imagine*. Orchestral version rather than John Lennon's original. Well, yes, he'd pay that. To have the words "there's no Heaven" may have affronted some of the family. Paulo had been raised a Catholic but there was no priest in today's mix. So don't push it.

Sarah was escorted out, her lads either side, holding her hands. That woman had just lost the love of her life and those boys had lost their father. And here was this old bastard doing his mean little review of the ceremony. He breathed an involuntary sigh and felt something like shame.

But he was over it by the time he had sidled across to the far side of the Condolence Room. He stood next to the doors, paper cup of orange juice in hand, watching the lengthening line of those offering their sympathies. The faces of Sarah and her boys were brittle masks. Leave them be. Just loiter a while to make up those obscure numbers and then quietly sod off.

The crowd was still shuffling out of the chapel. He had not seen Ted what's-his-name or the lovely with the tatt. They must have gone back out the main entrance. A couple he knew came through and joined the queue. The bloke spotted him and gave him an eyebrow flash. Contemplating whether he would wait to speak to them he became aware of someone at his side.

"Alex. Alex Johnson. How are you?"

The man's voice was quiet. It had a sneaky undertone he knew but couldn't immediately place. And when he turned to look into the pale blue eyes, he could not quite put a name to the face.

"I shaved the beard," the fellow said, acknowledging Oldie's confusion and the passing of a decade. Oldie's Ned Kelly beard was still in place. Nobody was going to be confused about who he was — except the wee kiddies in the mall at Christmas.

A long moment. The little prick had also shaved his head to disguise baldness. "Roger?"

"The same."

Oldie grinned to cover his discomfort. He glanced away and started to say something about long-time-no-see when — Holy fucking Mackerel! — Gorgeous was coming towards him. Or rather, towards the door next to him. She was leaving. He looked into her dark, serene eyes and wistfully imagined they bestowed the faintest of private smiles as she passed. Probably laughing at the ferocious shit-eating grin he'd put on for Roger. The name on her shoulder was in Cyrillic. Блонди. Blondie.

He smelt her. His eyes followed her.

"I, ah …" He swallowed and turned back to face Jolly Roger. Roger Kidd, the anthropologist.

Roger had also perved on the Vision's perfect buttocks as she walked away. He gave a perfunctory smirk, a gesture Oldie suddenly recalled with stifling familiarity. Some people don't change.

He'd also seen the tatt because he asked, "Still studying Russian?"

Oldie sighed — yes, he must have been at the night classes about the time he worked with Roger — and admitted that any formal study had long been abandoned. "Too old to really learn anything new," he said.

"At one time," Roger said, and deliberately smacked his lips in Blondie's direction, "I'd have run away from home for a bit of that. I wish I was twenty — thirty! — years younger and considerably richer. But here we are, coming up to the drop zone and having our noses rubbed in it. Dirty Old Men relegated to the sidelines, the periphery. Marginalized. Written off. Oh well, that's your lot, as the Christians say."

"Indeed. So ... I heard you were in Sunny Queensland?"

"Back here now. Permanently, I hope. Came back a couple of months ago. Did seven years over there."

"You make it sound like a prison sentence."

Roger ignored that and, asking how Oldie knew Paulo, turned to look over the crowd.

They stood shoulder to shoulder, men of a similar age at the funeral of a younger man they now discovered they had both known. They kept the conversation polite and small. Roger told Oldie that he had recently divorced — ex-missus stayed in Brisbane — and he had moved back into his old family home in Perth, where he intended to live out his days. Oldie told Roger that he had moved out to the Northern suburbs to be nearer Anna's school, that he was still with her and that they were as happy as larks together.

"She's a kindergarten teacher, isn't she?"

Oldie explained that the Girl was a Senior Teacher at a specialist unit offering intensive remedial teaching to children just entering the school system. The objective was to bring kids with language disorders up to speed so that they could then enter mainstream classes with the expectation of "fitting in".

"She's a little more than just a kindergarten teacher," Oldie concluded.

"Well, it's nice to hear of someone doing something useful for their money."

"Hmm. It is."

"My ex is talking about becoming a real estate agent."

"Oh," said Oldie, politely refraining from any further comment.

For a few seconds they jointly surveyed the crowded room, wondering how many of those before them did anything remotely useful for the money they were paid.

"Glad to see Paulo got a good turn out," said Oldie. "When you get down to it, I suspect there are remarkably few people who really care whether most of us live or die."

"Oh well," Roger laughed, "regardless of how many give a shit about our mortality, the question is: Do they wish us dead or alive? I reckon most people would be surprised at how many cunts quietly wished the rest of us dead and gone."

Oldie turned to look directly at the anthropologist, gave him a broad smile and asked what music he'd like played at his funeral.

"Mozart's *Requiem* — in full, if you don't mind. That would be the go. Along with something from the Rugby Songbook" And then he cackled, rather too loudly.

In response to the reciprocal question the Old Man snorted, "Something plaintive, something that won't leave a dry eye in the house. You know, applied at the right moment sentimentality will crack the toughest nut."

"Bastard."

"Well, you know, I try to be."

"Actually, thinking about it, I'd probably get someone to play the didgeridoo, have a smoking ceremony and lay on all the blackfella hocus-pocus — you know, something to reflect my professional status."

Oldie's smile coagulated before he caught the look in Roger's eye and realized his leg was being pulled. "Ha! A smoking ceremony in a crematorium chapel. That would be one for the books."

"Why not? They're being done just about everywhere now. Almost as often as this Welcome to Country lurk. Nice little earner for some people."

"Do I detect a ray of sarcasm?"

"You do. You do indeed. But, seriously, how can men of our generation and experience not be … ah, skeptical? But listen, if you think funerals are getting silly, have a look at what's happened with weddings. Jesus, it's not funny," Roger grimaced, "I've got two girls!"

Oldie laughed in sympathy and, moving right along, asked Jolly Roger about life in Queensland. "Is it true they drink their own bathwater over there?"

"Absolutely, they even quaff the stuff they've already pissed in. And are proud of doing so! Proud of it!" Then, as a casual afterthought, he quietly added, "Mind you, it's only a matter of time before they serve it up here."

"You reckon? Won't the de-sal program be enough?"

"Not really. They're still getting about fifty percent of the summer water supply from ground water. Pumping it out like there's no tomorrow. I thought you'd have your ear to the ground on that one."

"Not really. Only what I hear on the news."

"That barely touches the surface. The press in this town — this god-forsaken country — a bunch of lazy, useless pricks. Pricks without balls! They have no balls, none. All they report is what they're fed, the official waffle. The only balls that concern the local media are those kicked or batted. Even when a real cat somehow gets out of the proverbial bag, they'll do their bit to put it back in. Bloody worse than useless."

"You're not wrong."

Just when Oldie was starting to relax and even feel a dull glow of companionableness, the anthropologist did something quite unforgivable. "Actually," he said, "I'm glad I bumped into you." He then asked the Old Man if, as well as the archival research, he was still "in the book business" and would he care "to just have a look" at a novel he was writing.

It wasn't finished, of course. They never are. Fiction based on fact to protect the author (the putative innocent!) from being sued. It was, Roger assured him, a work that would "blow the lid off the shit that goes on with Native Title".

Roger rabbited and Oldie fended it off with a screen of professional hmmm-ings. A bad dream. Under no circumstances, he thought, must he let this man obtain his phone number. Somebody else's bad dream. Why do they all want to talk about their half-written books. Just get on with it!

Any hopes Oldie entertained of being rescued by a third party faded and he managed to get his sunglasses on. He was irritated. These bunnies never seem to realize that the very notion of fiction as an expository tool is, in itself, fundamentally a fiction. Didn't they know that trying to settle personal grievances through a novel was the oldest dead end in the book? How did we get to the point where there are more writers than readers, and the stale dross they turn out is about as nauseating as the relentless swill served up on cooking show television? We live in an age in which even the drivel is below standard. All 57 Varieties of it. Oldie blamed the universities.

"I blame the universities," he said, in the middle of Roger's rave.

"Eggs-zakly!" Roger's index finger shot up, rigid as a teenager's dick. "And I've gone into that, too. Believe me! One of my major characters is a lesbian academic who ..."

"Casting a wide net, aye! Ha ha! Anyone we know? Ha ha. A bit of the ol' re-tribbing-booshion? Settle a score or two? Always a temptation, but perhaps one best sometimes resisted. Usually just ends up looking petty, even spiteful. And, you know ... you don't want it to look like you're wiping your arse in public. Look, mate, let me just say a few words here." He whipped off the shades and with dollops of sincere eye contact explained that, as a part-time, freelance editor, he now dealt mostly with publishers of non-fiction — "history, in fact" — and that, when the time came, Roger should try to obtain the services of a particular agent in Melbourne, and that it was good policy not to show a book to anyone until it was finished. "The thing to value above all else is a reader's first impression. You only get that the once. Don't fritter it away. The other thing I'd say is this — a *roman à clef*, which is the literary term for the sort of thing you have embarked upon, is still a novel and is therefore governed by the imperatives of fiction. I know literature has more interesting and important things to do than to be talking about itself, but, well, the hard truth is that you just can't avoid artifice! And that means you sometimes have to compromise."

"Well, I …"

"I mean, in terms of technique. But beyond that, on an even more basic level, a *roman à clef* may work when the author is a public figure very publicly settling a score — you know, the discarded wife of a serving French President. But in Australia, frankly, your average reader — and, Jesus wept, don't underestimate how jaded Average Reader has become — couldn't give a shit that character B might be based upon some half-forgotten former politician who never *quite* got caught with his hand in the cookie jar or up some under-aged dolly's skirt. Could not give a shit. And think about this — in their search for meaning some of your readers could look in the wrong damned place. Your biggest problem could be some nobody you half know claiming they were the model for a particular character. That happens. And, ho ho ho, one of them might even feel obliged to sue you. But, yes, the ol' *livre à clef* … some young joker down at Freo has just done a novel loosely based on the Shirley Finn case."

"Does he finger Reg the Racketeer?"

"I haven't read it, but I heard the finding of the body of a murdered madam on the South Perth golf course is just the start point for what is primarily fiction. I believe it points at People in High Places, but to what extent some grubby Reg lookalike gets the nod I don't know. I take it you think he was behind it?"

"That seems to be the prevailing view."

"It does. But he's still alive, of course."

"But ga-ga. Quite ga-ga."

Oldie took that in before asking, "Where'd you hear that?"

"Oh ... around. Here and there. A journo by the name of Kafoops wanted an interview and got stopped by Reg's Missus."

"Hmm. So Kafoops is still around. I believe Mrs Reg is a proper piece of work in her own right. Well, as I was saying, if it's a novel, no matter what its genesis, there's got to be some internal dramatic tension to wind the thing up. You're wasting your time declaiming — things have to be *played* out. And, whatever you do, avoid moral pretensions and grumpy old man raves — avoid that shit like the plague. But I guess if you've got into it you must've already figured out all that sort of stuff."

"Internal dramatic tension and avoiding moral pretensions. Is that why *Power Without Glory* did so well?"

"Well, you're right, that is *the* Australian example. Long time since I looked at it, but I'd say the controversy over the libel case wouldn't have hurt the eventual outcome. Most of the major players were still alive and in the public eye when Hardy published that book. But, you know, that was sixty years ago. Times have definitely changed. Once upon a time everybody was sucking on bloody grapefruit for brekkie. Now — what do you know? — they're all eating damned blueberries and drinking go go juice and taking the name of antioxidants in vain. Times change and scandal just ain't what it used to be. Then, remember, there was a mini-series in the seventies — you have to wonder how well *Power Without Glory* would be remembered without that."

Roger pursed his lips, rocked gently on his heels and seemed preoccupied in digesting the sage advice that had just been bestowed upon him. Finally, he asked Oldie whether he remembered how they met.

"Ah, well, I think Steve what's-his-name probably introduced us."

"That's right. Steve Lyons. He was fronting for a property development outfit and he hired you to do the archives and he hired me to sort out the various traditional claimants. Old Billy Swan and me came up with the name Nibbelup. Nobody wanted to keep Chinaman's Swamp. Although I thought because of the old market gardens … well, never mind what I thought. Between ourselves, Billy and me used to call it Nippelup. Seemed like a good idea at the time. Billy was pretty sure it meant something. He contented himself with the idea that "Nibbelup" should be pronounced "Nippelup". Between you and me and the gatepost, in coming up with traditional names for new suburbs, I always wanted to see if I could get Cuddelup past the Nomenclature Committee at Land Administration. Well, ah ha ha, seemed like a good idea at the time. Anyway, I took the time to drive out to Nibbelup the other day. Been out there lately?"

Oldie shook his head.

"No?! You should, it's absolutely *fascinating!* Instructive! What a difference a decade and changes of government makes in this town. Subdivided from arsehole to breakfast. High-density housing. Neat as a pin. Some town planner's wet dream of the Holy Grail, no doubt, but to me … it just looks like Toy Town. I was expecting to see Noddy and Big Ears trundle around a corner at any moment. I know our work cleared the way for that project, but I can't rustle up any sense of responsibility for the result. Perhaps I should, but I can't."

"Well, no," Oldie began to agree.

"Hardly any graffiti yet," Roger rushed on. "But then, you know, give it time — sooner or later they'll shit in their own nest. You know the sort of thing, broken glass and flattened fast food containers on the streets, stuff nobody ever picks up just blowing around." He threw out his left arm to demonstrate how things blow around. "Oh yes, they *will* shit in their own nest. They always do. I dunno ... all this prosperity, yet people aren't exactly flourishing — in an intellectual sense, if you know what I mean — something in modern life seems to stunt mental growth. But, hey, what would I know? An amateur philosopher! Do you remember much about that job? I heard you still do archival and historical work for people. You wrote a very pithy little report for Steve. I've still got a copy. Do you still have your research notes? Liquid waste, remember? All that industrial eff-flu-ENT! Hell's bells, their fuckin' nest was shat in before they even got to it! They don't know it, but it was. Wasn't it?"

The Old Man squeezed out a laugh that advertised rather than disguised his unease. "I'd have to have a look ..."

"Well," said Jolly, positively beaming, "you see, that's one of the capers I've written about. I Kidd thee not! No pun intended!" He laughed at his own joke and slapped Oldie's shoulder. "But like I said — guffaw, guffaw — I changed the names to protect the innocent and poor old Billy's no longer with the living. Died five or six years ago. And there," he raised his index finger in emphasis, "you see, there it is. Who speaks for Billy now? What say do you think the dead have in anything, anything at all, in our society, in our culture? The living have the say. They may not want what Billy wanted, but they can say anything in his name. Hmm. Well ... I just spotted someone I'd rather avoid. Know what

20

I mean!? But listen, it was good to see you. I'll get in touch. Catcha later. Gotta fly!"

And he was gone.

The Old Man gave Roger a head start to clear the area, looked about the room one last time and made his own quiet getaway.

He walked slowly. Halfway back up the avenue he stepped onto the verge to watch another funeral go by. Only a dozen behind the creeping hearse. Family. Someone who had outlived friends. Nobody to make up the numbers. Nobody to be impressed by the expensive box, soon to be going up the flue. They do burn the coffin, don't they?

Who'd be there to see him off? Roger might turn up — just to hear what music was finally decided on. He tried to remember: Had Roger always had that philosophical bent? He knew in his bones it would not be too long before their paths would re-cross. He said he had heard the Old Man was still doing archival searches for people. Who'd he been talking to?

He had not let on, but he knew immediately what it was about Nibbelup that interested Roger. It was the old tip. All that rubbish, liquid waste and building rubble, dumped during the early 1960s into what was then a swamp and which was now a lake in a park where the locals stroll their dogs, power-walk their spouses, friends and lovers and so forth. Happy campers one and all. Just don't mention the sludge, the asbestos and the discarded drums of Christ-knows-what. And then, next to the park named after a politician there was a set of sports grounds; playing fields on which footy players could bark their knees, never suspecting what might be in the soil.

There's not a lot you can do when something bad really comes looking for you. You get on the wrong bus and it just happens to be the one with the bomb on it.

You have a blood transfusion and twenty-years later you are diagnosed as having hepatitis C, genotype one at that. You sink a backyard bore to feed the reticulation system in your veggie garden and your kid ends up on Ritalin. But, there you go — that's your bleedin' lot.

He reached the Railway Road entrance and turned onto the beaten track between the cemetery fence and the line of trees beneath which the cars were parked. Not long before he reached the spot where he had left Betty, he saw the woman with the Cyrillic tattoo half-seated, leaning against the tail of a silver coupe, the price of which would get you ten Bettys, black or any color you liked. The number plate was recent, but the car was three or four years old. A re-registered import. From another state or overseas?

It came to him: Ted Connell, former journo and now politicians' media advisor. Was she really with him? What a waste. He caught his breath as she adjusted her stance, leaning back ever so slightly to flaunt the firm fullness of her perfect breasts.

If the woman was aware of him walking by, she gave no indication. She was smoking a cigarette, lost in thought, waiting for someone. Ted, presumably. He was tempted to greet her in Russian — *Privyet* — but thought better of it. There was always the chance she was Bulgarian or some other Slavonic persuasion. Actually, he thought for the first time, those eyes had a hint of Central Asia about them. Her jet black hair looked natural, but he couldn't really tell. After passing her, he could see her reflected in the side window of a shiny, over-sized Patrol what's-it a few vehicles further along, but she did not turn her head and continued to gaze into the wild blue yonder.

She hadn't moved when he glanced at Betty's rear vision mirror as he drove away.

II

There they were on their evening stroll, just another overweight, middle-aged couple out there trying to do the right thing.

All the streets in their suburb were named after explorers. All the Streets, all the Avenues, all the Roads, the Drives, the Courts, the Places, the Ways — even the god-damned Loops carried the name of some old bugger who'd tramped this or that stretch of the wide brown land! Forty years back when the place was laid out, some joker got his paws on a copy of Ernest Favenc's *Explorers of Australia* and methodically worked through the contents page. It must have seemed like a good idea at the time, but for all the future residents would care, it might as well have been a list of apple varieties. When the Old Man and the Girl first arrived, and did their own late afternoon and weekend explorations of the neighborhood, he had told her stories about the explorers. He knew which of them had blood on their hands. Perhaps having an address in Pink Lady Way would have been a better idea than living in a street named after a killer called McRae. After all the streets in their immediate vicinity had been toured, and their stories told, they sometimes walked to the distant corners of the suburb — even as far as Warburton or Gibson — but age and routine gradually reeled them in and confined them to a set of walks that took them no further than a kilometre from home.

The Girl sensed he was working himself up to wax philosophical, though he was still some way off becoming full-on talkative. That suited her. At any rate, he wasn't being argumentative. Although he had definitely mellowed of late, he would always be a contrary soul, prone to hold forth and righteously work himself up. Perhaps it was aging, but lately he was more inclined to lapse into inarticulate frustration — with people, the world, with every damned thing. Things eluded him. Memory failed him just a little too often and his once certain facilities of speech and logic were no longer entirely reliable. The wit, however, although sporadic and perhaps not always as subtle as it once was, remained as acid as ever. He could be nasty.

After a day of a dangerously hot easterly, the sea breeze was in, flexing its muscles, excitedly swishing the heads of the rangier eucalypts for all it was worth. Pink and grey galahs hung upside down on swaying branches of wattle, busily working a feed out of the long seed pods. In the shelter of the back lanes, however, great vermillion and purple cascades of drowsy bougainvillea nodded over the asbestos sheet fences and in the lee of the brick houses full blown roses dozed.

Through the lanes and quiet streets they worked their way uphill to a small reserve of banksias dressed with their candle-like flower spikes, green turning to brassy yellow. They were on the crest of a limestone ridge, looking down across the suburb to a small promontory that hooked into the sea as an arm of reef and exposed rocks. In the lagoon a score or so kite surfers and sailboarders flickered on the beaten silver shimmer. Outlined on the horizon north of Rottnest Island, pale grey ships waited to enter Fremantle — cars from Korea

24

and Japan, clothes and practically anything you could think of from China.

Looking inland over a ruckled carpet of tree-lined streets and tile roofs rolling out over the rises and falls of the coastal plain all the way to the hills, they searched the folds of the Darling scarp for traces of smoke. Nothing. In that regard, the day had been a lucky one.

Far, far to the south a line of magnificent cumuli, surf white tinged with apricot, brooded and rolled away yonder through the closing chords of Richard Strauss's last song.

"O vast, tranquil peace, so deep at sunset!"

The park and sports grounds in the hollow behind the ridge were already in shadow, a deeper shade of well-watered green. Less than fifty years ago there would have been a seasonal wetland in that valley. Even now, in spring and autumn, pairs of migrating straw-necked ibises were still seen, pecking about, wondering what the hell happened to the old neighborhood. The heads of the old tuarts surviving down there, forking and spreading their enormous limbs thirty metres high and almost as wide, rose to take the light and the breeze. It is said the tuart is rapidly heading for extinction within its original habitat. He wondered what aerial photography from the 1960s would show. It would depend upon the time of the year the images were made — late summer parching had doubtlessly always been glaringly desolate in hi-res black and white. But lowering Perth's water table by pumping it out to fill backyard swimming pools and water golf courses probably hasn't exactly enhanced any tree's chances.

Even above the sound of the wind in the trees they could hear the smack of the bat and the shouts of the six or seven cricketers at the practice nets. The Old Man had not played the game since his school days and he never watched it on the box, but he occasionally amused himself by sauntering by a local club game on a weekend afternoon. He liked the way the flannelled fools took their game and themselves so seriously. Pity they also took professional cricket seriously.

"You know," he said, in all seriousness, gathering his thoughts, "someone has calculated that there are ten million people in the world writing novels."

"Gosh," she said, "I wonder how they worked out that number."

"Those are just the ones making a real go of it," he marched on, undeterred, "the ones who take it on in earnest. We're not counting the even greater multitude convinced they have *the* most original idea for a book. And, of course, the inevitable movie! This is not counting those who may get out a thousand words before they exhaust their brilliant idea's vast potential and are confronted by the reality that they actually have bugger all to say other than recounting one damned thing after another. Forget about them, at least they've sort of realized they've nothing to say, but there's still those ten million others banging away on their keyboards, scribbling in their acid-free paper notebooks. If they ever do get something into print — and I don't even consider the dark maw of on-line publishing — in all likelihood it will be because of one of the many available avenues of vanity or self-publishing. Then, in a parallel universe far, far away, the creative writing mob are farnarkling their efforts into university degrees that by some mysterious process *qualifies* them to become editors. Or, to get to the nasty reality of it, to then run their own courses on writing and editing. You know, it's the Gorky Institute of World Literature all over again."

He drew a breath and let out a dry bark of a laugh. "And then, in the middle of all this ... heigh-ho, heigh-ho, here comes Jolly Roger, keen as mustard to join the circus. Here he comes, talking about narrative structure and film rights. Film rights! I *think* he was joking."

"Of course he was," she laughed.

"Anyway, I told him to cut to the chase and write a proposal for a mini-series."

"What if he twigs you're taking the piss?"

Oldie shrugged. "Who's taking the piss?"

Roger had phoned that day. He said he would get in touch and he did. There was no point in even asking where he got the unlisted number. Roger Kidd knew how to find people when he needed them.

Apart from ostensibly picking Oldie's brain about matters publishing (when it came to e-books, he probably knew more than Oldie), he had certainly wanted to talk about that landfill site. Oldie was aware of and had done a bit of internet research into another case that had, on and off, been rumbling along for a few years; a housing estate on a former landfill on the eastern outskirts of Melbourne. The dump had started discharging methane gas, forcing the evacuation of hundreds of homes occupied by that politically sensitive demographic, "young families". Major law firms were involved. More than twenty million dollars of compensation was being discussed. So when he was asked if he'd had a chance to find his research notes from the Nibbelup job, Oldie was on his guard.

"Without refusing him outright," he told Anna, "I let him know it wasn't likely I'd find anything."

"Do you still have the material?"

"There'll be a copy on one of those old floppies in the stationery cupboard. All I need to do is find a machine to read them. Easier said than done. I guess I'd have to take it somewhere and pay for it. But there'll be a hard copy in a folder somewhere. Maybe at the back of one of the

27

drawers in the big desk. It's just a question of making an effort, of finding the time. But I'm not sure I want to have anything to do with this business."

"Why not?"

"Mainly because I don't know where it may go. I don't know what Roger intends to do with any of this. Maybe there's more to this than just material for a novel. What's behind this? Is it a land rights matter or has it to do with pollution? Or is it some venomous mix?"

He then ran up his professional ethics flag, pointing out that the work in question was commissioned and paid for by Steve Lyons, who was, in turn, acting for someone else. It was not Oldie's to hand out to the first Roger who came along. "If I do that sort of thing and it gets out it won't do me any good. You have to be careful about that sort of thing."

"But you've always said half the heritage consultants in this town regularly trade stuff that's a bit ... irregular. It's been years since you had anything to do with Lyons. Is he still in Perth? Did you sign a secrecy agreement?"

"I can't remember, but I think I would have."

"But your contract allowed you to share material with Roger?"

"Of course."

"So? Doesn't that still apply? If he then breaks his secrecy agreement — that's not your fault."

He smiled at her reasoning.

"Well, I wouldn't like to cause any problems for Steve. Some people found him a bit, I dunno ... oily. But it was just his way of doing business. He never did me any harm and he always paid promptly. Never questioned invoices or made excuses to delay payment."

"Has Roger worked for him lately?"

"Don't know. Don't think so. Last I heard Steve was based in Adelaide, doing some land claim site clearance work. The sort of stuff he was doing for developers and the mining companies here. He bought into a fish-farming venture at Eyre Peninsula. Anthropology, property development, aquaculture ... it's called diversifying! Steve Lyons is one of those people making money while they're having a shit."

"Well then?"

"Well what?!"

"Lyons has gone elsewhere and this would all be so irrelevant to him now. He's not going to care two hoots and if, as you say, Roger's novel is never going to be published ... but even if it was, very few people would make the connections, I don't see why you don't just give Roger what he wants. He would owe you and, you never know, one day that might be useful."

He shrugged and squinted to gaze up into the top of the sky. "And because," he said drawing out the words in a conspiratorial tone, "I really do reckon Roger is up to something. I reckon this is not simply a mere literary endeavour."

"Oh?"

He smiled into her frown. "When I saw him at Paulo's funeral, I thought I was smart to get in first and warn him off showing me his manuscript. But, you know, although he did ask me to look at it, he did it in such a half-arsed way as to pretty well invite my avoidance."

"So?"

"So, today I thought I'd test the issue. I offered to have a look at the thing and he," Oldie paused to fondle the moment, "now he, bless him, turns around and says ..."

"That he took your advice and would rather you not see it until after it's finished. The value of the first reading, first impression and so on. You wrote the script for him."

"I did indeed. Yep! Funny thing is, I'm still not curious to read his manuscript. So, if it was a bit of reverse psychology, it didn't work. Although I am a little intrigued about what he might entitle the thing. He told me he intended to recycle an old title, something from the nineteenth century. But he wouldn't tell me what it was. Anyway, he left me his phone number and address. Lives in Mossie Park."

"Do you actually know what went into that rubbish tip?"

"Nope! And I doubt anyone else does. Back then, mid-sixties, it could have been anything. Roger said something about some kind of liquid effluent. You know … ya good ol' sludge. I gave him the line that for history to be relevant to future generations it must be recorded accurately and, back then, what went into a landfill was not exactly regulated. But he … I just don't know."

"You think he's found something you didn't discover for Steve Lyons."

"My guess is that he's been to the State Records Office and didn't find anything. But he's discovered that the files I looked at ten years ago are now either closed or have been somehow misplaced. You know, lost. It sure as hell wouldn't be the first time stuff went missing there. So he wants to see what's missing by checking my sources against what's there today. But if he came up against Baba Yaga on the desk, and she was in one of her more obstreperous moods, he could not but believe he was being given the runaround, even if he actually wasn't. Christ, since she got her PhD she acts as though the SRO is her private domain. What is it with all these public servants getting these fucking useless PhDs in their forties? They think it means something!"

"Don't start," she said quickly, giving him *the* look. "It's their meal ticket. Like mine. Like ours. Leave it alone."

He grasped his hands behind his back and took another long look at the clouds piling to the south.

They now smoldered with the richer orange of evening. "Strauss wrote his last songs in the year I was born. I like that link."

"Golly gosh and double gosh. What *does* it all mean!? How many people, do you think, in this city have even heard of your precious Strauss?"

"More than you think."

"But less than you think. A lot less. This mob," her arm swept across the suburb, "are still into Bon Jovi, AC/DC or Bruce Springsteen and their kids are head-bangers — we hear them all about us on an all too regular basis, remember! The closest any of them get to Strauss is when some of the women give their mothers an Andre Rieu CD for Christmas. *I know!* Staff-room conversations."

He laughed. "Not *the* Andre Rieu!"

"The very one."

"Well then, that'd be the wrong Strauss. Still, I'd say a lot of them would recognize the opening of *Also sprach Zarathustra*."

"Only because it was in that movie. But, tell me, what happens next with Roger?"

"I guess it's my move."

"Do you have the time," her voice fell away, "for this sort of nonsense?"

"Yes, I know, I should be working on … finishing something. All the same, I'm a wee bit curious to see what might fall out of this tree if it's shaken."

"Something might fall on your head!"

"Narh! This isn't anything serious."

"You know this?"

"Sort of, I guess. As I said, I just can't recall there being anything significant in those old Public Works files. With that sort of stuff you could look at something … but without some other piece of information, you literally haven't a clue as to what it means. So, in that sense, I suppose you could say I don't actually know anything. Anyway," he took her hand, "we better get back. Max will be getting cranky about where his dinner has got to. Ah, the aroma of tinned fish guts in the evening."

"He was born under the sign of Pisces."

"So you say. As it happens, we, too, have fish tonight."

He had a feast or famine theory about eating. In nature there are seasonal gluts, sumptuous abundances — salmon, Bogong moths, lambs — and people periodically stuffed themselves. Later, when necessary, they could skip a meal or two.

It wasn't a particularly original theory and he didn't ever seem to practice the fasting part of the equation with the rigor required, but it did permit him to buy a heavy, lustrous fillet of fresh red emperor (twice as much as would have been deemed sufficient by a dietician), to egg and crumb it, grill it and serve it up with a few fried potatoes. For greens, sprinkle the spuds with freshly cut chives. Help yourself to the mayonnaise. Pass the salt.

After making appreciative remarks about the inch and a half thick slab of the pearly white fish, the Girl cut her portion in half and said she would save the "spare" piece for lunch tomorrow. He knew it would keep and be just as sweet eaten cold, but the message was that she did not agree with his exercise in excess. He was grateful she did not ask how much it cost. He would have probably lied about it.

She had made her point, but not so as to take the shine off his luxe.

"You only live once," he declared, in memory of that feast of excess they had when his father caught his big kingie.

What was he then — thirteen or fourteen?

They had so much fish and only the beach shack's tiny freezerless fridge. The whole family, all the way down to his baby brother barely out of nappies, had to stuff themselves in order that the fish would not go to waste. His mother even gave some away. Ye gods, when you consider what it would cost to buy a pile of really good fresh fish like that now!

As for crayfish!

But that's the thing. Thinking about what you paid for the thing is, one way or t'other, just going to distract from and sully the pleasure of stuffing your fat face like there's no tomorrow. And *that*, that really would be a waste.

That night, long enough after Anna had gone to bed for him to assume she was asleep, she heard him make toast, spread it thickly with butter and Vegemite, and start going through the drawers of his desk.

Sitting very still, tail curled neatly over his front paws, Max watched proceedings from the edge of the darkness just outside the Old Man's office.

Sidetracked by other things he dug out, it took the better part of an hour to find the Nibbelup folder. A quick read through the report confirmed what he suspected — there was nothing of consequence in it.

He got into the SRO's online catalogue and found that all but one of the files he had cited were still listed. That, of course, did not mean documents were not missing from the files that were listed. Pages could have been missing even before he had looked ten years back. Unless you paid careful attention to the numbering of the pages on a file you would not notice the occasional missing letter. He flicked through the notebooks in which he had penciled his research notes, and fanned the forty or so pages of photocopies he had done at the time. Nothing jumped out.

Nevertheless, he reckoned he could go into State Records and if Baba Yaga was on the desk he could fill a lazy half hour or so with another round of him and her trading polite insults while he bugged her with inquiries about lost or stolen files. It is a chronic botheration in many archives, but when a new electronic database is created without sufficient reference to the old card indexes the problem is exacerbated. Sid Wedge, Australia's most politically incorrect publisher, thought this had been done deliberately to allow a purge of files mentioning Aboriginal cannibalism. But Sid was loopy with paranoia — Oldie knew it was just ordinary bad management.

Hassling Baba Yaga was a cheap thrill. He knew that, but he still enjoyed it. The witch was obstructive by nature to all-comers, but nevertheless seemed to put in extra effort to thwart him whenever possible. She had always done that, but things deteriorated when, five years earlier, he did something for which she had never forgiven him.

Someone — Baba Yaga, apparently, judging by her sensitivity to the matter — had devised and authorized the purchase of flash new plastic ID cards. These were to be issued to researchers wishing to view documents from State Archives — and there were enough of the things manufactured to meet the estimated number of archive users for years and years. Clearly, creative thought, committee consideration and some substantial part of the budget had gone into those cards, which were also intended to be the very embodiment of the SRO's projected bright and efficient corporate self-image. But at the core of all that confident, tasteful design there was a hooly-dooly grammatical error.

Oldie wrote to the Government Minister responsible for Archives (along with Indigenous Affairs, Tourism,

Arts and Culture) and pointed out that confusion over the genitive case introduced an ambiguity that could have legal (and therefore financial) consequences. By sheer good luck it happened that the Minister at the time was a smart woman, one who actually understood that the error went against the logical foundation of language and, as such, could not be brushed aside as a mere matter of usage. The very responsible Minister wrote to instruct Baba Yaga to do another set of cards.

The witch therefore had reason to dislike Oldie, but since that episode all of her co-workers had treated him with an especial respect and courtesy. Funny about that.

It was late. He let Max out, had a long, steady piss against the lemon tree, and went to bed.

A little after five o'clock, just as the sky was starting to lighten, he and the Girl turned over, reversing positions so that she cuddled up to his back. He lifted his head on hearing what he first thought were the garden's reticulation sprinklers. It woke him because he knew this wasn't their rostered day and to be caught watering illegally, dobbed by a neighbor, would bring a fine he could not afford. It took a couple of breaths to realize he was listening to a passing shower falling through the plumbago hedge on the retaining wall outside their bedroom window. Rain, in the driest year since 1914.

"Hear the rain?"

"No," she breathed into his shoulder.

But they both knew her hearing wasn't so good anymore and he knew he wasn't dreaming. He felt her slip back into sleep. The rain became heavier for a few minutes.

Then he thought: The clue to what was dumped was who had done the dumping.

That flicked his Awake light on.

III

Once more little Black Betty buzzed forth and sped down West Coast Highway. The road steamed after another light shower and the sea was milky morning blue. Their months of accumulated dull dust washed off, the trees and shrubs shone. Vroom, vroom, said Betty, full of pep and go.

This time Oldie was going to Sir Charles Gairdner Hospital for a powwow with a surgeon about his gall bladder and some attached duct or the other. Five or six months back a three-night bilious attack landed him in Charlie's Emergency Ward, where he was rehydrated, given a couple of Panadol and sent home after the regulation four hours. As luck would have it, he came right and there had been no further attacks. Something called cholecystitis was mentioned by Doctor Lou. She even wrote it down on a piece of paper for him to put in his wallet and take home to look it up on the internet.

But his hep C status put another level of consultation and rigmarole onto the business and, after all the wheels had turned and then been turned again, after not one but two ultrasounds and visits to the relevant specialists he had finally, just last week, presented himself at the Nuclear Medicine Department for something called a HIDA scan. He spent an hour and a half keeping still under the scanner as a radioactive trace seeped through his liver and dripped into his gall bladder. It had all gone well enough, except that the venous catheter left a bruise on his arm about the size and shape of the compromised organ. He now copped such bruises practically every time he had a blood test. They were getting harder to hide. He did not derive, as he once would have, much consolation from the fact of the catheter being inserted by a beautiful Russian woman whose ID tag gave her name as Doctor Sweet. It was not much solace, but still, it was something ... the clear eyes of an angel with a sultry voice. It was hard to maintain a grudge in the presence of such loveliness. *Krasivaya, krasivaya, ochen krasivaya.*

Doctor Sweet! How on earth ...? Married name? He had told practically everyone he encountered about the aptly named medico. In much the same way that his gall bladder provided a good cover for the periodic tests required to monitor his hep C, the Doctor Sweet story was a nice distracting bauble to jiggle when he was asked how things were going.

So what hallucination would he have to report after this day's excursion into the haunted void? There would be something. As clever Nora said, real life never lets you down.

Driving past Karrakatta he had a vision of Blondie leaning against that silver coupe, smoking her cigarette and contemplating the tall summer sky. Even though her hair was as black as, he couldn't help thinking of her as Blondie. Apart from the tatt, he thought her face was of a similar cast as Deborah Harry's in her prime. Lovely, lovely, lovely. What on earth was she doing with that damned wanker Ted Connell? It was not the first time he had thought of her since the funeral. Wondered about her.

Wondered about himself. What could be more pathetic than an old clown's lust? What could be more fatally futile? And yet, and yet … he sought the far shore of Enlightenment. He had things to do, things to discover, to learn. He reckoned, in order to do that, he could shoo off the blowfly of lust.

A troupe of about fifty mourners were mustering at the main entrance. It looked like it was going to be a slow morning for the coffee shop. He slowed a little to scan the faces. Nobody he knew.

Further along, approaching the Aberdare Road lights, he noticed that the row of mature Norfolk Island pines towards the eastern end of the cemetery were looking decidedly disheveled. Even the trees were sick and dying. With little or no foliage on their limbs they looked like frightened broomsticks. Was that because of disease, the drought, age or just for having been planted too close together a hundred years ago? With Perth's sandy soils and strong winds, he wondered why more of the big pines around the place did not blow over. After a strong blow in Florida the authorities there had banned Norfolks in some coastal towns. He had one at three metres in a tub. The Girl had used it as a Christmas tree for a few years, but it became too much trouble to lug in and out of the house. It also shed piss-yellow stuff that discolored the carpet. It had outgrown its tub and must be root bound, so he ought to plant it out on his verge and let it have its head. By the time it grew big enough to fall and take out the house he'd be long gone.

Gone and long forgotten.

"Not my concern," he told himself, preparing to negotiate the idiotic ticket machine and boom at the entrance to the hospital visitors' car park.

He tried to find Betty a nice shady spot, but with so few trees left in the car park the small, creeping islands of meagre shade were all occupied.

He unpacked himself — big man, small car — and

steadied against the open door. Across the way, the eight-story bulk of G Block rose to stare down the sunshine. He had always been intrigued by the way its aspect changed according to the light and time of day. Right then it had on its bland oatmeal soap look, but come back in the evening, when it stood darkly against the twilight afterglow … then the thing definitely loomed, reverberating to a deeper chord. He and the Girl had to go there one rainy July night to identify their Jem. It was probably in there that he had contracted hepatitis C. He told himself it was just a building. But he could hear it breathing.

His appointment was in E Block, a place with its own trove of memories. The good ol' pain clinic. The good ol' pharmacy. Making the complicated walk-bus-train-walk-bus trip there and then the hour or so wait to get his oxycodone script filled. He had always seemed to get out of there for the bus-walk-train-bus-walk trip home just as the bus was drawing away, leaving him to a 20-minute wait for the next one. Every month for more than six years. Oh, yes, happy daze in the Promised Land of Shit.

On his way down the main corridor he saw a supersized cockroach stagger out from beneath a drink vending machine and, feelers whipping about, lurch into the middle of the thoroughfare. He stepped over it and kept going, but it was in the length of that stride that he decided he would avoid surgery. He heard an old woman following him gasp and start jabbing and thumping about with her walking stick. Ah, what sport! Remember the joke about the foot-stamping of flamenco dancing — the Dance of the Cockroach. *Très drôle*. He could have turned to take in the sight, but preferred to imagine it. Besides, the circus was perfectly reflected in the frowning faces of the elderly couple coming towards him. He smiled at them. It was not news that cockroaches

40

had the run of the place. There you go — he'd hardly stepped into the joint and he had a good story. Right again, Nora.

He had arrived early, but by the time he worked his way through reception, the waiting room and onto the chair in the corridor outside the surgeon's room, it was already half an hour after his appointment time. As a veteran of the public health system he expected such delays and always came with his own reading material. He had read most of the novels of Leo Perutz in waiting rooms — and would recommend them to just about anyone on the waiting room circuit. He was fortunate, too, in that he could generally tune out the tedious television chatter that had become mandatory in waiting rooms. Don't hospital staff ever notice that the places farthest from the screen are the most popular? No doubt they do, but that did not mean that Management, upstairs on Cloud Nine, would give a shit. In their own way, Management were as zonked in their space as the poor devils they had corralled in the enormous waiting room.

It was a timeless place. In all the years he had attended, the only thing to change in the waiting room was that the television screens had become bigger, louder. He looked around, the décor and color scheme seemed utterly familiar. But then, perhaps there had been small changes he had not noticed. His memory wasn't what it used to be. Who said elephants never forget?

Even though he was forgetting more things more often than he cared to admit, the shapes and weights of things once known somehow persisted. He may not have been able to find the piece that fitted the hole in his memory, but the shape of the hole was tantalizingly familiar. In cognitive terms, recall may carry greater weight than mere recognition, but he was grateful he could still sense the false note when he heard it. If he had to give a reason, he would say it just didn't add up. Others saw this as plain obtuseness, an indication that he did not fully understand what was being explained to him — and he would agree, with disconcerting readiness, that this was probably so.

At bottom, however, his non-compliance was simply because he felt it was safer not to trust people who were just a little too confident that you should trust them. Apart from the fact that he did not have a good track record with surgeons, more than half a century ago his great auntie Peg, after reading in the newspaper that a life-long friend of hers had died, said to him, to herself, to the empty teacups, to the quiet room with its ticking clock, that doctors bury their mistakes. He could not quite remember the moment when Peggy pronounced those words, not exactly, but he felt it still. He had remembered the memory. It had looped and stayed within him and it had shaped him.

So when the chipper chappy in the tweed jacket (complete with leather elbow patches for fuck's sake) looked at the ceiling and allowed that the tests were somewhat "contradictory", that there were "inherent risks" in meddling with his gall bladder and a duct running out of his liver, that they could, if he wished, monitor the situation with further tests in the new year ...

He fairly bolted — animated testament to the durability, the persistence of childhood impressions.

"Has anyone seen Gregor Samsa lately?" he practically shouted, beard swishing, gesticulating with inappropriate spritzig as he strode back out past the drink machine.

"I blame the universities," he said, loping across the road to the car park.

"See you later," G Block purred behind him.

"Don't get your hopes up," he shot back.

The car park boom lifted. Christ, it worked! Right! Let's have a few cards on the table. Time to figure out the lie of the land. Woo-hoo!

Before he and Betty ventured forth that morning, Oldie had checked out Roger's place on Google Street View — a nineteen-thirties brick and tile bungalow in a quiet street lined with mature peppermint trees. And now, having successfully alighted on the run from the medical merry-go-round, he was so full of beans as to be ready to take those extra steps of marching up to and loudly knocking on the front door. Presenting himself.

Apart from anything else, he was curious about Jolly's domestic arrangements.

The house was opposite a small park halfway between Stirling Highway and the river. There were no vehicles in the two-berth carport. The wad of catalogues and advertising shit in the letterbox looked fresh. Oldie parked over the road under a tree a few doors down and left Betty's motor and air-con running.

He watched the place for a couple of minutes. A curtain twitched in the house one up from opposite the car. Otherwise, all quiet.

Roger's was the most original, least renovated house in that stretch of the street. The place next door had been knocked through, with the back ripped out and an upper level stuck on. On the other side, for sale, there was a completely new piece of works, which the real estate agents described as a Tuscan villa. Tuscany … some place in Italy, wasn't it? Near Naples, by the look of it.

He dialed Roger's home number, tapped off as soon as the answering machine engaged, waited ten seconds and redialed. Still no pick-up before the answering machine. He cut the call. Roger's mobile went straight to voice mail.

He snapped his phone shut and took a slow, methodical look around.

Nobody in the park. Curtain over the road unmoved.

There had been no traffic in the street since he arrived. Apart from the carport, the front of the house was fairly well screened by the street trees and a few shrubs inside the fence. A high brick wall on the Tuscan villa side. No sign of anyone about on the other side.

He turned off the ignition, got out of the car and locked it.

As he crossed the street, he pretended to consult a small Spirax notebook he took from his shirt pocket. He frowned, going for the insurance assessor look. As if!

A couple of dark red concrete steps led up to the veranda. The steel mesh security door did not quite conceal the leadlight panes in the upper half of the front door. He touched the buzzer and heard the Big Ben chimes echo through the house.

Nobody answered, but he thought he noticed a slight change in the reflected light behind the dark glass panels of the door.

He held his breath and listened.

Nothing.

He tried the screen door.

Locked.

But inadvertently rattled it in releasing the handle.

A solid mass of snarls and deep, reverberating barks hit the lower part of the door. It was the Hound of the Baskervilles with the volume turned up.

Oldie damned near jumped out of his skin. He reeled back across the veranda, stumbled down the steps, loudly and obscenely taking the Lord's name in vain. The unshakable ferocity of the large, growling animal behind the door left no doubt it would do all it could to kill him, that if it got its teeth into him it would most certainly not just tear him apart, it would actually eat him. He didn't need to see it to know it was slavering at the mouth.

After running a decapitated chook circle or two in the front yard, the Old Man was across the street and locked in his car faster than the proverbial speeding bullet. Security video of the incident would have won a prize on Australia's Funniest Home Videos.

"Fuckin' Hell!"

Catch the breath.

"Fucking mongrel!"

Put on the seatbelt.

Talk about the fucking wolf at the frigging door! What in hell was that bastard? Sounded like a big Rottweiler. Maybe crossed with one of those Mexican drug lord Mastiff things. Someone sure wants to discourage intruders.

Start the car. Let the air-con kick in.

So much for the bright idea of figuring out the lie of the land.

Drive slowly up the street, over the rise to where the houses are highly salubrious and unpretentiously palatial. Fuck me Roger, how'd you get in so close to this? Yes, that's right, you said something about the "old family home". You inherited the place.

He parked at the picnic area high above the river. Got out and breathed through his nose until — pitter patter — his heart rate felt like it was finding its feet.

The river.

Now, that really did define the lie of the land in Perth. It was the first and last thing. Over 300 years ago a Dutchman stood somewhere here and gave it a European name. Almost 200 years ago the English built their town on a limestone ridge next to the mudflats separating the estuary from the sweet water. Oldie looked down at the Point Walter sand spit. Some scrubby stuff was growing on it. It had been a while, but a decent flood would sooner or later take care of that. After three decades of declining rainfall people had forgotten that in the right circumstances the Swan could turn on as savage a little flash flood as any Australian river. He had recently seen photographs of the 1926 flood, which overflowed Mill Point and washed away the North Fremantle railway bridge. And he remembered reading old newspaper accounts of a big flood back in the early eighteen-seventies. It could happen again.

Or, he supposed, the flood could come in from the sea. The Boxing Day tsunami sent a metre high surge along Perth's beaches. No real damage, though; and, in reality, a dangerously large repeat event was a long shot.

No, if he had to put money on the Force of Nature, the Act of God that would knock over Perth, it would have to go on the wind. One of these years a cyclone would slip around North West Cape, swing out into the Indian Ocean to gather strength as it drifted south, and then — kaa-fucking-*BOUM!* Good night, Perth!

BOUM!

Did he want to be, did he like being such a miserable, told-ya-so old bastard?

Not really, but he didn't exactly fight it. He had always explained himself to Anna by saying that there was just too much stupidity in the world. He wished he could ignore it, he tried, constantly, he really did, but there was always some fresh nincompoop spouting some truly innovative manifestation of silliness. Despite his bleak outlook, each new absurdity always caught Oldie totally unprepared. It would have been one thing if such stupidities had been aberrations, weeds in an otherwise sane world, but public discourse now seemed to him to be little more than whole crops of noxious weeds competing for space and light. And the microphone.

She occasionally checked him when his ruminations became too dull. The basic deal between them was that if he wanted her to listen to him then he had better not talk too much nonsense too much of the time. "That's enough now, stop brooding," she would say. And should she happen to use the same tone of voice with which she addressed her four and five-year-old pupils, he didn't mind, most of the time.

Most of the time.

Because there were times when it irked, when he thought she fell into the corrective demeanor and tone too quickly, a little too readily. He usually let such moments pass without comment, admitting to himself that she was entitled to the occasional display of mild impatience. He accepted it as an occupational hazard of living with a kindergarten teacher. He wondered how she would have handled the boys had she already been a teacher when they were growing up, going to school. But his wondering was irrelevant because Daniel had already left home when she started teaching and Jem was in his last year of high school.

Daniel …

It had been a week. He did warn them he would be on the road. Up the West Coast to Canada. At this time of year?

No news is good news. So they say.

At the edge of the cliff overlooking the river, along the path running through the lookout area where tourists stood to take their photographs, there was a waist-high stone wall, a parapet. It displayed a hundred or so commemorative plaques for former residents of the suburb. Nice little earner for the Council. People do like to see their name on things — park benches, stone walls, buildings, streets, towns, hills, celestial bodies … species of tape worm. Sauntering along the wall he saw his own family name. No relation, thank Christ, but irritating.

The river was like a nineteen-fifties travel poster — fresh air, sunshine, sails that were triangular snips of white scattered about on the sparkling blue waters. All that was missing was a smiling girl poised to launch a multicolored beach ball. She was no doubt reclining by the pool at one of the spacious houses perched on the rises of the lazy river's limestone banks. The cliff-top homes of the very rich in a wealthy country.

At Royal Freshwater Bay Yacht Club whole schools of bloody great big motor launches were lined up at their moorings. He could see people waltzing up and down the jetties, lugging gear and Eskies back and forth. On one of the larger boats preparing to set out an older, florid man in sensible shorts gave directions to younger men in silly shorts. A lithe young woman half emerged from the companion way and the skipper stepped over to hand her something from his pocket. A key?

Oldie caught himself before he started to build a narrative. He would be better occupied thinking about himself, making sense of his own situation.

It was understood between him and Anna that he would not ring her to discuss what had passed with the surgeon. There was no emergency, the news was not exactly bad. She had classes of littlies all day, so it could wait until he picked her up. Then he would tell her all about Tweedy's leather patches, the "contradictions" and Gregor Samsa's nimble antics. And when he told her, she would accept his decision to defer, to dodge surgery. He would tell her about their family name on the wall. He would even tell her about his unscheduled visit to Roger's. Indeed, retelling the day's events would be a useful life-goes-on restorative.

His situation: the trouble with his situation was that however he construed it, it came out at him dead within a few years. There was no way he would get his three score and ten. It is hard to maintain your equilibrium — particularly when you are a rather unstable fellow to start with — when faced with the certainty of imminent physical disintegration and mental deterioration.

Because there was no hope.

Or very little. Any drug to effectively deal with the virus was years away, over his horizon. As for a liver transplant — well, join the queue to take your chances on that one.

Not a lot of people knew about his illness. Daniel and Anna knew. A few of Oldie's closest friends knew, but generally he kept the matter secret. People behaved differently when they knew. More to spare himself than her, he hadn't told his mother, confused and deep in her self-pitying dotage. There was no point, providing he outlived her. Even so, there was pressure from several quarters for him to make the effort and fly to Melbourne to see her. He sensed it was inevitable, a ritual easier to do than not do. And better sooner than later, obviously. The holding pattern couldn't last forever. One day the trap of his disease would snap shut.

His dilemma was not merely the question of whether he would outlive his mother. There was also the business of surviving the circus of settling his mother's estate. What he expected to inherit would mostly go towards trimming the mortgage, but he had dreamed of pulling enough out of the pot to take a holiday in New Zealand. To see a few old friends while he was still more or less presentable. You can't just stand around waiting for the axe to fall.

It worried him that liver failure was not a pretty sight, and the option of stepping off the perch before the final stages was easier to consider in the abstract than to carry out. The question of when was the awkward, complicated bit.

The matter of how had settled, more as a stop-gap convenience than proper planning, to the eighty 5 mg Diazepam he had secreted at the back of the top left-hand drawer of his desk. Old Valium, a decade beyond their use-by date. Would they still have any kick? He suspected it would not be enough. He needed to find something else to augment what he had. It was something he would have to look into.

He peered over the parapet and down through the shrubs and small trees attached to the cliff face, all the way down into the river. It was deep. He had been thinking of climbing over and going down a way to have a piss behind the nearest bush, but the drop was just too precipitous for a man of his age and size. If he did get over, he'd never manage to hoist himself back up over the wall. It occurred to him that this place would be a grand one for someone wanting to finish things in memorable style. Just get a vehicle heavy enough to punch through the town worthies' wall and fly the long arc into the river below. Talk about making your mark, making a splash. It'd be remembered. By the locals, anyway.

But it was not his style.

He was not afraid of death. Pain or disfigurement, sure, but death itself was nothing. Nothingness. He had looked it in the face. At forty he had looked upon his dead father and at fifty he had closed the eyes of his twenty-year-old son. Both had been sudden deaths. Even as a child, when he had stood and looked upon that woman in the gutter, he had understood that death was as simple as a light going out. Life was there, and then it wasn't. Tears in the rain. That much, at least, was not complicated. There is no Death, only the dying.

With the woman knocked into the gutter, it was the behavior of the living that had held his attention and concerned him. As he remembered it, the body itself had not particularly shocked him. Perhaps he did not know what to make of it. Or perhaps it really did scare the living daylights out of him and he had simply forgotten, put it out of mind —repressed memory and all that claptrap. How would he ever know? How can anyone ever know such things?

More than half a century after the event he could see the lights reflected on the wet road and the big old pre-war Dodge parked askew, its lights on the Hume and Hovell memorial cairn, the town's modest cap doff to History.

He could hear his father suddenly exclaiming, "That's Alan's car!"

He and his two little brothers were in the back seat of the Austin A70, going home after dropping off Mum and another woman at the Friday night picture show. They jostled to see through the fogged, rain-streaked windows. Another car had stopped and three of four people were standing around. The front door of the house next to where his father parked was open and they could see someone on the phone in the hallway. He saw the bicycle on the footpath and he saw Alan Fanning, his face twisting in his hands, sitting on the bench near the memorial. The headlights picked him out like a character on a starkly lit stage. The boy didn't notice the body until his father walked across the road and, stepping over the deep gutter, paused and flinched at something in the shadow beside Mr Fanning's car.

His father told them to stay in the car. If he had only for once done what he was told ... but, no, he was a wayward child and after a minute he got out anyway and crossed the road in the drizzling rain, out of sight behind the Dodge. He came around the back and saw the woman in the long black raincoat. She was lying with her head towards him. One of the men had placed a jacket over her face. Her bare legs were left exposed. If there was blood he didn't see it in the dark. Her blonde, wavy hair gleamed softly against the bluestone gutter. The bike, its rear wheel bent to a right angle, lay on the footpath. But what the child that became the man remembered best, what had always stuck in his mind, was the full bottle of milk standing intact, balanced on the edge of the gutter, between the woman and her bike. It was like someone had just placed it there, with deliberation and great care.

He heard Alan Fanning sobbing, groaning, "Christ, Jim, I've killed the poor woman! I've killed her! I've killed her!" On and on. "I've killed her!" And his father quietly saying something as he sat there patting his friend on the back. Someone must have noticed the ten-year-old kid standing behind the Dodge because his father abruptly turned and quietly told him to get back in the car.

He did, and had the sense to tell his brothers no more than "a lady got knocked off her bike".

Alan Fanning had been a quiet man, a baffling mix of shy and taciturn. His young wife was just plain shy, and busy with their baby and a toddler. Unlike some of his father's other friends, Mr Fanning never sky-larked with the kids about the place. He'd say hello and maybe ruffle your hair, but he'd never pick you up by the ankles and spin you around like some of the other men used to do. And there he was, bawling his eyes out in front of everybody, his normally slick dark hair a mess. There he was, his world irrevocably knocked out of shape. The fixed had been displaced and the solid rendered fragile.

From overheard parents and the kids at school

he learned the woman was a recently arrived New Australian — some said she was Dutch and others that she was a Balt. There was a question as to whether she was married to a Dutchman or was just living with him. Someone said he was not the father of the woman's little girl, not the real father that is. It was universally agreed, however, that the bicycle carried no lights or reflectors. It was also rumored that Alan Fanning had been drinking after hours at the Freemasons' Hotel.

The town weighed the matter for a week or so and decided that even though young Fanning had had a drink or two, the fault must ultimately dwell in the fact of the woman riding a bike without lights on a rainy night. Wearing dark clothes.

Still, she had lost her life. She'd gone to the shop to buy a bottle of milk and she had been killed on her way home. And that little girl was orphaned. It was a dreadful tragedy, no question, but, well, when all was said and done it was an accident. The way of the world.

The Dutchman quit his job at the wood-yard and he and the child immediately went off to Melbourne and were never seen or heard of again. The police decided there was no point in charging Alan Fanning with anything — he was said to be chastened, a changed man.

But to have caused the death of another was not something easily put aside. The Fannings moved to Mildura to start a new life. There were Christmas cards for a couple of years and then people lost touch.

That was … fifty-two, maybe fifty-three years ago. Probably the year the Sputniks and Laika went up into the starry, starry sky.

His bladder interrupted his reverie, insisting it was time to go.

But where to *go*?

If that couple hadn't pulled in to sit in the bloke's car and talk — office romance on lunch break — he'd have taken the risk of pissing over the parapet. But there was something prissy about that tart in the car, just the sort who'd ring the cops and get him charged with willful exposure. With two escapes already that day he didn't think it wise to push his luck for a third.

He had passed a small shopping centre a few blocks before Roger's. He'd hang on until he got back there. He'd bloody well have to. That was something else Peggy told him, "It's no fun getting old". She would know. She lived to be ninety-three.

Vroom, vroom, he sped like a bastard through a kilometre of back streets.

He was quite the connoisseur of suburban shopping centres. He could read them. He saw them as reliable barometers of socio-economic levels, aspirations, demographics, the not-so-invisible hand and all that malarkey. The unexamined city isn't worth living in and if you want to examine the tea leaves and the entrails of society, then shopping centres are the places to haunt. For all their appearance of standardization, even the big supermarket chains catered for local tastes and a practiced, let us say, an experienced shopper — which Oldie was — could soon discern and interpret such variations. The gourmet and Asian sections were usually good places to start. While the fresh fish counter could be evaluated with a glance, the presence and range of organic produce required more careful monitoring. Moving into the general shelves, he would check to see how far up the quality range the store went with a particular product. Did they, for example, carry a brand of imported tinned mackerel that was twice the price but infinitely sweeter than any of the regularly available brands? And if they did, they probably also stocked those delectable but expensive anchovies.

He fairly smacked his lips at the thought of mackerel generously garnished with anchovies, all served up on thick slices of toasted white bread to soak up the oil and juices. And the hot toast would have been spread with that tasty organic butter from Denmark — the sweet one in the yellow wrapper. You betcha!

But first he had to park Betty and find the damned *piss-wha*.

The sun flashed off a car moving along behind the vehicles on the car park's upper terrace. Through the gaps he saw the silver coupe moving towards the exit up onto Monument Street. Even though he only saw the back of her head in the second she paused at the stop sign, he knew it was Blondie at the wheel. She had a passenger. An adolescent boy?

He half turned to get back in Betty to give chase, but he was already close to wetting his pants and had to find that toilet quick smart.

An ingrained knowledge of shopping centre layout fueled by frantic instinct had him standing at the urinal in under a minute. He spread his legs, pointed Percy at the porcelain and waiting for the drip to become a trickle and, finally, a stream … of sorts. Despite every care, he still managed to splash one of his boots.

"No fun getting old," he said to himself, doing his best to clean up with a paper towel.

He was answered by a long, strangled fart reverberating inside the far cubicle. "You got that right," said some joker with a croaky voice. Echoing off the tiles it sounded as spectral as the voice from the fucking crypt.

Jesus wept!

Without another word the Old Man washed his hands, snatched a wad of paper towels to avoid handling the door handles and got out of there. The paper towels were scrunched into a ball and arced through the air to land in a discarded shopping trolley. As sure as rotten eggs he wasn't hungry anymore. Gourmet to Go could keep their Black Angus Homemade beef pies. The inspection of the supermarket would have to be done some other time. He'd had enough excitement for one day and couldn't get home soon enough.

As he walked back through the car park a neatly groomed bloke about his age got out of a shiny new four-wheel-drive and gave Oldie a complacently friendly nod as he passed. This was a man in his early sixties who had never allowed his hair to grow over his collar but now sported a small stud in his ear; and who wore a T-shirt carrying the words "Grumpy Old Man". Grow up, Fuckwit, Oldie thought as, eyes narrowed, he returned the nod and hurried by.

Seeing such idiocy at such a time would have normally tipped his day over. But — what a hoot! — he had spotted Blondie once again! Now, didn't that just top everything that had come his way for the day?

IV

He heard Peggy calling him. It was definitely her voice. It roused her presence. Oral memory must be deeply embedded. Engrained.

"Be careful, Son," she said, with the urgency of having just caught sight of him high up a ladder, reaching out too far. When alone together, as they often were, she usually called him "Son". In that day and age it was not an unusual way for an older relative to address a boy, but in Peggy's case it carried a little more than would have been apparent to a stranger.

"Be careful, Son."

He was awake, with the Girl sleeping peacefully beside him.

It was light. He could hear doves cooing in the plumbago. Perhaps they had roused the voice. He had often listened to them during those high summer daybreaks as he lay awake in Peggy's bed, quietly waiting for someone in the house to stir.

It was family legend that young Alex ran away from home before he turned three. His mother was approaching confinement with her second child when Peggy, then in her early sixties and five years a widow, wrote to offer to have the boy stay with her in Melbourne for "a few weeks" — until the new baby was "settled". Trouble was, once his brother was born and Mum wrote to say Alex could return, Peggy kept finding reasons for him to stay. His parents even made the long drive up the Great Ocean Road from Apollo Bay to Melbourne. But Alex, spoilt rotten by his aged relatives, dug in his heels, refused to budge and demonstrated how unquiet life with him about the place could be. So Mum and Dad took their contented babe-in-arms home and left the very independent Alex with Peg and Jim and Bob until he got used to the idea of a little brother. That, according to the regular weekly letters from Peggy, was a slow process. He and Peggy contrived to extend his stay at Cameron Street until Christmas, four and a half months after his brother was born. Trams, trains, chocolate wafers, playing cards at night, smokin' seegars — who'd willingly leave all that? Trotting along holding Peggy's hand as she went her rounds shopping, he knew Sydney Road and the streets and lanes of Brunswick and Coburg better than some of the locals his age.

To some extent (it doesn't pay to be too precise about these things) he believed his interest in the past sprang from so much of his early childhood having been spent with old people. After his pre-school sojourn in Peggy's household he would spend many of his school holidays there. And not just at Peggy's. One way or another he spent a lot of his childhood away from home. From when he was seven, a good part of his long summer holidays was spent on his paternal grandfather's small dairy farm in Gippsland. His grandfather had taken up the farm when compulsory retirement meant he had to climb down and give up driving steam trains. It was in that little farmhouse outside Rosedale that Nin, his gentle, frail grandmother, had taken matters in hand and taught the boy his alphabet. He was always a late bloomer.

Later, as a teenager, he was farmed out to holiday with the numerous rural cousins on his mother's side.

But there was always a couple of days, a week now and then, "in town" with Peggy, even if he had to share her with his brothers.

Peggy shared her house with her brother Jim, two years her junior, and their sister Anne, known as Bobby, who was two years younger again than Jim. All born in the Empire during the reign of Queen Victoria, they were surrounded by things of that and the Edwardian era. They sang lilting old songs to themselves and talked to one another of childhood friends and family. They told the boy stories and gossip about a world he did not quite understand was long gone. On one level he understood some of the people spoken of were not there, but the distinction between dead and alive was not always made and the people mentioned were all, one way or another, contemporaries. They were people who could perhaps one day call in for a cup of tea and a scone or two.

Sometimes they did — there was an old fellow, one of their Tasmanian cousins, who turned up one day out of the blue. He looked very much like Jim, but he talked different, somehow. Perhaps that was because, as Alex was later given to understand by Bobby (quietly, out of the side of her mouth), he was from the Catholic side of the family. Ah-ha!

Peggy was the only one at Cameron Street who had been married — a Melbourne & Metropolitan Tramways Board Inspector named Jack Tonkin. As a young man Jack had been to Western Australia, where he worked on the Kalgoorlie pipeline. Stories about Perth, the river, the pipeline, the heat and the tragedy of C.Y. O'Connor were told in Peggy's house long after Jack Tonkin's death. Told in his memory.

The union between Jack and Peggy did not produce any children. Even before Jack's death a couple of years before Alex's birth. Jim and Bobby were boarding with

Peggy. Jim and Bob both still worked part-time and both had long-term "companions". Jim used to stay weekends with Stella, a widow, and Bobby took her annual holidays on interstate bus tours with Ern Spence, railway signalman and bachelor.

Ern had visiting rights on a Friday night to make up the numbers as Bobby's euchre partner. He played cards and received supper on the understanding that he took his leave by eleven in order to catch his tram home. Spen-oh, as Jim called him behind his back, had a room in a big old house overlooking the North Melbourne shunting yards, where he worked. For a humble railway worker, Spen-oh had been around. He had been to Pompeii. And he had been to Japan sometime in the nineteen-twenties or early thirties. The funny thing, which Oldie only noticed in his own old age, was that Ern Spence had much the same distinctive voice as the renowned Japanese actor, Chishu Ryu, the Old Man in *Tokyo Story*. Oral memory. He had the same lean physique, too, only more bandy-legged. Oldie liked Spen-oh, who told him stories and fed him what accumulated to be a fine stack of pre-War *National Geographics*.

As for Stella. Well ...

There was a story ... a story that long before any time anyone could really remember there had been a certain incident that caused Peggy to banish "that woman", forbidding her to ever again set foot in her home. Peggy was five foot nothing and Stella was a big, intimidating woman, so the showdown must have been memorable. The few times Jim took the boy to Stella's house she was nice enough but he sensed she would rather he wasn't there. Perhaps she didn't like the way the kid tended to stare at the big, black mole beside her nose. Little Alex watched his manners because he loved Jimmy, an unfailing supply of shillings and good bedtime stories.

The Old People all had their own rooms and double beds. Alex slept with whoever he liked, but because Jim retired early and told stories the boy usually slept with the man. These days that would be labeled as "inappropriate". Back then the only issue was Jim's snoring, so loud the neighbors across the lane could hear it. But young kids are heavy sleepers, deep dreamers. The boy would put on his pyjamas and climb up into Jim's high bed with the starched linen and the bolster pillow. Jim would turn out the light and they would lay there in the dark while the long, convoluted yarns about lions and tigers, tethered goats and Cap'n Jim Corbett unfurled. Occasionally there'd be a stampeding, rogue elephant to be shot (Jim's stories always ended up with the beast slain, usually in the nick of time by the hunter's last shot) but the main attraction was usually a lion or a tiger. The tigers were always man-eaters and especially cunning ones at that.

Jim never told one of his stories without first asserting that it was true. This was an important part of the ritual. He would sometimes strengthen his case by citing the specific book or magazine in which he had read the account. These documents were kept in the bottom of his wardrobe, somewhere behind his first-aid kit with its little brown bottle of mercurochrome. Oldie could remember his father giving Jim, for Christmas he supposed, a book about the Kruger National Park in South Africa. The old fellow was delighted, studying the map on the endpapers and the black and white photographs inserted throughout the text. Material from that book no doubt found its way into his stories. It may have been where he picked up the word "kraal". For a while there a lot of his stories had kraals in them. Jim was always good on generating a sense of place, of explaining the lie of the land as it were.

With his emphasis on truth, Jim explained that tigers were not native outside India and, more vaguely, Asia. He was most emphatic that they were not found in Australia. Nothing to worry about there. But then, opening a crack of doubt, not all of Jim's tiger stories were set in India. The boy had been mightily impressed by one about a tiger that escaped from an American circus when a train was derailed in the Rocky Mountains. That tiger led its trackers a merry chase across hundreds of miles before it was mortally wounded in a terrible fight with a grizzly bear. The tiger killed the bear but she (the most dangerous wild animals were always females) suffered a nasty gash on the shoulder, which turned septic (no mercurochrome) and left her so weak she could hardly walk. In those circumstances it was only a matter of time before the hunter and his Indian tracker caught up and cornered the half-crazed animal on a cliff high above a raging mountain torrent. Tigers do not give up, and she still had enough power and determination to charge the hunter and his Indian tracker on their horses. The pack-horses were so badly frightened that one of them broke its lead and fell off the cliff into the river below where it disappeared and was never seen again. With their lever-action, high-power repeating rifles, the hunter and the Indian fired repeatedly into the maddened, rushing tiger. It dropped dead right at the feet of the hunter's horse, which had been trained not to flinch — and of course didn't.

True story.

Jim was reliable, but when it came down to choices the kid knew that Peggy was sure as eggs right about Stella. Any woman who used perfume that strong had to be suspect.

He probably never again trusted another soul as completely as he did Peggy. He believed what she told him. One wet night after witnessing the heart-racing spectacle of a house fire further up Cameron Street, and worried as to how a house could catch fire and burn so quickly in the rain, he asked Peggy about the possibility of her house doing the same. Tucking him into her big bed, she explained that the fire had been caused by faulty electrical wiring, but the man had come and looked at her house's wiring just a little while ago and he told her it was as good as new. Besides, her house was painted with a special paint that didn't burn, a paint that actually stopped fires. It cost a bit more and some people couldn't afford to use it, but Jim knew a man in the paint business who gave him a good price. She said it with such perfect off-handedness that he fell asleep in absolute peace of mind.

He believed her, but sometimes he wasn't quite sure he understood her. Peggy had once intrigued his young mind by confiding that she wondered what the people in her dreams thought of her. "You do such silly things in your dreams," she said.

So why was it that now, almost three decades after her death, she woke him with a call to be careful?

As he had done almost sixty years before, Oldie lay still and listened to the doves in the cool of the morning. He knew it wasn't a good idea to put too much store by dreams, but her voice had been so startlingly clear, loud enough to wake him and immediately recognized.

It was Saturday and he had turned off the clock alarm. Even so, the Girl would soon wake, make their breakfast and get into the weekend newspapers. They did not take the papers during the week, and she did not miss them, although if he brought one home and left it on the table she was soon engrossed — she just couldn't help herself. Weekend papers and their numerous supplements were her indulgence. And now *The West*

Australian, The Weekend Australian and *The Financial Review,* all tightly rolled in cling wrap, were ready and waiting on the front lawn.

His Saturday breakfast never varied: a dessert spoon of psyllium husk mixed with yoghurt followed by fish oil capsules and vitamin B tablets washed down by cranberry juice followed by toast and jam with good strong heavily sugared coffee. During the week the toast and jam were replaced by rolled oats and prunes, regardless of season.

"The older I get," the Girl said for no apparent reason, "the more I appreciate the importance of routine. It's a useful discipline."

The remark went straight over his head. After checking the cartoons, book reviews and the posh real estate pages, he told her he would be working that morning and took himself and his second cup of coffee off to his room.

Sid Wedge had sent him another manuscript. Oldie scrolled through it, a memoir of a Latvian immigrant boy growing up in the golden weather of Perth in the nineteen-fifties. He randomly looked at a couple of sentences here and there, wanting to know if the man's words made sense in themselves. The book had twenty chapters. He read the opening paragraphs of seven of them, then the closing lines of the preceding ones. Back to front, back and forth, he hefted the weight. Eyes half closed, he gauged the texture with his finger tips. There were about ten good photographs — enough. One was a humdinger for the front cover.

Finally, he printed the third chapter and set to work with a bright red pen.

An hour later he knew what he was up against.

He would phone the old fellow to ascertain just how amenable he would be in negotiating the obstacle course of turning a manuscript into a book and getting it into print. Then, if all seemed hunky-dory, he would give a quote for his services. He had already discovered the old fellow was well-heeled.

It was work. And it could, without too much insult to his intelligence and injury to his soul, be handled routinely. Like knitting.

Unlike the reviewing of books.

One day he might get around to writing an essay on the detrimental effects of prolonged book reviewing. It is one of those activities in which there is a constant pull toward the routine, the formulaic; and the real discipline of the craft is in resisting that pull. But no matter how you try, in the end the job erodes the raw, elemental pleasure of reading. Oldie had written about 250 reviews over a decade and a half and it had cost him. How much, he would never really know. Financially, it hadn't come within coo-ee of paying for his time and knowledge. And then, in the small town of Perth, even a half honest review sure as hell didn't win many friends. He knew all that before he started, but he was surprised and deeply dismayed to discover just how many people could turn really fucking nasty really fucking quick over even the mildest criticisms of books that should never have been published. The wound was one that had not healed with time.

Oldie came to Sid Wedge's attention when he gave one of his publications a bollocking in *The West Australian*. Sid immediately threatened to shoot him with his recently acquired antique Colt Navy cap and ball revolver, but about a year later he approached Oldie in the SRO reading room, told him he had been right about that particular book and offered his hand. It was the start of a lively personal and professional association.

Sid had been known (once in a blue moon) to foot the

editorial bill, but he usually got the client to deal directly with Oldie as a freelance consultant. He enjoyed working with Wedgie, most of the time. Decisions were quick, clean and generally right — and there was always a whiff of helter-skelter and sheer bloody ratbaggery about their collaboration.

Apart from cleaning up manuscripts, Oldie wrote the blurbs and press releases, liaised with the typesetter, designer and publisher. He always made it clear from the start that he was not a publicist, although for the right client he would offer, for what it was worth (not much, usually), an introduction to a couple of newspaper review editors he still knew. He slugged away for bugger all, but he liked the work and he was good at it.

Or he had been.

Lately there had been a couple of embarrassing slips. Stupid, obvious things he would have once spotted immediately. Now they were being brought to his attention by the typesetter.

He was tired. His eyesight, memory and concentration were not what they used to be. He suspected the deterioration of his eyes had something to do with his fading mental powers. Whatever the physiological basis, the result was that his interest in the wider world had narrowed, lessened. There was only so much with which he could be bothered. Aging: the balance between resistance and submission, rebellion and resignation.

But then, some days, it seemed more like his attention had shifted to other things, or that he was trying to somehow discover and focus on what was of ultimate value to him. The harder he looked, the bigger the puzzle. Things danced before his eyes.

Physical decline was an expected and clearly visible road, but mental decline — or, more precisely, cognitive deterioration — that had not been so clearly envisaged or anticipated. It frightened him. There's always another bend around the bend.

The phone rang late in the morning. Anna answered and Oldie heard her ask who was calling.

She met him in the passage. Holding the handset at arm's length, she whispered that it was Roger Kidd. She gave Oldie her best quick, bright smile, kissed his neck below his right ear and brought the phone around to hold it before his face. He hesitated. Still smiling, she tilted her head, quizzical. He looked into her eyes but didn't smile back as he took the phone from her.

"Roger. Old chap. What can I for you do?"

Roger let out a dry cackle before, in a level, businesslike voice, said he assumed Oldie had something for him, otherwise why had he called at his place at, ah, 1:07 pm yesterday. The precision of the time and the short pause before he gave it let Oldie know Roger had a security tape.

"What kind of dog is that you've got down there?"

"A Rottie. Name's Tyson."

"As in Mike?"

"Yeah. That'd be the one. Look, mate … sorry, I would have warned you if I knew you were coming. You know, baked a cake and all that."

"You seem to be very security conscious."

"Can't be too careful these days."

Be careful, Son.

There was a moment's wait before Roger resumed. "Well, like I said, I'm really sorry old Tyson gave you, ah, a bit of a start. Come down again and I'll introduce you. He's not as bad as he sounds. He'd only ever have a go at someone who broke in or, you know, actually laid hands on me. Had him a long time. Brought him

67

back from Queensland. His bark's worse than his bite, as they say." He forced a laugh at once deprecating and apologetic. "So, anyway, what brought you to my neck of the woods?"

"Spur of the moment thing. Just happened to be in the vicinity." Oldie let a beat pass before adding, "Just thought I'd see how far you'd got with that Nibbelup landfill business. I'm assuming those cheerful souls at the SRO have not been as useful or helpful as you would have wished."

"Oh, I'm sure they would if they could. But yes, the place does seem to be a bit disorganized. Understaffed and underfunded, like everywhere these days. I'm told they don't have sufficient space. Stuffed in more ways than one!"

"And you reckon that's why files are missing?"

"Well ... could be. Could be. People could take pages out. But, on the other hand," he laughed, "you could, if you needed to, even put something in! Think about that for a lark! Anything's possible."

Which is why, Oldie thought, you'd like to be a little more certain about what was there when I looked ten years ago. And I no longer remember.

He was about to say as much when Roger cut in and, pronouncing his words clearly, said, "Interesting tactic, what? Leaving stuff in the archives. Sort of like, you know, the living using the dead as ventriloquists' dummies. Not that uncommon, one way or the other, when you think about it. You could argue that's the basic methodology of any costume drama you see on the tellie. And, listen," he rushed on, "I really am writing this all up as a novel."

"I never said you weren't."

"No, you didn't. But you thought it. Come on, old son, you thought there's gotta be more to this than some old bugger having a belated crack at the literary masterpiece he should have, would have written thirty of forty years ago if he really had it in him. Listen, *I'd* be thinking that if someone else came to me with such a yarn. I understand your caution. *I'd* be cautious."

Both men let the following silence fill itself out toward something like a standoff.

"So," Oldie said at last, "how, um, far ..."

"You know, it's interesting, how when you get into the thing, you sort of get carried away. Pretty soon you find it takes you into stuff you may not have expected to, um, deal with. You have to think about things you didn't expect to think about. Questions arise. Do I stay on one track or can I explore some of the side roads? And," he laughed, "which is which, anyway?"

"I thought you were more or less relating events as you'd witnessed them."

"I was. I am. But ... listen, Alex, excuse my inherent paranoia, but some things are probably best discussed in person. Like I said ... can't be too careful. What say I return the visit and I take you to lunch at Hillarys? Some place at the boat harbor. You choose, but I'd rather not do anything involving chopsticks. As Spike Milligan said, chopsticks are one of the reasons the Chinese never invented custard."

Oldie laughed. "I've not heard that one before."

"That's because I just made it up. Anyway ... we didn't have a chance to catch up properly at Paulo's funeral. Too busy checking out the talent."

They agreed to meet by the Lang Hancock memorial at the Hillarys Boat Harbor tourist mall the following Tuesday, exchanged email addresses and were just about to hang up when Oldie said, "By the way, I called in at your local supermarket after I left your place and who should I see ..."

He checked himself. Anna was listening to him as she read her newspapers.

"Who did you see?" Roger's voice flattened with a sudden wariness that startled the Old Man. Later, he would remember how Roger sounded then.

"Well ... you know, the party ... at the funeral."

"The party at the funeral ..." Roger repeated, then sniggered as the penny dropped. "Did you speak to her?"

"No. No, I didn't. There wasn't an opportunity."

"Is that right?" Jolly had recovered enough to be fairly giggling. "Well, what can I say? As just another in the long line of men who reckon their wives don't understand them — what can I say? Yes, she's in my neighborhood. And you reckon you saw her first! But I'll tell ya for free, her name is Carol. Carol Dubois. She's Canadian. Used to be a model, mate — what d'ya reckon? — a fucking model! Sort of posh, but not put on, if you know what I mean. Good breeding, as they used to say. Lucky old Ted found her in London three or four years back. She and he have some sort of small video production outfit — mostly online promotional stuff by the sound of it, but looking to get into something bigger. She's in her mid-thirties, whereas good old Teddy's quite a catch at a mere fifty-three. I suppose it is a question — well, let's be frank, a fucking mystery — about why she followed him to this particular god-forsaken end of the earth. People always have their reasons."

"Whoa, Roger! What have you been up to? How do you know all this?"

"Ha, ha, still waters run deep, don't cha know."

"Have you spoken?"

"Listen, I'll tell you all about it over lunch. I'll just say this, there are people out there who derive great pleasure in secretly blighting the lives of others."

"That's a pretty, um, stark view of the world."

"Too right! And here's another tip: Watch out for the prissy ones — the natty dressers — they're the worst, the sneakiest. There, that should whet your appetite. And here's another thing Spike said: Sex goes; memory goes; but the memory of sex — that never goes. But, listen, duty calls, I'd better go. See you Tuesday. Remember, it'll be my shout. Seriously, I mean it, I'm kinda cashed up and feeling lucky at the moment. Long lunch. Catch up properly. Plan a bit of sabotage and ... whatever. So, see you about twelvish."

And he hung up.

"Well bugger me!" the Old Man breathed into the buzzing handpiece. "Runs deep right enough ... but hardly still."

Anna looked up as he put back the phone. "That all sounds a bit cloak and dagger."

"Hmm."

"The party at the funeral," she said, making air quotes with her index fingers.

The clumsy gesture annoyed him. More than it should have.

"Ah, look," he drawled, not quite disguising a sudden surge of testiness as he moved to leave the room, "I don't know what Roger's up to. He said, 'Still waters run deep'. Is that cryptic enough for you? I can only wait for all to be revealed when he takes me for a feed at Hillarys next Tuesday."

"A business lunch! Half your luck!"

"Yeah," he relaxed a little, "might be quite pleasant."

"Don't let him make you drink!"

"You know I can handle that sort of situation," he snapped back at her, then abruptly stalked off up the passage towards his room.

The Girl pulled a long face at Max, who, from the comfort of the sofa, had observed all that passed.

"What do you reckon?" she asked him, privately.

Maxie gave her his slowest, cat's whisker-short-of-a-yawn blink and looked away. Dismissing the matter. Losing interest fast. People!

There are credible theories as to why some things are remembered but not others. There were explanations to be had — Oldie had read and sort of understood them — but it nevertheless worried him that he could not remember the name of that girl in the woodshed at Helen Boyd's birthday party. His first sexual kiss, and he couldn't recall her name. He was not even sure he would recognise it if he heard it, but he did remember and was quite sure she was Helen's cousin, a tall, clean-limbed country girl who came to school by bus and so was not normally seen about the town after school or on the weekends. He must have been fourteen going on fifteen, and she was the next year up in school. It was after dark and about a dozen kids were playing hidey in the bushes and sheds and shadows of the Boyds' backyard. He and Norman Grey got into the pungent darkness of the woodshed with her, put their backs to the door and took turns tongue kissing her. She and Norman started it and he took his turn. Other than being excited, he didn't quite know what to make of it, but later, out in the yard with the others, having supper (cake and coke) and pretending nothing had happened, he looked at her and wanted to do it again. It never happened. She had moved on.

Now, even if she was still alive, the girl that she was, was long gone. Would the old woman using her shopping trolley as a Zimmer frame even remember those rushed embraces with a gangly boy who moved away later that year? Anything could have happened to that girl and he would never know. It would be a mind-boggling, zillion to one fluke for him to discover who

72

she was and what became of her. He supposed the only way was to find Helen Boyd, and ask her. To go back to that country town and ask around. Apart from the fact that there was no real point to the exercise, it was a task about as fraught as discovering whoever it was that *may have* taken kickbacks to allow dumping of nasty shit into landfills around Perth back in the early sixties. Which, as it happened, was about the time those Brylcreemed lads were learning the business in the woodshed.

Still, he couldn't quite leave it alone. Why was it that he could remember Helen and Norman's names, but not that girl's? He remembered her, what she looked like, her manner, but not her name. He'd known it once, he knew that. Known it for years, but not any more. The first girl he had ever kissed. You weren't supposed to forget such names.

There's only one first. There was only one Yuri Gagarin.

Now, the world was stuck, grinding itself down. He had become accident prone, a tottering old fool, dropping things, bumping into things. Always so damned tired — ageing is a process of energy declining as mass increases.

Oh, for a bit of lead in the old pencil, some heat in the meat.

It was Sid Wedge who told Oldie that Roger Kidd had been found dead.

The publisher phoned around midday on the Wednesday to discuss what Oldie wanted to do about the old Latvian's manuscript. After getting that business out of the way they settled into one of their regular rambles around whatever happened to be on their minds. They were both seriously into gossip.

For no other reason than for something to say Oldie mentioned that he had been stood up by Roger and asked Sid if he knew him.

"Lives in Mozzie Park? Been in Queensland? Recently divorced?"

"That's him. You know him?"

"Only by repute. My mate Don Kenna knew him and … I was talking to Don about an hour or so ago. Anyway, sorry to have to be the one to tell you this, but the reason he didn't turn up is because he's gone and topped himself."

Oldie opened his mouth, but no sound came.

"Alex? You still there?"

He found an affirmation and forced it out.

"They found him late yesterday afternoon," Sid went on rapidly. "The neighbors heard the dog barking, been at it all day. So the cops went round, looked through the windows, broke in and found him. They're not yet saying officially how or where exactly he did it, but it was a hanging. Don heard it from the ex-missus. So … how well did you say you knew him?"

At first he answered Sid's questions briefly, awkwardly, but gradually he found his voice and was soon prattling on about his dealings with Roger in considerable detail. Before he knew it he had told the publisher all about Nibbelup, the old hazardous waste tip, the suspicion that files were missing from the SRO, Oldie's belief that Roger was interested in something more substantial than just writing some damned pissant novel and the fact that he had emailed Roger and left several messages on his answering machine after the broken lunch date.

"If you left messages … I'm surprised you haven't had a visit from the cops. Early days, I guess, but I reckon they'll want to check you out. Do you reckon someone might have, you know, helped him along?"

"What…? How do you mean?"

Even those acquaintances who, in hindsight of course, claim to have had an inkling that some soul was "at risk"

74

are profoundly jolted by suicide. It cannot be undone and the breezy courtesies and civilities of daily doings are revealed to have been but a brittle, thin veneer. In seeking explanations people consider the possibilities of terminal illnesses, total financial failure or perhaps even imminent public exposure and disgrace. It was just like Wedgie to reach for the most extreme possibility before anyone else thought it let alone dared voice it.

Oldie was still floundering about, seeking a footing in the churn and wash released by the news of Roger's death. He was too preoccupied and bothered to properly take in and react to Sid's off the map suggestion. "Murdered!? Nah ... that dog ... I mean, he'd eat anyone who even looked like raising a hand to Roger."

"Not if it was locked outside in the backyard — which it was. That's what alerted the neighbors. The dog was usually in the house and had a pet flap to come and go as he liked. But that must have been blocked or locked."

"Look, apart from the dog, I'm pretty sure there was at least one security camera that worked around the place."

"Well, OK, I dunno, I'm just asking. You're probably right. As of when the ex-missus spoke to Don no note had been found. I guess the cops will look at what's on his computer. Maybe they'll do that before they talk to you. Mind you, the way our Plods do things — not exactly known for barking up the right tree, let alone finding their way to the right neck of the woods. How much are you going to tell them?"

"Well ... I suppose it depends on what they ask."

"That's right. See what they have to say. Don't lie to them, but if they don't ask, keep out of it."

"Look, Sid, this is a bloody nasty shock. It's all a bit too sudden and I need to think it through, to gather my thoughts sort of thing. I'll give you a call when I've got my head around it." He was about to say Goodbye and hang up when he added, "Maybe it'd be better if you didn't say anything to anyone about, you know, the possibility."

"So you think it is a possibility?"

"No ... not exactly. Um. Look, I just think we should find out more before we ... speculate."

Although Sid readily agreed, as he returned the phone to its stand Oldie had the feeling the hares would be running all over the paddock before the day was done.

"Roger would have put his dog out himself," he said aloud. And completed the thought that had Tyson been locked in the house with Roger's body the cops would have had to shoot him to gain entry. Roger would have thought of that. Wouldn't he? He must have. Obviously, he did.

The alternative didn't make sense.

But then, half an hour later, it sort of did. Roger had said he was flush and he sounded up. He said he was feeling lucky. And three days later he goes and hangs himself?

But then, moods swing, unexpected news arrives ... people are impulsive.

He found himself looking out the window, waiting for a police car to quietly pull up. The thought struck him that if cops did happen to be at the house when the Girl arrived home from school she would panic. Ever since they turned up at the front door the evening Jem was killed, a police car parked outside someone's home always ran a ripple across her pool of grief. If they were outside when she got home she would be afraid that someone else had been rawly plucked from this world.

Her fear would be for Daniel. His latest email, received two days ago, had been from some place far from the tree named Livingston, Montana, where "they" had taken a cash job sorting out the IT at a medical clinic. Winter had taken hold and as soon as the present job was finished "they" intended heading for Mexico.

They? Mexico? Better not to dwell on such vague information.

But the cops did not turn up. Not that afternoon and not in the days that followed. When they had not shown themselves by the weekend Oldie concluded that Roger's death was not regarded as suspicious or worthy of even a perfunctory investigation.

Roger's sudden death was, however, a troubling mystery to him. What was it Roger said at Paulo's funeral? Something about them being dirty old men, relegated to the sidelines, coming up to the drop zone. He knew that dreary feeling of being finished — of being finished *with* — of never being anything more than he already was. Written off. It was a knowledge they shared.

But then, the last time he spoke to him, Roger didn't sound as though he thought he was finished. He had *un*finished business. He was doing things. He said he was cashed up. He sounded cheerful. Feeling lucky. And even if it was in some degree just an excuse to get together and chew the fat, there had been something Roger wanted to talk about. There had been something. Something he didn't want to discuss on the phone. *Can't be too careful.*

Whatever which-way Oldie turned it, Roger's suicide didn't quite make sense.

When he and the Girl discussed the matter that night she reminded him of the brother of a friend who, about twenty years earlier, had hanged himself with a tie in his walk-in wardrobe. The fellow's older brother, a businessman facing bankruptcy and possibly criminal charges, had hanged himself a few weeks earlier and it was said that, in trying to understand his brother's act, he was just sort of trying it out. He and his wife had had a few drinks. She'd gone sleepy-byes and heard nothing.

Misadventure.

Playing around with hanging is far more dangerous than many people realise. Once the blood flow is cut and the person passes out, their body weight will do the rest. You don't actually need a big drop. You can hang yourself from a door knob. People do that.

"But once someone's so far gone as to be mucking about like that," she said, "they're pretty well there. Aren't they? It's just a matter of time."

"I suppose. But we don't know what it was with Roger. It could have been anything."

"Or practically nothing."

"Perhaps he just couldn't face the circus of another god-damned Christmas!"

He was trying to make a joke, but she did not smile. Most of their friends and family preferred to believe his loudly professed loathing of the festive season was an affectation. She knew it wasn't.

He did not mention the sinister kite Sid Wedge had flown.

V

By nine o'clock the temperature was already nudging thirty-eight and the sky was an exhausted pale blue. The mighty sun smote and glanced off the sea as from a lead mirror. A steady north-easterly pushed fires along somewhere back in the hills, grey hazing the horizon with smoke. Before the day was over the wind would pick up and homes would be lost.

Far out to sea a three-masted barquentine stood in full sail, a hallucinatory shimmer in the morning glare. Oldie thought about how, out there in the offing where the big sharks cruise and the deep water begins, the land's parched breath had been cooled to a refreshing breeze leisurely luffing the sails and caressing the tanned limbs of the vessel's healthy young crew. He thought of how at day's end a young man would taste the salt on the lips, the breasts, the buttocks and inner thighs of a perfectly formed and aroused young woman. Until quite recently such erotic daydreaming would have afforded him a few minutes of drowsy pleasure, but now it gave way to a blunt pang as his head filled with the sound of old George Burns crooning Sonny Throckmorton's "I wish I was eighteen again, and going where I've never been."

It pissed him off to be choked up by such sentimentality, but in his condition he was vulnerable and just had to cop it.

Decades ago, Oldie's synapses hard-wired those lyrics to memories of riding all night in the cab of a truck up through Central Australia, up The Track from dinner at the Tennant Creek Hotel to an early breakfast at a Katherine service station. The air was so clear the stars on the horizon blazed as bright as those in the zenith. In those hundreds of more or less straight miles they saw only a few other night travellers, a couple of trucks and cars coming south. He and the driver could pick out the glow and then the gleam of an on-coming vehicle's lights when it was yet ten to twelve miles out. That was in January 1969 when, although actually already twenty, he was still just a kid on the run and going to Darwin — somewhere he'd never been. Funny thing, the song didn't come out until at least a decade after he made that all-night journey north.

He met the Girl in Darwin. She and her friend shared a room in the house next door in McMinn Street, a row of old fibro houses later blown to Kingdom Come the night Tracy came to town. He had a flash — the Public Bar of the Darwin Hotel, the most popular disc on the jukebox was Eric Burdon and the Animals thumping out *We've Gotta Get out of this Place*. Chances were a big table of a dozen or more over-landing hippies, stuck in Darwin while they earned some bread, would be raising their glasses to roar out the chorus line: *If it's the last thing we ever do!* He knew he had that one right. No crossed wires in that memory.

He'd been back to Darwin in the mid-eighties, for a month at the end of the Dry. It had been an interesting but melancholy adventure. He had not been back since. That reluctance to disturb, to compromise his memories was one reason he had never gone back to New Zealand. And although it was not the primary reason he had not visited his mother in Victoria for a decade and a half, he told himself, by way of excuse, that it played a part.

The snide voice of a Federal politician assiduously selling away his own and the nation's soul as he crapped on about asylum seekers cut across Oldie's reverie. He changed Betty's radio to the Classic FM station and landed in the middle of some lush orchestral romp. The sort of stuff his friend Champagne Richard, with delicate condescension, referred to as film and circus music. For now, in this moment, it would do.

Oldie knew Roger's parents were dead, and gathered from the death notices that the memorial service was being arranged by the only surviving sibling, a sister. Sid Wedge came up with the information that Roger's ashes were to be placed in the grave of a brother who died young, which was why the service was to be at Fremantle. Apart from wanting to see who turned up, Oldie was curious to observe how the salient fact of Roger's "voluntary death" was handled. He guessed the tactic would be to proceed as though the deceased had died in an accident. A life cut tragically short, and so on. On the strength of his limited acquaintance with the man he reckoned that line would not have met with Roger's approval. But there you go — funerals are for the living.

He had hummed and har-ed, hemmed and hawed all week over whether or not to attend the service. At bottom he never doubted he would, but it was in his nature to just have to be seen to be going through the motions of hemming and hawing. Why keep it simple? Anna saw through his gammon and showed her impatience by pricking him with the thought that he seemed to be developing a morbid fixation with funerals. To her further exasperation he readily admitted to the charge, claiming that in his circumstances this was entirely natural. After a murmured quibble over the use of the word "entirely" she let the matter drop.

Sid Wedge did not re-visit his foul play scenario, but

did express open suspicion about the police failing to contact Oldie. "It makes you wonder," he said slowly, almost as though speaking to himself, "what's behind it." The publisher was a notorious conspiracy theorist and Oldie, thinking he was facing the prospect of that magic moment when the pattern in the carpet would reveal its *true* significance, swallowed and changed the subject. One cannot solve a mystery by invoking something that is even more incomprehensible.

It was because he took it as seriously as he did that Oldie refused to enter into speculation with others about what had happened to Roger. Apart from anything else, it was premature. It was the way of things, he believed, that if anything was to come to light it would not be until after some of that proverbial water had flowed under the bridge and people's attention had wandered elsewhere. But it was a big IF and so, in the meantime, he would go to the funeral and see who else made their appearance. He believed Roger would not have begrudged him the entertainment.

Coming through City Beach he turned the air-con up another notch. He looked at the clock and realized he would be lucky to arrive at the cemetery before start time. It would be a close run thing and he wasn't sure what parking was like near the crematorium. He seemed to have got himself mixed up in some sort of convoy of container trucks heading for the port. The bastards were hogging both lanes at the Oceanic Drive lights. The Old Man looked at the huge wheels less than a metre from Betty's side and felt vulnerable. In broad daylight the driver could see he was there, but in a rainy twilight with lights reflecting off all sorts of surfaces, the peril increased.

Especially for a kid on a motorbike racing to see the love of his life.

Just ask G Block. It handles a lot of those who die on Perth's roads; or beside them, in those waiting gutters. G Block is more than willing to tell you all about the perils of the road. Yes, it knows a thing or two. It can give you a comprehensive list of workplace hazards. And, were it to really stir itself and have a rummage around the office, it could come up with a cleverly illustrated, multi-lingual pamphlet detailing the lurking risks and menacing possibilities to be found in and around the average family home.

Of course, there are dangers less tangible. There are matters on which G Block (apart from the occasional sly wink) maintains a complicit silence; matters too diffuse to be defined beyond a heading such as Causes of Self Harm. The diagnosis Depressive Illness is all very well, but it cannot tell others that the decision of a new neighbour to cut down all the trees on his property in order to install a swimming pool may prove fatal to the quiet, seemingly cheerful old bloke who had lived in the shelter of those trees for decades. Or it might have been no more than that year the shopping malls were hammering the Christmas carols an extra week too early.

Truth is, Oldie had been telling those who asked, he did not know Roger Kidd very well. Not really. And should anyone inquire, he would add that he did not know what Roger had been working on when he died. It would be the old "Sorry, mate, no idea" routine.

Should anyone actually mention Nibbelup, he'd play it with a straight face if not quite a straight bat. "Hell's bells, that was ten years ago. Why do you ask?"

In the eight days since Roger's death, the Old Man had been elsewhere, beavering away on the old Latvian's book, a well written, interesting story revealing a rather dark family secret. A generation ago one of the major publishers would have given it a go, but now, despite (or perhaps because of) all the official prate about multiculturalism, books about post-war migration struggle to find a market. Those directly involved were too old to do much reading beyond their newspapers while their children, although not exactly uninterested, had other concerns. All the same, Oldie and Sid Wedge agreed it would be worthwhile getting the manuscript into print. Somewhere down the track it would play its small part in distilling a fuller and more accurate historical record.

Not bad, not too bad at all, and it paid the bills.

Or, to be honest about matters financial, it paid some of the bills. Without his wife's income the Old Man would have been destitute, on the street, as his mother had constantly predicted throughout his tiresome adolescence. She had told him, many times, he would end up in the gutter. He took no consolation from the fact that his mother's age gave her a dated image of gutters, but he did wryly note how few real gutters remain in our towns and cities. Gutters of the kind that drunks fell into and where they occasionally died have been replaced by plain curbing and underground storm water drains. He wondered whether that gutter in the town where he grew up was still there.

Regardless of the depth of gutters and their modern replacements, the Girl's salary paid the mortgage and put food on their table. He was, officially, her dependant and, what's more, a mighty big eater. She shouldered the burden without rancour and even left him, a dyed-in-the-wool spender, to handle the household budget.

Which, all things considered, in his opinion, he did well enough. He did all the shopping and he did the cooking.

She did the dishes.

Sometimes his clear luck made him uneasy.

He wondered if it was all just too good to be true. The financial dependency undoubtedly fostered a physiological one — he knew which side his bread was buttered on — but he had learned to push his qualms aside, to draw a breath, get on with it and worry about the morrow when it came. Beyond making sure he had the Lotto numbers in every week, there didn't seem to be a lot else a man in his situation could do. You can put your trust in faith all you like, but when the blow comes it'll be purely luck if it misses you. Miracles are for the weak-minded and the faint-hearted. The meek and the mild.

He had about as much of a head for business as he had an aptitude for things mechanical: Fuck all. He had tried, for years, to drum up paying work. It was a bloody hopeless undertaking because, apart from everyone being an editor or researcher these days, such skills as he had were not much valued or appreciated in the Golden West or, as far as he could tell, anywhere else in the Great Southern Land.

Not in the times in which he lived.

Despite such disregard, he was absolutely certain, to the extent he was indeed a social misfit, that it was society rather than him that had made the wrong call. His confidence in his abilities rested upon that most reliable of foundations — a plain understanding of his own secret limits. That, and a willingness to do the hard slog of attending to the details, meant that those who trusted his judgment got their meagre money's worth.

Not that they always saw that or were prepared to admit it even when they did.

His critical faculties were as strong as a hammer and, as Stan the Man observed, the man with a hammer sees nails everywhere. The odd thing was that, while this trait was primarily inimical to social success, it didn't exactly get him much business either. What couldn't be overcome was the simple fact that he was one of those unsettling smartarses who, too often, turn out to be right; to have, behind the glib wit, nodded towards some truth no less uncomfortable for not having been said openly. It is just a matter of arithmetic that smartarses who don't suffer fools gladly inevitably piss off many more of their fellow citizens than is good for them.

As far as doing something else, like night filling at Woolworths or whatever else the Certified Yobs at Social Security (or whatever it is called these days) deemed a real job, he was now well beyond anything involving regular hours and more than an ounce of physical exertion. Too old, too fat and altogether too damned pig-headed. He was not about to entertain notions of a new career as a cleaner. No one would get their monies' worth. Beyond that, as soon as he mentioned he had hepatitis C most employers would start looking for an excuse to let him go. He might as well tell them he had AIDS or leprosy.

Regardless, Anna Girl still loved him. If he sometimes pinched himself about that, it was a bedrock given, over which others shook their heads and asked what it was that she saw in him. Of course they had not known him when he was young and brilliant and had a bright future.

Not that he would ever concede he gave or had ever given the smallest dob of steaming shit about what people thought.

So, he asked in his Betty-borne reverie, had the end of Roger's marriage anything to do with his death? Almost certainly not directly. But perhaps in some private, tangential way? What crimes of the heart had been in the mix? It was unlikely anyone would ever know. Not even Roger's ex.

Oldie reached for the former Mrs Kidd's name and

couldn't find it. He must have seen it in the death notices. He had the feeling he may have briefly spoken to her on the phone all those years ago when he and Roger worked together. He drove through Cottesloe, eyes narrowed, hyperventilating in an effort to remember.

He stared at the blank but nothing flickered.

Yes, the public truth of it was that Oldie had not known Roger Kidd very well.

And yet, he did know *something* of Roger. They had not just crossed paths, a connection had been made. Although Oldie had been a bit leery of the bloke to start with, he had somehow warmed to him. While most of Oldie's childish generation hurtled headlong toward senility, Roger seemed to have learnt something. Oldie had been looking forward to their lunch. Two old bastards past caring, they could have shared a few hours of simple bonhomie, gossip, frank revelations and tall stories with a dash of the good ol' plottin'n'schemin'. To be entirely honest, he had even been looking forward to clarifying Roger's real interest in the secret history of Nibbelup.

One thing he did know. Had things gone the other way, good old Jolly would have turned up at his funeral. He'd have been there to make up the numbers and see the show.

Driving through Cottesloe he passed the spot Mike K once pointed out as the site of the heartbreak of his life. There had not been any nonsense songs at Mike's funeral. Steve Kakulas, stooped and ninety-five if he was a day, sang the responses to the priest, his fluttering voice lightly finding its way into every corner and roost of the Orthodox Church. Half an hour after the service ended and Oldie was going down William Street, there was Steve back in his grocery shop, behind the counter, white apron on, ready for business, the incarnation of the everyday dignity of routine and of knowing where everything belongs.

Sitting in the traffic on the lights at the East Fremantle end of the bridge, he looked back at the packed rows of pleasure craft ranked along both banks of the injured, sullen river. The fantasies, sentimental and otherwise, sustaining such a stubborn waste of resources are clearly very powerful. Mind boggling — as in boggled minds. The big glass houses, the flash cars, the useless boats, the aimless travel, the 1000-thread-count Egyptian cotton sheets and a hot shower twice a day — all the razzle-dazzle. How could it not end badly? They had already, and not just metaphorically, been caught with their pants down.

People seemed to think of life as a game of musical chairs and hoped they would have a seat when the music stopped, but this Old Man, he plays for keeps. With a knick-knack, paddy whack, give a dog a bone, this Old Man ...

This Old Man, he liked having a gr-groan.

This Old Man, he wrote his own tombstone.

He had thought about asking Doctor Lou about a script for Happy Pills. Something to cheer himself up, to stop him from forgetting himself.

But Doctor Lou was not likely to give him anything without extracting a stack of Health Management concessions and promises. She'd go on about his weight, again. Now that would be depressing.

And his blood pressure. 161 over 87. Sitting still.

But then, just thinking about the damned fool neighbor and his never-ending renovations! Or that brainless young prick down on the corner thumping out industrial strength bass whenever he fucking felt like it.

So it goes, just another old bastard trying to bluff his doctor.

Well, so what? Fuck it, he thought in a shining bubble of clarity, when everything smells like overripe bananas, stale sweat and fresh brown shit, you have to clear a space, make room to feel you've retained some charge of your existence.

He arrived a few minutes late. The heat mugged him as soon as he opened Betty's door. It pressed and swaddled him, hindering his breathing. He took off his jacket and tossed it on the back seat. A hasty glance around the almost full car park behind the crematorium did not reveal any vehicles he knew. But then, most of the mourners had parked around the corner, near the entrance opposite the golf course. He noticed there was an above average contingent of rough and ready four-wheel-drives, several carrying out of town plates. Professional associates — always a sure way to make up the numbers.

It suited him to slip in at the back, to read the crowd from cover, checking out who was there. Should he wish, or need to, he could quickly make himself scarce afterwards. On the other hand, it would be useful to renew a few acquaintances in the archaeological and anthropological fraternities. You never know, a job or two may come from it, something to throw at all those inevitable dentists' and vets' bills. Not to mention the latest water bill, on which the decimal point had apparently been misplaced.

The West Chapel was full but not to overflowing. He could see the backs of the heads of those he took to be the sister and her supporters; and, seated across the aisle, the ex-wife (Fiona?) and the daughters. They sat still as statues with a couple of fidgety boyfriends (husbands?) in attendance. The bloke giving the vapid eulogy had known Roger since they were at university together. He anxiously droned out all the right things while avoiding the main event. Oldie's gaze drifted over the congregation and found Steve Lyons standing against the far wall, at the quick getaway position. Steve hadn't changed much in ten years: tasteful dark suit, not an exquisite silver hair out of place, as sleek and as affably pleased with himself as all get out. He looked like Fernando Rey in his suave prime. While those around him fanned themselves with the Order of Service (must get one of those), Steve was the picture of relaxed attention as the speaker stumbled through the minefield.

Suave. One of those old-fashion bloke things. Steve Lyons had nailed it. Oldie didn't even try. He saw all too often how most blokes who reach for *suave* just end up looking a goose. But Steve, you had to admit, did pull it off without effort — which, of course, is the only way to do it.

The very un-suave emcee/celebrant (Where *did* they find him?) waltzed out the usual banalities, the sister bravely attempted to impart some dignity by reading something from Proverbs about wisdom, and then one of the daughters started explaining to everyone just how good a Dad her father really was — but the sobs came, her face fell off the map and she had to be led away. It was fairly clear that this was not a funeral for which there had been any requests or directions left by the deceased. No *Requiem*. No rugby songs. No damned didgeridoo-doos.

There were two mobs of blackfellas, old men, seated three a piece on opposite sides of the aisle near the back of the chapel. Oldie didn't recognize any of them, but he could not get a good look at their faces. Maybe some of them had come over from Queensland. He would watch to see who spoke to them afterwards. Steve seemed to be alone. While the daughter was having her heartfelt say, someone moved in their seat and Oldie caught a glimpse of Ted Connell's rugged profile, seated in the middle of the pew two back from the family.

So Connell knew Roger well enough to come to his funeral. Who did Connell work for these days? Which Government Ministers did he have most to do with?

The last time Roger talked to Oldie he had reeled off quite a bit of stuff about Ted and Blondie, information apparently acquired from personal acquaintance. Yet at Paulo's funeral Blondie had walked right past Roger as though they were strangers. Probably was the case back then, but somewhere or the other, someone had since said Hello to someone.

Or so he surmised.

Oldie ran his eyes over the gathering once more. Blondie wasn't with Connell and she didn't seem to be anywhere else in the chapel. There was a fairly strong showing of middle-aged suits on their lonesome, men who had probably taken the morning off work. A few blotched faces seemed vaguely familiar, but apart from Steve Lyons there was no one he knew well enough to talk to. That's what happens when you don't use Facebook or Twitter. He wondered what Roger would have made of this lot. Past caring, as the Aged Care Professionals say.

Hail, hail, the gang's all here.
What the feck do we care,
What the feck do we care now?

If Roger Kidd's death was suicide, then Oldie understood the reason could be as ephemeral as a trick of the light, a rainbow as fatal to the man as those poisons that leave no trace. One of those things nobody else could quite see.

Consider the glittering shards of shattered memory. The large, obviously dangerous pieces can be found and, carefully, over time, gathered up and disposed of. But the tiny, barely visible splinters and specks are another matter. Scattered like broken glass across the floor of a life, they only become apparent when, even years later, a sudden pain pricks the soul and spots of bright blood bloom on feet and hands.

Above all, it was the timing of Roger's death that worried Oldie. It seemed petty, but they had an appointment, and Roger had broken it.

They emptied out of the chapel to some muzak rendition of *Abide with Me*. Didn't the band play that as the *Titanic* did the old slip beneath the waves routine? Oldie guessed the funeral director had been left to her own devices on that detail. All teed up, Sweetheart, just press Button B. At least Roger (or, at any rate, his memory) had been spared the indignity of some silly, maudlin ballad. Or, God help us and count your blessings, *Amazing Grace*. That was something, at least.

He stood aside and watched the condolence line softly shuffling through its paces. First stop was Roger's sister, then, at some distance, on to Fiona and the two daughters. The older women were pale but dry-eyed, the daughters flushed and teary. Steve Lyons, Mister Urbane, positively seized the hand of the daughter who addressed the gathering, held it between his big mitts and, with ineffable sincerity, looked into her eyes to assure her of something important. Something, Oldie imagined, along the lines that the lithe young woman and her sister should know their Uncle Steve considered it to be his duty and it would be a privilege … and so forth. Oldie inspected mother and daughters for family resemblances. The girls had their mother's willowy stature. They stood like her. Graceful. If there was something of Roger in them it was perhaps around the eyes. But you had to look for it. Once again, he found himself pondering the fascinating mysteries of genetics.

The two groups of blackfellas came down the line separately, keeping to themselves, and presented with quiet formality. One lot had an obvious minder, an anthropologist by the look of him, who paused and said a few words to the widow before shepherding his clients out the door. The second group stood together out of the way to take tea and a biscuit. Nobody approached them and they left as soon as they had finished their cuppa.

Oldie was a little dismayed at how few people he knew, but looking about he became aware that he was not the only solitary man of indeterminate age and occupation skulking around the edges of the room. There were four or five such unobtrusive observers. One beefy, neatly mustachioed bloke was ostensibly checking his phone for calls. It dawned on Oldie that a little exercise in surreptitious photography was going on over there. Damn it, what kind of devious, tacky bastard photographs people at a funeral?

A cop?

He looked like a cop. If Mister Mo was a cop … that wasn't good. Not good at all.

Hmm. This was definitely something to steer clear of.

Of course, looking like a cop didn't make him a cop. Or even, to be charitable, a bad man. But if he who wasn't necessarily a cop was nevertheless taking pictures, then that wasn't real good either. No bloody good at all.

Mister Mo was making like he was talking to someone on his phone, but his squinty eyes continued to flicker around the room, watching everyone in it. Oldie waited until he was looking the other way and then shifted his own position to be partly obscured behind a trio of middle-aged women taking their tea and bickies. As soon as Mo's gaze returned to where Oldie had been, he was hunting for him. When he did locate him a few seconds later Oldie met and held his eyes. That's right, Pal, he beamed across the room, you've been made.

"Got ya!" he said, for the plain pleasure of saying it aloud.

Even as Mo looked away and continued his phone conversation as though nothing had happened, the Old Man knew that drawing unnecessary attention to himself hadn't been the smartest thing to have done. Oh, well, so fucking what?

"Mister Johnson?"

He turned to face a largish, owlish woman in her early fifties who had appeared at his elbow. Black silk dress, paua shell brooch and a string of pearls. Classic blue rinse perm. She stared, unblinking, unsmiling, her head inclined to one side.

He was about to make a generic affirmative noise in his throat when he was grabbed by the shoulder and given a playful shake — Steve Lyons, glowing bonhomie at Oldie, at Owl-woman and at some startled joker just passing by. "Hoping to see you here, old boy," he said, then, in one smooth step, slicked past Oldie, extending his hand and introducing himself to the woman. Yes, being suave isn't just about dress sense.

Mrs Owl responded with matching aplomb, even conceding a brief, tight smile. Although she gave her name, Oldie didn't catch it and for the life of him wasn't inclined to ask her to repeat it.

She let go Steve's hand and, rotating her head on the axis of her solid shoulders, immediately fixed her attention back to her purpose. "Mister Johnson," she said, "Brenda would like a quick, private word." She inclined her head at the shortening queue attending Roger's sister. "Perhaps in a minute or so, when she has been freed up a little over there."

"Of course," he said, nodding as though he knew what it was all about.

She blinked at him with slow deliberation and, without another word, took herself off.

The two men watched her go before Steve turned to Oldie and said, "So ... bad business about Roger."

"Not good. Hmm, listen, I didn't catch that woman's name ..."

Steve puffed his cheeks and half shrugged. "I thought she said Sophie something. I thought you knew her. She seemed to know you."

"Never seen her before in my life! Friend of the family, apparently. But, look, while we're doing a spot of the old ID checking and who's who ... over my right shoulder ... against the wall, the bloke with the mo, blue shirt, on the phone ..."

Steve narrowed his eyes and peered where directed, but even after he had Oldie repeat the description he still gave a little frown and said he couldn't see the suspect. When Oldie finally turned to look for himself he saw that the man was gone. Nowhere in sight.

"Well, no matter," Oldie returned a lame grin to Steve's inquiring if bemused gaze. "How the Devil are you? Still in Adelaide? I heard you're now the Big Fisherman."

Steve did his decorous chuckle. "Well, not *that* big. I've shares in a mussel farm and I'm a minority shareholder in a southern bluefin tuna operation, down there off Port Lincoln. Think in terms of a feed lot — they catch the fish and fatten them. Feed them pilchards and formulated pellets, whatever they are," he laughed. "I leave the running to those who know what they're doing. I'm just a silent partner in a fishy business. Found my vocation! And, yes, still in Adelaide. In the Hills. I ... ah," he lowered his voice, "I came over here on business, family business, so I thought I'd, um, like to see poor old Roger off and, ah, pay my respects. I saw him and Fiona a few times in Brisbane, but … tell me, what's the story here? When did you last see him?"

"About a month or so ago. First time I'd seen him since we worked for you. Saw him at a funeral, as a matter of fact. Funny thing, I asked him what music he'd like played at his funeral. He said he'd like a dirty song, something from the Rugby Songbook." Oldie stared hard at Lyons. "Good old numbers like *Why was he born so beautiful*? Or *Arseholes are cheaper today*. Do you know those?"

"Can't say I do," said Lyons, a barely perceptible crema of embarrassment on his voice.

"No, me either. I had to look them up on the net." Oldie sighed. "I suppose he was joking. I guess we'll never know."

"Yes, a sudden death. It's most distressing, most upsetting. For those left to carry on. It really is," said Steve, his voice rebalanced to a glowing aura of perfectly modulated solace.

And before he knew it Oldie was spilling the beans, gabbling out the whole sorry business of Roger's proposed literary endeavour and how that was associated with an interest in the archival research related to the Nibbelup job they had all worked on all those years ago. He told how he and Roger had planned to meet for lunch. He said that the last thing Roger had said to him was that he was cashed up and feeling lucky, but at the point he was about to broach the possibility of something "suspicious", Uncle Steve's big paw firmly shepherded him out of earshot.

Oldie shut his mouth and damned near bit his tongue.

God Almighty, he was such a pitiful blabbermouth. Done to impress, it always had the opposite result.

And he knew it. Knew it, but more times than not just couldn't help himself. Pitiful.

From the other side of the room it looked as though Lyons was comforting a friend momentarily overwhelmed by a sudden burst of grief. It would have sounded that way, too, to anyone standing next to them. But Oldie's antennae quivered when Lyons wondered aloud, just a touch too offhandedly, what on earth could have interested Roger or anyone else about Nibbelup after all this time.

"Dunno," he muttered. "I deleted all that stuff years ago and have pretty well forgotten most of it. He didn't speak to you about it?"

"No. No he didn't do that. I wish he had. I'm intrigued ... but as I said, I've had no communication with Roger since he came back to Perth. When he said he was cashed up ... what, um, what do you think that was about?"

"Didn't say."

"Hmm. Yes, a sudden death. Always unanswered questions. Loose threads. And you see, unfortunately, now I'm pressed for time. Back to Adelaide tomorrow morning. But I'll be over here fairly regularly and we should keep in touch." Like a magician's trick, a business card materialized between the finger tips of Steve Lyons's extended hand. "Actually, do me a favour, seeing that I am indirectly associated with, ah, that I have something of a minor interest in this Nibbelup business, if something were to come up, I would appreciate it if you could keep me in the loop."

As Oldie squiggled his own email address (complete with diacritical marks) and phone number on a page torn from his notebook, Lyons asked him whether he supposed Roger's sister wanted to talk about the dead man's literary work.

"Dunno. Can't think what else."

Handing over his scrap of paper to Lyons, Oldie saw Ted Connell heading for the exit. The fucker winked at him. There was no doubt, Connell looked directly at him and winked.

The Old Man slipped the business card into his wallet without comment. If he was wondering what Connell was up to, he wasn't about to let Lyons know. "I better say my few words to Belinda," he said. "Let me know when you're in town again."

As they shook hands Lyons said, "Brenda."

"How's that?"

"Brenda," Lyons jutted his jaw at Roger's sister. "You just called her Belinda. Her name is Brenda."

"Oh. Yes. Thanks. That could have been ... ah, a whoopity-doo and a half."

Lyons gave Oldie an indulgent, beneficent smile, tapped him on top of the shoulder and applied a friendly squeeze before releasing his hand. Oh no, thought Oldie, turning away, not another bloody Freemason!

He mustered himself, went over and said all the right things to Brenda. She seemed like a nice woman, but he couldn't help thinking that her preternatural calm and too even voice had to be drug induced. She thanked him for coming and told Oldie that her brother had told her that he had been looking forward to working with him on his book. She wondered whether Roger's manuscript "stood a chance" of being published.

His confusion must have shown — Sophie the Owl-woman, standing stock still at Brenda's elbow arched her eyebrows. He saw now that her eyes were different colors. The left was dark brown and the right was hazel. She'd make anyone nervous. When he explained that he did not have and had not seen Roger's manuscript, and why this was so, Sophie took over Brenda's side of the conversation. "So you think it's still on his computer?"

"Well, I suppose ... either that or on some external hard drive. It must be." He stared back at the women. "Why wouldn't it be?"

"We were hoping you would know what the document was called," Sophie said.

"No. Sorry."

"We'll have another look," Sophie said to Brenda.

Brenda revived and once more thanked Oldie for coming to the funeral and for explaining things to her. He was being dismissed.

"You've not found it?" he ventured.

"Not yet, but we haven't looked properly. We don't know what he called it and there is a small tub thingy full of thumb drives. A friend of one of my nieces is going to, ah ..." Brenda gave him a helpless, lost look as her reply trailed off.

Something in the way Sophie pursed her lips warned Oldie not to persist. He was aware of a couple standing behind him, waiting to pay their respects. Drawing him away, Sophie asked if she could have a contact number. "In case something comes up."

He retrieved his tatty notebook from his hip pocket, tore out a page and scribbled his details. She dictated her mobile number and directed him to contact her, not Brenda, should anything turn up his end.

He thought he should say something to Roger's wife, but she had moved away. Steve Lyons was gone. As, apparently, had Mister Mo — the Man Who Never fucking Was. The crowd was thinning out. Time to split.

The air temperature outside the chapel was scorching, a full fifteen degrees hotter than inside. It was so hot he could hardly breathe. Like a furnace.

He winced as he glanced at the building the other side

of the Chapel. Oh, sweet beJesus! A damned sight hotter in there. Poor old Roger was probably being sent up the chimney right then. How long did it take? How did they keep everyone's ashes separate? Wonder how they deal with the smoke. Some kind of catalytic converter?

He had Betty's doors open and her motor running to rev up the air-con before he noticed the card under the windscreen wiper. He got out and plucked it free. A sloppy fountain pen scrawl, "Pls give me a bell. Best, Ted."

Well, well. Never a dull moment. How did Ted know Betty was Oldie's car?

He looked around. Nobody he recognized. The place was clearing out. He didn't manage to get hold of an Order of Service after all. If there was a wake, he wasn't invited.

As Buster Keaton once put it, "In the enemy's country — hopelessly lost, helplessly cold and horribly hungry." Except, of course, for the temperature ... but, yes, he was hungry, in a habitual, ambient sort of way.

He climbed into Betty, flicked on the Classic FM, turned up the air-con fan, belted up and buzzed off, heading for downtown Freo to buy himself a proper ice-cream.

To keep in form, he drove halfway down a tree-lined, suburban street, parked in someone's driveway, made a show of consulting his street directory for a couple of minutes, then reversed and went back the way he had come. As far as he could tell, he was not being followed.

But then, what would he know? He may have practiced tailing cars for a caper — detective work, it is addictive, isn't it? — but what did he know about, say, tiny tracking devices? Or whatever else was used these days to know who goes where? All he knew was from old movies, and the snoop profession had surely geared up since the days of *Stakeout*.

VI

Anal bleaching. Aye-*nal* bleaching. There it was, in black and white, on a large board hanging in a shop front at one of the mall's busiest intersections. Anal Bleaching: $159. Although printed in the same stylishly light sans serif lettering as the several dozen other items listed, it nevertheless sort of leapt out at you. Yes Ma'am, step right up, bend right over and we'll get down to business. *Arseholes are cheaper today*.

He had left the Girl at home reading through a folder of the latest batch of jargon soaked mumbo-jumbo, stuff she had to "assimilate and share" with her colleagues the following day at one of those Professional Development Days teachers are required to regularly endure. It was a bit rich having to cop a two-day seminar first week back after the summer holidays — at the very time when real work had to be done — but that's the way the gung-ho nitwit powers that be called it. He had muttered a few warming up remarks about the poison of academic poppycock but she brusquely let him know that another rave from him was not going to solve her problem. Not today. She was just going to have to read the drivel and get her head around it enough to bluff her way through. In the meantime, could he not (it would be a *really* big help) just leave her to get on with learning her lines. Thanks.

So he shrugged and took himself off to the big supermarket in the very big mall, to buy some fruit and veggies, to wander about practicing his ogling and attending to the seeing of what was what. And there it was — anal bleaching. Yes Sir-ree! Plain as the snuffling nose on your face. Advertised. For all the world to see.

He stood and he stared.

Who said there was nothing new under heaven? Clearly, the earth had turned on its axis. What would Yuri Gagarin have made of this?

Anal bleaching. He would have to look this one up on the internet, my word he would. But even if he didn't yet know what, precisely, it entailed, he had the basic idea. Had it in a flash. It was pretty well self-explanatory. But then, further down the list of Total Body Beauty's chic services, he saw — *vajazzling*, from $120.

Vajazzling?

He mouthed the word to himself but nothing surfaced.

He considered what that "from" indicated. Something variable, open-ended? Well, these days, it was all open-ended. An open slather.

Someone brushed by and he noticed the steady flow of people around him. He stepped back a few paces to move out of the traffic. A circa 40-year-old woman with too much makeup and one of those faux toffy accents walked slowly by, talking too loudly on her phone, "The finals! Oh, darling, that's wonderful ... Mummy is so proud ... yes, of course, darling, of course you can ring your father ... the *finals*! You *are* a champion! I love you!"

Oh dear, he thought, that can only end badly.

How many of these women streaming by knew what vajazzling was? The younger ones, those with tattoos across their exposed rumps and studs in their nostrils, they would probably know. Those pubescent girls working on their smirks, they would know. *Va*-jazzling. Something to do with *vaginas*? He mouthed that word to himself. He'd ask the Girl if she'd heard this term uttered over a cuppa in the staffroom. On second thoughts, perhaps it might be better just to go straight to Google, with SafeSearch clicked Off.

A social observation as an aside: In the English speaking world, there are very few young men (those born, say, since the fall of the Soviet Union) who have seen a full minge. Not with the naked eye, in the flesh, that is. Probably much the same demographic (include the girls) who have never had to step over a proper street gutter. He wondered ...

Wondered and, too often, was confused. Just the other day, he had some kind of Pygmalion experience when he made eye-contact with a clothing mannequin. For a split second he wondered why the blue-eyed girl standing by the shop entrance was staring at him. But there it was — a dummy whose eyes followed you.

As an officially designated Senior, with the magnetized plastic to prove it, he knew that getting old is more than the simple, everyday spiralling down into physical decrepitude. There is a social aspect. It is just a fact of life that the culture, the world in which he was raised and felt more or less normal has been replaced. Subtly and almost imperceptibly it was eroded. The things, the attitudes he and his cohort once took for granted had gradually become passé, redundant. It has always been so. He understood his own disgraced generation, but he did not fully understand the freshly baked lot coming through. Although, after all was said and done, he reckoned that some things stay the same, even when manifested in new clothes. But, *nota bene*, that's the best case scenario.

It was a dilemma. He did not know which was worse,

attempting to keep up or simply giving up the chase. The first involves an unhealthy degree of pretence, while the second usually slipped into an equally unwholesome wallowing in an imaginary, sentimentalized past. All that putrid garbage of puerile old Rockers' comeback concerts and so on.

Poseur or has-been? In these benighted days in which we live, that is the question. Not an attractive choice. Either way, disgust and tedium are unavoidable.

The consolation, as he saw it, was in staying close enough to the chase to observe and take amusement from the spectacle. He allowed himself the small conceit of thinking of himself as an old fox following up behind the hunt. At a safe distance, of course. A matter of distance and perspective. Take anal bleaching, for example. For some old dear in her seventies, who would need the matter explained to her, it could never be other than a perversion, a grotesque and disgusting aberration. For the young honey with the electric blue hair it was just another aesthetic option in her catalogue of self-image. But for someone in the middle it could be a source of amusement.

And Blondie? Ah, now, Blondie ... yes, now that brought him to a question worth asking: What would be her opinion on anal bleaching? On vajazzing?

Vajazzing?

He squinted across the thoroughfare at the beauty parlour's bill of fare. Whoops, sorry — vajazz*ling*, with an "el". A certain something in her voice pushed Oldie towards believing that Blondie most likely knew what was what with anal bleaching, vajazzling and any other such peculiar practices as yet to be discovered by him.

She had left a message on his answering machine the previous afternoon. When, more than a fortnight after Roger's funeral, he had not phoned Ted Connell,

Carol Dubois called on behalf of her colleague, smoothly asking Oldie would he mind calling her "when he had a moment". And who gave her (or Ted) his unlisted number?

He sure as hell had a very specific moment when he heard her voice. Whatever Canadian was left in it was refracted through the cut crystal of London posh.

He hadn't yet returned her call. The thing was that Blondie left her number, not the one on Ted Connell's card. She thereby offered him the choice as to with which of them he preferred to do business. What significance would attach to his choice? And what judgments would that preference invite? The thing was — Blondie's voice went straight to his balls and expertly weighed them.

And the big thing is — no matter how decrepit and how far past it a man knows he truly is, that man still needs to believe he might yet taste one last drop of life's sweetness. What's more, and this is the main thing, that man *wants* that need, that hunger. He has to be able to imagine and believe that it is still, somehow, possible. He heedlessly yearns for it with all his heart, even though he knows the daydream is only going to last a few floating moments.

He would ring her.

Tomorrow.

Soon.

He and Sid Wedge had one of their long, rambling talks on the phone. Trying to stay on dry ground, skirting the swamps of conspiracy, he was after any information the errant publisher had on Ted Connell. Sid had asked around, but came up with nothing other than the information that Ted's first wife had caught him out in an affair with a fellow journalist, divorced him, got the house and two kids, Ted buggered off to London, worked for some public relations outfit "or some such shit", then came home with the girlfriend — to wit, Ms Dubois. She then had her commitment to the relationship tested when Ted's ex-wife died of cancer and Carol was called upon to help Teddy Boy look after his teenage kids. As far as Sid could learn, there were no real skeletons in Ted's closet. "As a journo," he said, "he's your average time-serving arse licker, never trod on anyone's toes. Nobody bigger than him, at any rate."

After discussing a few manuscripts that had turned up in Sid's mail and having a mutual whinge about noisy neighbors, they drifted onto personal matters. Oldie mentioned that, after years of delay and excuses, he had more or less agreed to travel to Melbourne to see his semi-demented, aged mother.

"Better late than never," said Sid, with what Oldie sensed was a trace of disapproval over the matter having been left so long. The sentiment, if Oldie had read it right, surprised him. Wedgie was a constant surprise.

Better late than never?

Not always, Oldie thought, keeping it to himself. Not always.

One thing he did get, unequivocally: there was not a lot of point in subjecting others to a dreary account of why he did not get on with his mother. It's like discussing ailments — people have their own problems to deal with.

If pushed, he might offer the opinion that intractable personality clashes between parent and child are not, in fact, uncommon. Often as not, it's nobody's fault. Just something that has to be managed. Often as not by a third party, such as an accommodating daughter-in-law.

"I ran away from home when I was three," he told people. "What more can I say!"

What pity he felt for his mother was on the other side

of the glass. What pity he may feel for himself could not be known until after her death. Perhaps that would be her final gift — to outlive him.

Sometimes he looked into his mother's eyes in the photograph taken at her sister's wedding. It was a clear, high resolution image, taken by a professional photographer. She was twenty-four and very beautiful. Looking straight into the camera, her open, not quite smiling face tinged with curiosity, her steady gaze reaching across his lifetime to touch him with an intimacy he had never directly experienced with her. She once told him that a few days before that photograph was taken she had discovered she was pregnant with him and was suffering morning sickness.

There you have it, he thought, the antipathy started before he was born.

It was Anna, of course, who had saved the airfares and car hire. She stood ready to book the tickets, sort out insurance and car hire, find Max a place to stay and do all the things Oldie simply did not understand how to do. All she needed was his agreement to the scheme so that she could arrange to take part of her long service leave during second term. That would allow them to be away all of April and into May.

He raised the idea of, once in Melbourne, popping over to New Zealand for a couple of weeks. Do the South Island: Christchurch (see their old friend, Mike), over to the West Coast, Hokitika, back through the Haast and down to Invercargill, up to Dunedin then through the Mackenzie Country back to Christchurch. It would be an adventure.

She calmly told him what he knew. They had neither the money nor the time.

What she needed, she told him, was for him to take some responsibility, to resolve to behave and not quarrel with his mother, to do his best to make the trip as pleasant as possible for all concerned.

He pursed his lips and said he would try to do his best.

Well, OK, in the meantime, what he could do, she said, was to plan some excursions, road trips out of Melbourne. They could afford a few nights in motels. He could show her some of the places of his childhood and growing up. They could also strike out and go somewhere they'd never been. She told him that would be their adventure.

Lickety-split, clickety-click, he got on the interweb.

"Max von Mewler! Maxie bin Laden! Where that cat be at? Ah, Maxie, you old devil, you've been spoilt rotten. Just look at that — fish guts in virgin prawn jus! Mmmm! Very tasty, my fine-furred friend. Tais-tee!"

"Maa-wouw," Max agreed, too busy bolting down his evening meal to say more.

"Glad you like it. I mean, we both know you're quite capable of pulling that old sniff and walk routine. Even from ones you *previously said* were your favourites. Oh yes, I remember. You've even walked from those expensive ones that big fluffy white Persian you fancy on TV endorses. You remember her. What was her name ... Natasha? Yes, I think so. A bit of all right was Natasha, aye? You won't wanna try walking away from your din-dins when you're in boarding school. That's right, boarding school for four or five weeks. If you don't eat what they give you, they'll just toss it and then give you another serve the next day — and by then, old chum, you will be only too happy to scoff it down."

Max ignored Oldie's chit-chat and chomped on regardless. Natasha's got nothing to do with it, Boofhead, it's all about how fresh the fish was when it went into the tin and how long it has been in the tin. Boarding school? What the fuck is he on about?! He knew the Old Man was crapping on because he was anxious over the Girl being late. To make matters worse, they'd just heard an ambulance wailing up Marmion Avenue and, presently or soon, she would be driving up that hectic road. Oldie had had a few close calls himself when, in a two-lane stream of heavy traffic travelling at a touch over the eighty K speed limit, some jackass misjudged the gap and shot out from a side street. Anyone with any sense would be nervous about that road at this time of day.

Having lost their son in a traffic accident, Oldie and the Girl always tried hard not to be overly late. They gave each other ETAs and did their best to stick to them. That morning she had made sure to tell him she had a staff meeting after work. She said she would be home about five-thirty, but by five-forty the "about" had been expended and the old fool was fretting. It was not something he could control.

He'd spent most of the long, hot day alone, trudging along at the seemingly endless task of indexing someone else's book, with no one to talk to other than Max. No phone calls, no mail. He had started to dial Blondie's number but hung up before tapping the last digit. It had been four days since she left that message on his answering machine. He'd replayed it half a dozen times, but he still wasn't ready to call her back. He wanted to meet her somewhere, but wondered whether he was chickening out. On the other hand, if he didn't call her, bloody old Teddy might return to the fray.

He was, he told himself, busy with work. Indexing, reading, Googling ... one thing led to another. Or, as often as not, the other thing led away from the original matter, up the garden path to chase some well-known bunny down a long and winding burrow.

And yesterday he'd had the damned half-yearly hep C blood tests and abdominal ultrasound. The radiologist was a middle-aged Indian woman who gave no indication of his result. Sometimes they would quietly tell him things were "much the same", but when they didn't he'd learnt it didn't mean it wasn't, just that they were observing the protocols of their profession — it was the specialist's job to tell him. As for the taking of his blood, that was always a shag around and, once again, a wretched phlebotomist wounded him, leaving a nasty bruise in the crook of his arm, something it was better to hide than to explain.

So, with those particular hoops having been jumped through, it was a three week wait to see Vladimir Mayakovsky, Chief Hepatologist, for the results. He'd learnt to cruise it. One day the news would not be good.

One day.

He would call her tomorrow. This time, definitely. He was telling himself he was pretty sure he could not actually help her (and Ted), but there was no harm in meeting for a coffee and, playing it by ear, passing the time of day with a beautiful woman. He wondered if she knew it was him she had seen talking to Roger at Paulo's funeral. He wondered.

He told himself such a meeting would be an adventure, a harmless treat. Pathetic, but there you are. He would tell the Girl it was about discovering what Ted Connell and his associate were after, perhaps making a useful contact and, just maybe, even scoring some work.

All of which was true enough, but he was fragile and would have liked a few minutes of molly-coddling masquerading as grown-up conversation — tacit approval — before getting into the business of preparing their evening meal. Only now, with Anna running late, there would not be time. They would chat a little during their meal as they watched the news, but by then they had passed the stage when the unloading of his daily hassles sounded like a casual, offhand thing. Recounting whatever small revelations and bright ideas he may have had during the day didn't seem very important as they watched people's homes destroyed by fire, flood, wind or some dire combination of the aforesaid calamities. And that was before they even got to the international news.

The dining room air-con had been rattling and roaring away most of the afternoon and that room was relatively cool when the Girl finally arrived just before six o'clock. One look at her told him something more than being hot and tired was bothering her. Saying only that she had a headache she dropped her basket on the floor beside the dining room table and headed down the passage to the bathroom for a couple of Panadol. He opened the bottle of mineral water he had placed in the freezer, poured her a glass and silently handed it to her when she returned.

"People!" she said with deep disgust. "I honestly don't know if I can keep doing this."

He leaned back against the bench and crossed his arms, passively inviting her to vent her spleen. But she just shook her head, dismissing everything and nothing. She handed him the empty glass and said she needed to lie down for a while before she could even contemplate facing a meal.

She had half turned to go when she looked back and quietly asked, "No mail?"

He shook his head, knowing that all she was really interested in was some word from Daniel. They had not heard anything in the six days since a brief email announcing "they" were still at someone's holiday cabin at Lake Tawakoni, an hour's drive east of Dallas, and that Mexico probably wasn't going to happen "any time soon". Florida and a last space shuttle launch had been mooted.

"No news is good news," he said, as lightly as he could manage.

"So they say."

"Well, I'm sort of relieved he's not going to Mexico. We could call his mobile if you like. Later on tonight. It must be three or four in the morning there now."

"Let's see what tomorrow brings," she said as she lifted her top over her head. She extended her arms towards him to pull the garment off.

"Skin a rabbit," he said in the same brisk voice his father used when Oldie was a kid and, at the end of the day, they accomplished their collaborative act of quickly pulling off a pullover.

Her slacks fell around her feet and she stood in her underwear.

"That's better," she sighed. Their eyes touched.

"Kids play up in the heat?"

"Kids, parents, the Department ... everybody. Actually, the kids, despite all their problems, are easy compared to the others. It's just ... people. I'm so tired," she sighed, turning towards the lounge room and the couch.

He knew she would need about an hour of undisturbed rest to find some semblance of equilibrium. He had seen her like this before, too many times. The hot weather was an aggravation, but the actual grievance came from somewhere else. Kids and parents she could cope with, mostly; but when she mentioned the Education Department he knew that, once again, some highly qualified dunce had devised yet another innovative obstacle to teaching, some barefaced insult to intelligence and common sense. He followed her to grab the phone handpiece, taking it back to the kitchen, closing the doors behind him. He considered whether Butter Chicken on steamed rice was the best meal for a tired, cranky Girl. It would have to do — the chicken thighs were already thawed and diced. Chop a couple of sticks of celery into the mix just before serving to give it a bit of crunch, finish off each serve with a scatter of pine nuts. With the sauce out of a bottle, it was a dish that did not leave a lot of washing up.

He fingered the phone keypad, considering giving Blondie the call then and there. Get it over with. But the piece of paper on which he had written her number was in the lounge room. Well, OK, then he'd call her tomorrow. Definitely.

He turned on the radio and found the news station rabbiting off sports results, as usual. He rolled the dial back to Classic FM and there was Handel's *For unto us a child is born* just getting underway. *Unto us a son is given,* pomp, pomp, pomp, *and his name shall be called Wonderful!* Clever old George Frederic. Boy, could he fizz along! He either cheered you up or mellowed you out. Knew a thing or two about lofty wigs and damned fine coats, too, did George Frederic. Oldie always did have a thing for those elegant, embroidered dress coats of the eighteenth century. He would argue that men had never dressed with more style than back then. Not that anyone ever asked his opinion on such matters.

The hum of the air-con and the steady bounce of George Frederic created an effective sound screen against the various acoustic invasions of privacy the neighbours thought it their right to inflict. As a student in Melbourne and as a hippy working as a wharfie in Darwin, he had inflicted his fair share of loud music on hapless neighbours. He wasn't proud of it. In fact, the memory of a distraught middle-aged woman in her dressing gown banging on the door of the house he shared in Carlton made him cringe with shame more than forty years on. But he *had* grown up. The turkeys he had as neighbours were old enough to know better, yet they continued to behave as though they were silly bloody teenagers. Although as individuals they bored him shitless, their collective crassness, the relentlessness of it, did have a certain end-of-the-world fascination. It didn't exactly excuse them, but he did understand they were frightened people. The deeper the denial, the louder the parties. And yet, somewhere behind the donkey-braying bluster, they were afraid, waiting for the axe to fall.

In the kitchen Oldie dangled a fatty scrap of chicken in plain sight of Max. The cat's rush at the morsel belied his advanced years. Many a young cat could take a leaf out of Maxie's book. The low throaty growl with which he pounced upon and tackled the meat as it hit the floor did not need subtitles.

The unsettling possibility of being outlived by a sixteen-year-old cat didn't bear thinking about.

It was folly and he knew it, but he could not help wondering what people would remember of him. Not immediately afterwards, but in twenty or so years' time, when memories had mummified into polished stories and fixed images. Some of those future lenses would distort him to the edge of recognition, but surely someone would retain a moment, some glance met or word heard, that echoed something of what he felt was his true self.

But what is True Self anyway? Many, most people, are careful not to display it. They think, often rightly, that it makes them vulnerable. Better to have a persona that can deal with what life throws at you. What it throws in your face.

Until, that is, something slips through and what we should call the soul is touched.

As often as not when he remembered his father, it was the sight of him sitting there patting Alan Fanning's back, quietly uttering words of comfort to calm his friend. He had never seen his father like that before. He saw a younger, rawer man — as he had been during the war, perhaps; before his watching son was born.

He wanted to believe that what he saw that winter's night had been truly fixed by the circumstances of the moment. If that were so, if memory was indeed anchored on a reality, that would be a comfort as profound as any religious consolation.

But his own experience had shown him, with certainty, that memory *was* mutable, that it could confound even the clearest mind.

Not long before Daniel went overseas Oldie asked his son what he remembered of Peggy and Jim, the only ones of the Old People still alive when he was born. He had been taken to visit them several times between the ages of two and five and he did, indeed, have a vivid memory of Jim, of a particular moment.

According to Anna, who also remembered the incident, it happened when she took the children home to Australia for a visit. Oldie was not there, having remained in Auckland and at his job. One evening Oldie's father had taken Anna and Daniel to Cameron Street (Jem left sleeping in the care of his grandmother) and the thing happened at the end of the visit as the three of them were preparing to leave. Daniel was then still a couple of months shy of turning three, so it was apparently his oldest memory of Jim. Surprise entailing alarm and astonishment must be good cement for memory, a bit like Peggy's paint story to Oldie.

As they gathered themselves up to leave, Daniel asked Peggy if he could have one of the oranges in a bowl on the sideboard. An intelligent, confident, silver-haired, good-looking child, the first of a new generation — Peggy would have given him the orange if it was the last thing she possessed in this world.

Jim, who by then was using a walking stick, led the way up the wide hallway through the centre of the house towards the front door. Daniel, orange clutched against his chest, followed a few steps behind; his mother and great-great aunt, arm-in-arm, a little behind him. Oldie's father brought up the rear, probably bearing an old biscuit tin filled with cakes or scones Peggy insisted her guests take "for later".

Jim quietly cautioned the child, eighty-five years his junior and a tenth his size, to stand back. A big man for his generation, he required elbow room to manoeuvre himself and his stick as he went through the operations of turning the big rattling key, drawing the big clanking bolts and turning the big brass knob in the centre of the heavy wooden door. Daniel stood still in the middle of the hallway, his wide-eyed attention fixed, as Jim positioned himself beside the slightly ajar door.

Holding the door firmly with his right hand, obscuring the narrow opening with his body, Jim suddenly thrust his walking stick through the gap, banging it between the door and its frame. Intently watching something outside, he stamped his foot and boomed, "Get back!" with his loudest, deepest voice.

Everybody froze. Anna said later that she thought there must have been a dog outside. She said Daniel flinched but did not step back. She did not notice what Peggy's reaction was.

"Get away! Get out of here! Go home, you cheeky monkey! Go home! Go on — get off!" Jim continued to growl from deep in his throat as he banged his stick about, never taking his eyes off the unseen danger in the darkness outside the door.

Finally, Jim opened the door enough to thrust his head out and look around. After an extended moment he stepped back, but still held the door so nobody could see outside, and half turned to address Daniel.

"It was that monkey who lives up the road," he explained, his voice quieter but threaded with indignation. "He wanted your orange! He can't have it. That's your orange! Isn't it?"

Daniel said, thirty years later, that it just never occurred to him that the old man could have been joking. He held his orange to his chest with both hands and whispered a "Yes". If there was a fleeting twinkle in Jim's eye or voice, the child missed it.

"All right, then. Well, he's gone now. I sent him on his way. He's a bloody cheeky monkey." And with that the big old fellow swung the door wide open and stepped across Peggy's beautifully polished brass doorstep onto the broad, wooden front veranda.

Jim stood at the top of the two steps down to the garden path that led straight to the white picket front gate. He looked up at the sky and drew a deep breath of the night air. "Come on," he said, turning back to Daniel, who hesitated on the safe side of Peggy's gleaming doorstep. He held out his hand for the child, "Come on, we'll open the front gate together."

Daniel took Jim's hand and, walking stiffly to the pace of the old man's amble, went down the path. He kept his bugging eyes on his grandfather's car, parked against the curb directly opposite the front gate. He did not dare look into the shadows of the hydrangea bushes lining the fences either side of the front yard.

Despite Anna's insistence that Oldie was not there that night, and his rational knowledge that she was right, the story had somehow been classified in his consciousness as a memory. He recalled it as something he had seen and experienced himself. He had considered the possibility that Jim pulled that trick on him or one of his brothers when they were young, but the memory he had of the event was from an adult perspective, not a child's.

No matter how obvious it was that Anna must have told him the story after her return, and no matter how much he held in mind that his intimate and long knowledge of the place and people involved had facilitated the transference from story to personal experience, the moment when Jim stamped his foot and beat about with his stick was as inextricably his as Anna or Daniel's.

There had been occasions when he had heard people claim to have personal experiences that were directly contradicted by incontrovertible archival documents. In a few cases it was obvious the claimants were consciously lying, but in many others the confusion, perplexity and pain generated by the confrontation with the historical evidence convinced the Old Man that genuine phantom memory was involved.

People experience phantom pain. So, why not phantom memory?

VII

They arranged to meet in the city, at the State Art Gallery coffee shop. She said she had been told about his beard and would recognise him. Neither of them openly stated what they wanted to talk about. Roger Kidd's name was not mentioned, but "on-going research" was. Oldie lied and said he had to go into town anyway to examine documents in the State Records Office, just across the plaza. He toyed with the idea of really going into the SRO to pester and upset Baba Yaga, but, as it turned out, he did not indulge himself in that simple, wholesome pleasure. Blondie said, truthfully, that she wanted to have a look at a couple of colonial era sketches in the old courthouse wing of the gallery.

He shampooed his beard, polished his leather boots, put in the dental plate that provided him with an upper left incisor, wore his best relaxed fit, long sleeve black shirt, shoved a book and a few folders into his leather satchel (along with a couple of large bandaids and some cotton wool, in case he bled) and told Anna he had to go to the archives. He said that, as far as he knew, Ted and Carol would both be there to meet him for coffee.

"Good thing our names aren't Bob and Alice," she quipped.

But he didn't get it. Not until he was well on his way into town on the train. Too late. "Ha! Two steps!" he blurted, loud enough for the woman sitting two seats in front of him to look up from her texting.

Still two steps ahead of you, Buddy Boy, the Girl would shake her head in weary disbelief whenever he didn't get one of her jokes. Holding up two fingers to reiterate, she would say, "Two steps, Bud."

But she believed his fib about Ted coming to the meeting. So, ha ha, two steps in the wrong direction!

The train pulled up the slope out of Warwick station, crested and picked up speed for the six K straight down to Stirling. He enjoyed this part of the journey. After the morning rush and the school kids were out of the way, an elderly gent on his Seniors Pass could score a window seat to himself, comfortably distanced from the few other passengers. Sometimes he read, but mostly he just looked out the window and, clocking along, non-stop down the centre of the freeway, simply relaxed, watching the traffic, sunlight dancing on windscreens, the trees on the embankments, the skyline, daydreaming.

Slowing into Stirling, the train passed the spot on the northern lanes where Jem had his accident. Road works a few years later realigned the access lanes, changing the streetscape and blurring the Old Man's memory. The changes had not softened his sorrow, but he had passed the place many hundreds of times and had learnt to live with it.

As you do.

Sometimes he ran his mental video of that night, but memory had worn its own ruts and gradually settled, concentrated into a set of brief visual clips, gestures, words, fixed images. He used to say to people, on the anniversary, that it seemed "like yesterday". Even now, when he set his mind to it, it could seem that way, sort of. But most of the time, when he was on his own, going about his business, and he happened to think of it, it actually felt like a long time ago, something like the approximation of eternity.

Even so, some things remained disturbingly tangible. He remembered the moment that night when the boy passed him as he was leaving the house. Jem quickly reached out and lightly gripped the Old Man's wrist. It was not a gesture he had ever made before. Nothing was said. A fleeting smile, a touch, and he was gone, into the rushing wind of the night, into the darkness.

An hour or so later the cops were knocking on the door. As they must have done that cold night that little girl's mother died in the gutter. As they did for him and Anna thirteen years ago next winter.

Thirteen years. And they still had Max, Jem's cat.

No one wants to die young, but then again, everyone resists getting old. No one grows old anymore, they just get old — old and decrepit. Their days shrink and dry up, they kick the bucket and their bodies are disposed of. End of story.

The train was already pulling out of Glendalough and running down to whizz along the side of Lake Monger towards Leederville. The broad, grey surface of the shallow lake remained much the same whatever the season or time of day, but the surrounds had been landscaped and rehabilitated beyond recognition; particularly along the eastern side, where the construction of the railway and north-bound lanes of the freeway had required a slice of the lake reserve. There'd been a fair bit of land claim monkey business over that deal. Roger had probably known about that caper. Was that in his book?

How many hundreds of times had he and the Girl walked around Monger? For two decades of their middle years it had been almost a daily ritual. They must have walked that two-mile circuit at least three thousand times. When the boys were young they had often come along, running about and charging on ahead to chase the ducks or to be chased by the swans. The swonks, as they called them. They'd stood quietly and patiently to see the long-necked turtles gliding in and out of the shade under the jetty. He and the Girl amused themselves in observing the other regular walkers and joggers, commenting on their appearance and giving them names. One hapless, middle-aged gent, self-consciously trying to keep his weight under control in just-a-little-too-damned-neat casual clothes was dubbed the Claremont Serial Killer. There was the tall, thin English woman — sleek-headed, no chin, sharp nose — she and her spitting image three teenage daughters were The Geese. And then there was Ginger Meggs, the Ballerina, Big Poofta (complete with tiny poodle), Sad Sack, the Old Bodgie and his missus, Honey Bunch. Oh, happy days.

One way or another he had acquired knowledge of that lake and its history. He knew a few of its secrets.

Assuming Blondie wanted to talk about old rubbish tips and their legacy for the aquifers of the Swan River coastal plain, she would need to hear some of the things he knew about Monger's Lake and environs. Let me tell you! You wouldn't *believe* what shit — and I mean that literally, the night carts used the northern end — was dumped there in the twenty years following the war. But such real, biodegradable, organic shit was the least of it. More than one old Bodgie would have to admit that he and his mates used to dump stolen cars there. They'd push or drive the vehicle into the bulrushes and then start a fire — hilarious. And then there was the official vandalism. One old fellow reckoned that just after the war the museum chucked away a whole lot of old muzzle-loaders, no value then and excess to their needs — de-accessioned, as they call it these days. The guns were ferried out in a row boat working from a long gone jetty on the southern side and scattered about to settle into the deep mud of the lake floor. Dozens, scores of Tower muskets, the last of the Brown Besses. The old joker who told that story said he was one of those who actually did the job. Said he and the other lads took turns standing in the prow and harpooning muskets at imaginary whales — hilarious. Didn't want to brag, but reckoned he was the champion of that sporting lark. But, you know, anyone could get rid of anything at the landfill on the eastern side, anything, and then, when everyone got all ecological and "sustainable" and the place was rehabilitated to buggery in the late nineties, the whole bloody mess was churned up and exposed for all to see. They'd expected something, but — Christ! — did those prize Bozos at the Council get a *nasty* shock! Even though shards of blue asbestos and the broken rims of corroded drums were clearly visible through the tonnes of mulch covering the newly formed banks, even though startlingly vivid rainbow slicks appeared on the newly created billabongs every time it rained, the whole business was still covered up. When it comes to keeping things nice and quietly buried, nobody does it better than local governments.

He'd heard there was an old flood drain connecting Monger to the Swan. He wondered about that. The river was a good four K away, south through the city; more than five, if the drain went east behind Perth, through the Claise Brook drainage system to feed into the river at Burswood. It was one of those things he had always meant to look into. Like the Osborne Park drains that had been dug north of Monger in the nineteen-twenties. There had been some sort of controversy about them. He was pretty sure there had been press allegations of incompetence, some frivolity about drains that ran up hill. He couldn't remember the details but thought he might still have a file on it, somewhere.

There was, too, a story that the car repairers and painters over in Osborne Park used to dump all sorts of dodgy stuff into the drains and that it was from them that heavy metals — chromium was mentioned — got into the water table. That source of pollution was cleaned up in the eighties, but the stuff could hang around for years and anyone using bore water on their veggie garden could do some real damage to themselves and their kiddies.

The train bounded along, merrily, merrily, smoothly swaying, tumble-rumble over the Vincent Street bridge. He looked back. Even under a cloudless summer morning sky, Monger's surface was a listless grey. Bye-bye lake. Bye-bye swonks.

Yes, lots of stories.

And that wasn't even counting the blackfella ones. He could tell Blondie that Midgegooroo's brother had been shot there in May 1833, just a week or so before Midgegooroo himself, bound to the gaol door, was executed by firing squad in Perth. Wouldn't it just be damned funny if some of those old guns that did for those poor old blackfellas had ended up in Monger's mud? Oldie had also heard, from a usually good source, that there were Aboriginal graves near the lake, but he hadn't been told exactly where. Sometimes, out of sheer devilment, he told people they were on the rise at the southern end, probably on the land the Catholic monastery sold off for an expensive property development back in the late eighties. He didn't know that. Not for sure. But it was a convincing demonstration of how something lurking in the *hachure* of History could step out and bite the present on the arse. Just like in that movie, *Poltergeist*.

He wouldn't tell Blondie the Lake Monger burial story. Not yet. Stick to what she was interested in — water and old toxic tips. There were enough authenticated burials in awkward places without making up more. There was one in the grounds of Perth's Government House, another behind or maybe under the Albany Town Hall. It should be noted that, discovering suspected, vaguely located burial sites is an art in itself, a talent that, in the right circumstances, can earn you some money. Brown paper bag cash money. After dark money. *Nalichnye dengi.*

Of course, if you wanted blackfella business mixed up with water business, there was all that surreptitious hanky-panky about the mythical Wagyl's wrigglings at Monger. The Wagyl's calling card was a clump of bulrushes, so there were after dark plantings. Followed by before dawn removals. Brown paper bags of hush money all over the place. And a good time was had by all.

Maybe he had better not tell her too much about that either. At least, not let on how much he had been involved. There were legal issues. And it might look like he was trying too hard to impress. He had to watch that. At one time, when he was younger, before all the illness and memory loss crap, he had been an adept conversationalist. He was quite the verbal acrobat, a genuine flippin' trapeze artist. Then, he always had the *mot juste*, the pertinent anecdote, the nail-on-head argument; he could think as he spoke. Now, he ran the risk of running off the cliff and peddling air, *à la* Wile E. Coyote. Or saying something a little too familiar, even plain inappropriate. Especially around attractive women of a certain age. The confidence of his youth was now misplaced, a liability. He knew the smart ones didn't like it and yet, time after time, he let himself slip.

Just couldn't stop himself. Later, alone, he'd recall those moments of buffoonery and cringe. Wilt.

No, he wouldn't do that today. He would listen and respond with care. He didn't, he reminded himself, know anything about this woman. A Canadian with a Russian tattoo — clearly, a sophisticated woman. Or, at any rate, one who had been around.

The train descended into a concrete trench and entered the tunnel beneath the city. Heading down, wheels screeching on the camber, it made a drawn out ninety degree curve before the carriages straightened up, aligning, to slide on a low rumble into the fluorescent cavern of Perth Underground station.

Oh what a multicultural world we live in! Just look at that cavalcade flickering by along the platform. Young faces from just about everywhere. Truly, a fantastic carnival of the exotic striving for beauty through novelty — dyed hair, tatts, piercings, mardi gras costumes worn as clothes.

He was old enough to remember when, only a generation back, seeing an Asian face on an Australian street would have drawn a second look. Sometimes he thought about what the Old people — his Old people: Peg and Jim and Bob, Nin — what they would have had to say about all this change. He knew they would not have liked the scale and speed of change. But would they have accepted it as somehow inevitable, a continuation of the vast changes they had already witnessed?

But Holy Smoke, just look at that dark beauty! Abyssinian? The Queen of Sheba is alive and well. She must have got on at Glendalough. How come he didn't spot her before? You'd go years before seeing (in the flesh, that is) breasts that stand so firm and proud on such a tall, slender woman. And Jesus wept — no visible means of support! — just look at the way she is dressed!

Although a purple headscarf with silver thread frames her serene face, there is nothing modest about the rest of her attire. And the whole damned show carried off with such natural poise.

His longing was incurable. The allure was implacable, pitiless. Shamelessly, he jostled to get directly behind her on the escalator, left a step between them, and gazed spellbound at those sublime buttocks tightly wrapped in a gossamer black skirt as he followed her on the long, breathless assent up out of Subterranea, rising, rising to brim and spill off the escalator into the sparkling, sunlit street. She walked away, careless of her power, down the broad pedestrian mall, quickly slipping into and through the whirl and stream of the crowd sauntering by on its collective business.

Deafened by lust, pining for something he had never had and never would have, he stood and watched her go. At his age, to be stuck with, consumed by such demons. It was dreadful. But then one day she, poor woman, may very well stand where he did, scathed in her turn by desiderium.

The bubble burst. In a rush of burning air Woland and his henchmen swirled up to disappear behind a high gleaming tower. The Old Man's skin prickled. He felt heavy. His legs ... were weighted with small, neatly sewn sandbags tied around his knees. His mouth was dry. A hot wind was roaring inside his ears. He knew he was wearing his sunglasses, but there was such a glare ... lurid yellow spots were dancing.

He steadied himself.

He was not going to faint. Nothing so dramatic today, thanks. Just a touch of the vapours. Call it delirium.

He breathed in, held it and then slowly exhaled through his nose before lumbering off through the Murray Street mall. He would buy a cold drink and a hot sausage roll and sit on a bench in the shade outside the post office. The pigeons would give him the beady eye and peck around his feet while he contemplated the physics of the big, heavy granite marble rolling upon the water. He had the better part of an hour up his sleeve. He would gather his thoughts. Get his wind back.

Memory can get you into trouble. Remembering what it was like to be eighteen doesn't make you that age.

But then, do we live to grow old? Is that it? To grow old in the hope of acquiring wisdom and understanding?

Good luck with that!

What, in all honesty, could he say he had learnt?

"Never trust the bankers," he whispered to himself. "And be very wary of doctors."

Amen.

He got there ten minutes early to do a recce, but found she was already seated at an outside table, head back, sunning herself. She was wearing blue jeans and a plain white T-shirt, the sleeve of which covered her tatt. He wanted to ask about that. He took in her mop of jet-black hair, but she was definitely Blondie. The smooth wide face. The ripe cherry lips. He assumed she had dyed her hair blonde at some stage of her life. Sort of the reverse of what Godard did with Bardot in *Le Mépris*. He thought he might ask her, sometime, whether she knew about that. Maybe it was a decade or two too far back, ahead of her time. God, Godard had gone eighty! And Brigitte ... well, no, it was too long ago. Best shut up. It would just seem like he was showing off.

A moment after Oldie spotted Carol Dubois, before she saw him, she gave a slight start and leaned forward to pull her chirping phone from her bag. Oldie slowed to watch as she then fished out her business diary and commenced writing.

Concentrating on her call, she didn't indicate she had noticed him until he stood before her. His eyes were no longer good enough to make out the numbers and names she had just written, especially when, having removed his sunglasses, he was making a little show of not looking. The shadow pip of a nipple ... he could not avoid noticing she was not wearing a bra under her T-shirt. He licked his lips and stared at the items on the table: her black, patent leather tote bag and, protruding from it, an unsealed Manila envelope containing a document about an inch thick.

Oldie's heart sank, fell straight through his bowels and kept going. Another manuscript! That would ruin everything. A lesser man would have dropped to the pavement, into the foetal position, bawling, cursing, kicking and screaming.

But, hang on! Let's not panic. Bloody Hell! What if ... what if that's Roger's manuscript?

Listening to her caller, she looked apologetically at Oldie and gestured for him to sit facing her. Her expression was somewhere between a pout and a smile, more around her mouth than on her lips, which (of course) he found very fetching. She raised a finger and opened her mouth to interrupt her unseen interlocutor, but closed both hand and mouth and looked down at her notebook as the chatter from the phone suddenly intensified. Oldie sat, placing his black, patent leather satchel on the spare chair, next to her tote bag. He saw that she noticed.

Snap!

He looked around. He hadn't anticipated they would be sitting outside, next to the main pedestrian thoroughfare between the city and Northbridge, in view of anyone walking over from the station towards the State Library and the SRO. It was odds on that one of the

129

many researchers and aspiring historians he had dealt with over the years would see him. He knew that more than half of them would sit themselves down, expecting an introduction and a full account of whatever business was being discussed. They would all want to be helpful, to share their knowledge. They were like that.

The prospect made him nervous, restless. He looked into the dark, cooler interior of the cafe. Plenty of good tables in there.

Carol's face alternated between smiles for Oldie and frowns over the angry buzzing coming out of her phone. Her murmured stream of conciliatory phrases didn't seem to be having any effect. There was clearly a problem, somewhere.

Thinking it better to give her some privacy to deal with the situation, Oldie started to rise, intending to use the circumstance as an opportunity to move inside and have a look at what was on the menu board. She didn't look up but her hand shot out to lightly touch his wrist. The tips of her fingers rested a moment on his skin before she withdrew to rest her hand on the table beside his arm. They remained in their fixed proximity as Carol cut in on the woman, insisting she listen to her, and then explained, politely but allowing no interruption, that although the issue was vexing "for all of us" she was "absolutely certain, confident" it would be sorted out that afternoon. Without drawing a breath she went on to say she was keeping someone waiting and straight away worked her way into and through the necessary adieus. In one continuous motion she turned off her phone, snapped it shut and dropped it into her bag. She threw her hands above her head, puffed out her cheeks and let out a rich laugh.

"Come on!" she declared, slapping the table top. "Let's go inside, out of the way. I really need a good strong coffee."

She insisted on paying and, without asking if he wanted it, added a Melting Moment apiece to their order. Instead of taking the chair opposite him, she slipped in beside him on the black leather banquette behind the table. She half turned so that her knees came close to his, but when he discreetly eased away a few inches she did the same.

Something about the light inside, reflected through glass, momentarily recast her. The white skin, red lips, black hair ... Snow White. Nah, he retracted the thought, Snow White was miles too pure.

Stirring in a lot of sugar, she conveyed Ted's apologies for not being able to make it, and then caught the Old Man off guard by asking how well he had known, not Roger, but Paulo.

He explained that, having met through mutual friends, he and Paulo had taken to meeting a couple of times a year for coffee, to discuss literary and related matters, an informal book club of two.

She nodded and quietly said, "I can see that. He was a very nice man. I heard he was writing a television comedy before he became ill."

"Yes, based upon his time as a public servant. But he did not discuss it with me. Not in any detail, that is. I've no idea how far he got with it. I can't imagine having chemo is conducive to writing comedy."

"No. It would not be." Her voice was low and she did not look at him.

He wanted to ask how well she had known Paulo. But he held his tongue and let his silence form the question.

"I knew him through my stepson's school. Paulo was very active on the Parents' Committee. He was one of those people who always turn up, who do the work. Until the cancer got a hold. That's how I knew it was serious — when he started missing meetings and functions. He had always been so reliable. A lovely man," she concluded as she raised the white cup to her red lips.

"And Roger?"

"Oh, I didn't know Roger Kidd." She put her cup down on its saucer with hardly a click. "I only met him the once, a week or so before he died. He came around to see Ted. They had some mutual acquaintances from when Ted worked for the newspapers. Years ago, long before I came out here. When he came, I knew I'd seen him somewhere and then he told me he'd been at Paulo's funeral. That's how your name came up. It was Roger who told us about you. He spoke very highly of you. You were friends?"

"Friendly. We worked together ten years ago, but I hadn't seen him since. Not until he approached me at Paulo's funeral."

She waited, but he just sat there, stock still, his eyes half closed, staring at the passing parade outside in the bright sunlight. He sensed rather than saw her cast him a look out of the corner of her eye. "I'm sorry," he finally said, turning to look her in the face, "I'm missing something here. Didn't Ted know Roger well enough to go to his funeral? And, I don't understand, what was it that Roger told Ted and you about me?"

She looked at him carefully. "I thought, I mean, we assumed Roger had spoken to you about our meeting. If there's been a mix up I apologise. He said he was going to ring you."

"He did ring me. But he didn't want to discuss things on the phone. So we arranged to have a meal together. I spoke to him on the Saturday. We arranged to meet on the Tuesday. He never turned up."

She blinked, briefly looked away, and then turned back to ask him whether he knew what Roger had wanted to discuss.

He ignored her question and, keeping his gaze and voice level, pushed on. "I was sitting there, at Hillarys boat harbour, waiting. Ringing his phones. Waited an hour, got myself a feed of fish and chips and then went home. I realised later he was already dead by then. Funny thing, I emailed and phoned, yet the cops never got in touch with me. You'd think ... you know, as a matter of routine, they'd contact all those who had dealings with Roger in his last days. Did they talk to you or Ted about him?"

He saw the flicker of uncertainty in her eyes. "No, they didn't ... but we only saw him that one time he called around, and there was no other contact. Why should the police be investigating?"

"I dunno," he shrugged, "routine, wouldn't you think? I heard he didn't leave a note." He paused to instil significance. He liked being in control of the conversation, of holding cards she sensed were there but couldn't see. But he also felt her becoming wary, stepping back.

"Anyway, you were about to say why Roger mentioned me to you."

"OK then," she took a breath, "here goes. Ted and I are looking to produce a documentary on the water situation in Perth. Mainly focussed on desalination as a solution to declining rainfall, but a related issue, as you know, is the potential pollution of the water table ... and Roger said you had done some research. Look, I'm sorry," she shifted quickly on her seat, "what you said about the police ... I don't understand, are you saying there was something, something ... *odd*, about Roger's death?"

He could hear it in her voice, she was thinking of bailing out. He decided to chance his arm, to spill the beans and then invite her to help him count them all up. He told her of Sid Wedge's suspicion of foul play.

"I've heard of him. But isn't he a bit crazy? Conspiracy theories and all that stuff?"

"Absolutely!" Oldie's face lit with delight. "Oh, yes, he has definitely got a kink in him. Mad as! Jewish World Conspiracy. September 11. You name it. Global warming is a con. I'm not joking! And look, although I agree with him that we are all being poisoned by what we eat — too much fructose! — and the pharmaceutical industry rules the medical profession and all — Wedgie always goes that extra light year too far. I remember one time hearing him go pretty close to claiming the cure for cancer is drinking sheep dip or some such thing. Oh yeah ... mad as! But, you know, I've got to admit, I've had some fun working with him. There's what I call the helter-skelter element. And he's always at war with the powers that be. There is, what you might call, an *abiding* rancour. He's been known to write to politicians calling for the public execution of Arts Department officials. I mean, you have to take your hat off to him for that! As a publisher he is, well, limited. But, trouble is, so are the rest in this town. At least, excuse my French, he's not a bloody academic."

She smiled and he, trusting soul, looked deeply into her eyes.

"As for Roger," he continued, "I have to say, he *did* seem on a roll when he called me. And, you know, I was looking forward to seeing him. A couple of cranky old bastards putting the world in its god-damn place." He paused to push his half drunk coffee away and regarded the passers-by. "These days everybody has their own *life narrative* — I believe that's the term. This is not just writing memoirs stuff, this is what people live by, self image stuff. People are actors, and god-damn method actors at that," he let out a dry laugh, "you know, playing the lead roles in our own particular soap opera. Facebook and all that shit. But then, and this is where it gets sticky, we also have to play support roles, cameo performances, in other people's soap operas. And that requires variations of the persona for different audiences, different situations. I think we actually *need* to do this, that it's stimulating and healthy, that it gives us a vital sense of control and independence and all that palaver. But the upshot is that we have secrets. Necessary, *essential* secrets. Necessary as much for emotional well-being as for practical reasons. And so, we create different compartments within our lives. We have to. So ..." he lowered his voice, "anything is possible. But, suicide? Well, I don't know. I guess we've all known someone. It can come at a person suddenly, in ways that cannot be anticipated. Like a traffic accident."

Tenderly, they inhaled each other's silence before he continued.

"I don't know how far Roger went beyond what I originally gave him and Steve Lyons. By the way, have you talked to him? After all, Steve paid for the research in the first place. Or, to be entirely accurate, his client did."

"Who was that?"

"Some faceless corporate outfit with a set of initials for a name. A. I. something Holdings. I can't remember. Probably long since wound up. Roger and I were always arm's length on that. It didn't concern us. They were just the property developers for Nibbelup. I suppose we could look it up, but I have no idea who was behind it, who Lyons was dealing with. Actually, he probably dealt with their lawyers rather than them directly. I take it you haven't spoken to him?"

"No. Do we need to? Ted may know him from somewhere."

Oldie pursed his lips and shook his head. "It would be better coming from me. If need be, I'll talk to him. He was also at Roger's funeral. Quite a few interested parties at that funeral ... but, anyway, I spoke to him there and he said he'd keep in touch."

"Is he likely to be a problem?"

"I don't see why," he replied. "Steve's a businessman. These days he's into aquaculture — fattening up tuna in sea cages. They feed them pilchards. Back in the late nineties, before Steve got into it, there was a virus that decimated pilchards all along the south coast. Not sure if it was ever proven, but suspicion fell on pilchards imported to feed the tuna. I don't know, but it is possible Steve got into the business on the back of that scare, when more cautious investors were going elsewhere. That'd be just like him. Anyway, regarding Roger, he may have found something more than I did. I don't know. Or, to put it another way, he may have discovered the significance of something that was under our noses all along. This business is like that — the apparently insignificant detail can rear up and become the key to everything. Circumstances change, and the trivial is suddenly invested with consequence. For what it's worth, and I never had the chance to tell Roger this, I think the way to approach this is to find out not so much what was dumped — I mean, we know it'll be asbestos or heavy metals or something equally tasty — but to find out who did the dumping. That would be my approach. Who did the dumping? Which companies? Who owned them and who managed them? And then see what connections can be made. As you probably know, a former manufacturer of asbestos building products is in strife over dumping stuff next to a Catholic orphanage down there on the Canning River. That case is in court and it has probably got a few old boys daydreaming about what they were up to in days gone by. So, who else was dumping stuff down there? Or at Lake Monger? Or down at Spearwood? Or, in the immediate matter at hand, out there at lovely, it's-a-great-place-to-raise-kids Nibbelup. My guess is that some prominent public figure — back in the day when they were just another player making a buck — had some connection to a company engaged in illegal landfill activities. You know," he laughed, "like the Mafia do in Italy. What's it called? The Camorra, in Naples. But then, let's not get carried away here, the locals, whatever their inflated opinions of themselves, are not your actual Mafiosas! At least, I hope not."

"But you don't know that." She was frowning, worried.

"Well, no, I don't. Not really. You're right. But, look," he reached across and touched her shoulder to reassure her, "don't get me wrong. I'm just saying, the locals might bend the rules and break a few laws along the way. You know, demolish a heritage building without permission. Have the occasional suspicious fire. That sort of thing. But they're not habitual, violent criminals. Basically, Perth style is to pay people off. Or, if that doesn't work, run a smear campaign. They're pretty good at that. It's cheaper and easier than bumping them off. It is possible, but I doubt it, that some people *may* have been interested in what Roger was doing, but I really, seriously doubt anyone was going to ... do him any *harm*. Shirley Finn aside, it's just not the way they deal with stuff here. As far as I know, he really didn't have anything *that* sensitive. If there had been anything suspicious the cops would have contacted me. To keep up appearances, if you follow my drift."

"Shirley Finn? The madam found dead on the South Perth golf course?"

"That's right. Shot in the head. Winter, 1975. Ancient history, although there are a few interested parties still breathing. Funnily enough, Roger and I talked about that at Paulo's funeral. There's a novel out about it. It's now well and truly an urban myth, but there always was a rumoured political side to that affair. They reckon Reg Pascoe was behind it but that didn't stop him going on to become State Premier. Reg the Racketeer, the bagman. I daresay more could come out one day. Perhaps after Reg kicks the bucket. Who knows?"

"But doesn't the Finn case show that people in power here *are* prepared to kill to protect themselves?"

He gave a little, plosive puff. "That was a long time ago. And really, who knows what personal considerations may have been in play. There was a lot of smoke, so there was a fire — but where, exactly, that's not clear. Why some rumours get legs and others don't is a good question. If there's some underlying disenchantment or belief to fuel it, a rumour is easy to run. Drop a few hints, in strictest confidence, to the right tattletale, let them join the dots and before you know it the dogs are barking on the street corners. Always remember, people are inclined to believe a story, especially when they have had a hand in telling it to themselves."

He tried to gauge her reaction, but she gazed out the window, preoccupied. After a while he finally asked about her and Ted's interest in Roger's research.

"The thing is, he approached us. He rang Ted and then came around straight away, within a half hour. He lived near us. Said he'd heard we were interested in producing a documentary and offered to help with the research. Which was *great*, but we had the idea that the desalination story would have more interest for the global market — which, let's face it, is where we'll have to go to finance and sell it. Even so, he *did* tell us a few things that intrigued us and, you know, we thought we ought to check them out."

"Intriguing things. Like, some toxic landfill sites — covered up, in more ways than one? A whiff of official corruption? Documents missing from the archives?"

"Yes."

"And he told you I knew about all this and may have further material?"

She nodded.

"With regard to the financing of your documentary ... I wonder if that means corporate sponsorship? De-sal plant manufacturers, for example?"

"We would look at that. Of course. Would you have a problem with that?"

"I guess not. Who told Roger you were making a documentary?"

She shrugged. "It could have been any number of people. It's not a secret."

"And he and Ted knew each other from before?"

"They did, but they'd not seen or spoken to one another in years. I'm not sure why he went to the funeral. I don't think I even knew he was going. Spur of the moment curiosity. To see who turned up. Ted's like that. He knows so many people and I had just been interested in how Roger could help us get the project up." She abruptly stopped and sat still to let the moment swallow itself before she continued. "That sounds rather heartless. Sorry. It came out wrong. Let me explain. Ted and I set up our production company when we came out from London. He did a bit of work for UK media as a freelance stringer — yours truly behind the camera — but there's not a lot of real news here as far as London is concerned."

"The business may have done better with you in front of the camera."

"Oooo," she cooed, "a flatterer!"

He shrugged, with all the nonchalance he could muster.

"Well," she went on, "maybe so, but not enough to make a go of it. No, we needed regular income and with his connections in this town, it was going to be

Ted who did that. As it happens, his work is pretty full on at the moment. So I do the running around and deal with the daily bits and pieces. Today, among other things, I'm trying to source some mid-nineteenth century images of Perth. And later on, as you may have gathered," she pulled a face, "I'll have to clean up after a botched printing job and smooth a few feathers."

"And I suppose, with Ted's job and all, he has to be careful about any perceived conflicts of interest."

She didn't miss a beat. "He does. We keep that in mind with everything we do. It's a delicate but manageable situation. Should a real problem arise, Ted would have to make a decision."

He looked at her, the question on his face.

"His job or me!" She positively chortled as she lifted up her bag and took out the Manila envelope.

It contained his ten-year-old report to Steve Lyons and copies of documents it cited. As he leafed through the pages she tackled her Melting Moment. "I love these things," she said.

There didn't seem to be anything he didn't know about, but without going through it systematically he could not be sure anything was missing. He told her this and asked what she knew about the novel Roger said he was writing.

Her bewilderment was genuine. He believed her when she said she had never seen or heard of it.

"Well, I'm not sure whether I'm relieved or disappointed. Frankly, I'm a bit burnt out looking at people's manuscripts. But he did tell me, we discussed it, and he told his sister as well, that he was working on a book ... a novel based on this stuff. She thought I had it. Asked me about it at the funeral. From what he told me, it was a *roman à clef*, a novel with a key, which is ..."

140

She raised her index finger and wagged it in mock reproach. "I *am* Canadian," she said. "I went to school in Montreal. French is *known* to me. I had a bi-lingual dog. As to the literary terminology, my mother was a lecturer in the Department of English at McGill. An English lecturer who always insisted I read anything French in the original — *La Chute*, not *The Fall*. She was, dare I admit it, an academic, no less."

And then she gave him her low husky laugh and her half-closed eyes shone with the lights of ancient campfires.

"Ah, well," he murmured, scrambling to collect himself, "I believe McGill is a bona fide university. Yes, I have that on good authority. They are few and far between, but such places still exist. It's just the jumped up rubbish we have here that gets up my nose. You know, Crawley Tech, as a mate of mine refers to the University of Western Australia."

"OK." She leaned towards him. "Here's another idea. Roger's novel may have been semi-autobiographical and contained things — personal matters — the family don't want to be known. The sister, the ex-wife, whoever, may have been just checking to make sure you don't have a copy. End of story. You say there wasn't a note, but perhaps his book was one long suicide note; a reckoning, a settling of scores. It wouldn't be the first time that's happened, would it?"

He wanted to say he had thought of this possibility, but he hadn't. And that was obvious.

"I'd also say," she went on, "and I mean no disrespect by this, but from my one meeting with him, I had the impression Roger Kidd was one of those people who like to cultivate an air of mystery around themselves. Such people often ..." she hesitated on a slight frown, "have a need to make themselves interesting."

He was about to politely demur, to point out that Roger had actually been digging where a few bodies may very well be buried. But as he opened his mouth she raised her index finger and said, "I'd just ask: Was Roger a sphinx without a secret? Someone who'd rather lie than admit they had nothing to hide?"

"Well," he half smiled, "I guess that's one of the things we need to find out."

"Yes, so then," she returned the smile, "I don't know what your rates are, but do you think you could perhaps check out some of those old business connections you mentioned?"

"Of course. It's just that ... I could spend a lot of hours at fifty bucks an hour and find bugger all. I reckon the best I can do quickly is perhaps find evidence that files have stuff missing. You know, in that era as pages were added to files they were numbered. So you can usually see if something is missing. Mind you, I have heard of appropriately numbered pages being substituted from other files. But, really, even when you know it's been buggered with, what does that give you? The Big Nuffin'. And that's on top of a situation where anything illegal was probably not written down, not intentionally at any rate. You know, with his connections and background, Ted could probably come up with a few likely names just by asking around. Discreetly, of course. Someone may know something that doesn't actually incriminate themselves and be willing to, you know, show off a little as to how well informed they are. I'm not actually from Perth. I didn't go to school here so I don't have easy access to the old boy networks. You will have noticed, the mentality here is small town politics, the essential dynamic of which is personal loyalties."

"Believe me, the personal obligations factor is not a distinguishing feature of small town politics only.

Chicago is not a small town. Besides, wouldn't you agree that personal loyalties are what hold together criminal organizations, such as the Mafia?"

"True," he inclined his head to concede the point. "All the same, Ted is probably in a better position to narrow the field. And then, do you actually want to go down this path? Like you said, desalination is your main story."

She tapped her fingernails on the table, considering what he said.

"Let me talk with Ted. But even if he were to suggest a name, you'd be the best one to find the records to tie it all together."

He indicated that he understood.

"Now," she reached for her bag, "can we go outside and sit somewhere where I can have a cigarette? Remember, I'm a smoker. You saw me smoking by the car after Paulo's funeral. I thought you were going to say Hello that day."

When he expressed surprise that she remembered him, she replied, flatly, without any smile or flattering inflection in her voice, "You have a memorable face."

He was about to joke that he wasn't sure "memorable" was flattering when she clarified, "The beard. Photogenic."

He jerked his head back and gave her his quizzical stare.

"Seriously, let me take your portrait." Her hand shot out and the backs of her fingers lightly brushed, touched the beard where it rested on his chest. "Perhaps I can place you for some advertising work."

Before he could respond she asked him whether he did much writing "of his own".

"A little. No, not really. Occasionally. Nothing worth talking about. There are far, far too many writers these days. Did you know, there are presently at least ten million people in the world writing a novel? That's not an exaggeration. Ten million!"

She grimaced. "And the bulk of them ..."

"... are rubbish! But, guess what? That doesn't preclude many of them, far too many of them, from being published. 'Fraid not! Because, wait for it, the Wonder of the Age is upon us! Electronic self-publication is *the* growth industry and here comes *every*body. There's just too much noise now. You know, I'm not sure Roger would have understood or agreed, but in our shameful times I actually think that keeping silent is an honourable thing to do." He shook his head in consternation. "It has to be better than being rejected, unread, by some bored editorial assistant brat. Deleted!"

As they walked across the plaza to the low limestone retaining walls serving as seats around the lawns and trees outside the museum, she asked where he was from and how long he had been in Perth. Without much prompting he told her that forty years ago he met the love of his life in Darwin, followed her to Perth, where they married and then ran away together to live in Auckland for a decade. It was a safe, romantic story he knew women of a certain age liked to hear.

Restless women.

He had an inkling of what Roger was on about when he raised that question about her reasons for coming to Perth with Ted. You just knew, as Peggy would have said, that she was a woman with a past.

"So, indulge me," he said, "I'm curious, what's with the Russian tatt?"

"Oh," she glanced at her shoulder and arched her eyebrows, as though surprised by both his question and that her adornment might be showing. "Oh, that," she patted her sleeve. "That's a long story. I've had it a long time. Youthful hi-jinx back in Toronto," she half laughed.

144

"Call it a keepsake."

Finding a spot a little apart from others, they perched on the low wall under the shade of a plane tree.

"Did you ever dye your hair blonde?"

She gave him a wide-eyed incredulous stare. "Of course! Doesn't every girl, at least once? Especially one whose natural color is mouse. In fact, I once did an ad as a blonde. In London, for car batteries! Yep, batteries. Don't ask! A girl's gotta do what a girl's gotta do. But let me tell you, TV, print media, billboards — people recognized me on the street, so I went black. But, hey, it sure the heck paid the bills for a spell."

"Always a consideration."

"Kept me off the street," she said, matter-of-factly, putting on her sunglasses.

"Ever thought about revisiting blonde?"

"Sure. Or redhead."

"Strawberry blonde!" he blurted.

Did she wince?

She brought out a beautifully engraved, silver cigarette case. It flipped open smoothly and snapped shut with the perfect *click*. He had time to notice the engravings were long-legged birds in flight. Storks, probably. She toyed with the cigarette for a couple of seconds before putting it between her lips. She had a lighter in her hand but did not use it.

"So," she murmured around the cigarette, "you're one of those who think sugar is the addiction of our age?"

"Sugar?"

"Before, you said fructose. That's a sugar."

"It is. So fructose converts to fat, stimulates appetite and, yes, it's addictive."

She lit her smoke. "I really should get going," she inclined her head towards the old courthouse. "I want some historic images of Perth to show how quickly this city has grown on this fragile environment. In less than 200 years, a sprawling metropolitan area, much of it paved. So I want to show it as a village, a town and so on. Growth. Toronto, Melbourne, Chicago — many North American and Australian cities have the same developmental trajectory. In Perth, most of that growth has been in living memory. Since the nineteen-fifties. Many people here haven't just inherited the urban sprawl, they've experienced it."

A pair of elfin school girls in the uniform of one of Perth's most expensive school hurried by, grinning as, in a subdued, conspiratorial voice, one told the other something with great animation. Suddenly the listener screamed with mirth. "Oh my Gawd!" she shrieked, "What the *farck*!" She then repeated her remark even louder and playfully punched her friend's shoulder. People a hundred metres away turned to locate the source of the disturbance. The excited girls rushed on, oblivious.

Oldie and Blondie exchanged a glance. "Girls," she said, with a slight shake of her head.

"They all seem to have me down as an easy mark for the spare two dollars for the bus routine," he told her.

She turned to look at him. "Yes," she said with a slow smile, "I can see that. And don't tell me you ever refuse them."

"Not often. But I want to tell them it's a bad habit for young girls to get into. The sad thing is, they don't know any better but, you know, really — asking strangers in the street for money? And they seem to target dirty old men at that."

She shook her head and wagged a finger.

They sat together in easy company while she smoked. He told her there were a number of good sketches and paintings of colonial Perth in private hands and gave her the names of some people to talk to. He also mentioned a painting of Perth and the river foreshore in the eighteen-sixties, a large, detailed canvas depicting the town as viewed from the spot where the war memorial would later be erected in Kings Park. It was on display at the Museum at the Benedictine Community at New Norcia, an hour and a half's drive up Great Northern Highway.

When she said that, despite having lived in Perth a few years, she had not so far managed to see New Norcia he replied, "Get Ted to take a day off and take you up there for lunch. The meals in the pub are pretty good. And that hotel, on the rise there, it looks like something out of *Gone with the Wind*."

She stubbed her smoke and flicked the butt into a deft arc that bulls-eyed into a bin. "OK. Sounds like a great outing. But in the meantime, I've got to be elsewhere." She stood, took off her dark glasses and offered him a bright smile and her hand to shake. "I am glad to have met you, Alexander. Really, I am. I'm sure we can work together. I look forward to doing so."

He nodded agreement and held her hand a moment longer than decorum required. He wanted to tell her he would like to be her friend, but could only manage a strained "See you later". He stepped back, gave a small wave, turned and walked away in a rosy glow.

Thank God he shampooed and conditioned the beard! Without thinking he reassured himself by running his hand down its soft and shiny flow.

He went back to the station via Kakulas Brothers', the only place he knew where he could buy tinned saury. True, they were just the dwarf Atlantic ones, and to the ignorant eye looked like Spanish sardines in oil, but they were sweet and tolerable on toast. Ah … if only he could find someone selling smoked Pacific sauries. Next time he had Betty for the day he might run around a few of the Asian food shops. Why was it that there were a zillion lines of tuna in the supermarkets, but never one of saury?

While he was at it, he might as well get some of the Greek's Turkish delight. The pistachio one. Take a few chunks of it home to the Girl for dessert tonight. Yes, and grab a few extras for the train ride home.

He checked his notebook to make sure he still had Owl-woman's phone number and thought about how best to shake that tree. Not too directly, obviously. Anna had warned him about the possibility of something falling on his head.

He dutifully waited for the lights to change before he ventured to cross William Street. No sense in taking unnecessary risks.

VIII

The rain drifted in from the sea before sunrise, rousing the scent of the lavender at the front of the house. He raised his head in the grey light and heard the faint dripping of the roof gutters. Prematurely forecast several times in the previous week, the only rain had been pearl and gold curtains trailing down the distance of the ocean horizon at sunset. Now, finally, light but steady showers whispered over the coastal plain. With the dams at less than a quarter of their capacity, the driest, hottest summer on record seemed to be readying to relent. Better get those gutters cleaned this year.

He turned and stretched on his back. Anna rolled towards him, snuffling but sleeping soundly on. It was too hot and humid to cuddle, but he let the back of his outstretched hand touch against her knees. There was more than an hour before the radio switched on and they would tumble into and through their morning routine of showers, breakfast, coffee, toilette and getting her off to work. The annual virginity popping season had ended and another school year was underway.

There was a question of how long she could continue to work. Each year seemed longer and harder for her. She freely admitted that even if they had not been going East in April she would have had to take the time off anyway. The term "burn-out" had entered their discussions and she was making noises about cutting back to a four-day week. He couldn't argue against it.

But then, there was no getting around the fact they still had a burdensome mortgage with the banksters and her (along with everybody else's) superannuation had been so white-anted as to have become about as substantial as a cardboard cut-out. By the time she came to collect, it would hardly cover the power and water bills. Never mind the Council rates.

They needed an inheritance, a bumper lotto win or some other trump everything windfall. With both their mothers alive and living in their own paid for homes, the first option should eventually come through. But even though the old dears were well into their eighties, they looked like they would last a while yet and a few years in a care facility would put the bulk of the family legacy in someone else's bank account. The Lotto ... well, best to just grit your teeth, keep the faith and buy next week's tickets. As for the windfall scenario, so far that had not exceeded having once picked up a fifty in a mall car park. Sweet enough, but not even a full tank for little rattle&hum Black Betty. Besides, with practically everyone using traceable credit cards, he couldn't remember the last time he picked up even small change.

Meanwhile, back at the ranch, he'd had bugger all work, generated bugger all income, and just feeding him was a major drain on their budget. One good thing was that he hadn't been throwing their dollars down the sinkhole of a superannuation scheme for him. That was the silver lining — not having to plan for and ultimately face old age in an increasingly vicious world.

It was easier for him, given that he was the one with the ticket and flight plan taking him out over Roger's drop zone. That scenario, obviously, excluded any unforeseen twist in the ribbon of Fate. He hardly dared think of what would become of him should a runaway bus or a melanoma be dropped into the script to claim Anna. The world is brimming, ready to spill with stories about the ribbon of Fate becoming entangled in the whirling spokes of Destiny. Or is it the ribbon of Destiny and the spokes of Fate? Either way, you never know what's around the corner and, in the random-bolt-of-lightning stakes, he and the Girl were equally vulnerable.

That kind of inverted Gambler's Fallacy hardly worked as a consolation because, all the while, he had folded into his hand the dark ace of the disease living within him. Day in, day out, it gnawed away, eating him alive. He'd re-read Susan Sontag in order to wrangle the rampant metaphors back away from the space in which he tried to live, but somehow the struggle only confirmed their strength. Mostly, the disease prowled as a living thing (which, of course, it was), but at other times the persistence of it seemed mechanical. Then he imagined the cuff of his jacket snagged in some slow moving but relentless machinery, and that he was being drawn into something that would mince him. Although he acknowledged the whole metaphor thing could be a complicated route — ah, the sweet perils of Aristotelian verbosity — he held to the notion that a description was often the best approach to a causal explanation; and that, with a bit of Platonic luck, explanations tend to keep the demons tethered, in their cages.

There were no such reassuringly philosophical nostrums to neatly handle the matter of how she would fare after he died. All he could say was that her character was her destiny and he would have to trust in that.

The rain had stopped and the sky was clearing. The dawn chorus was underway. He heard the kookaburras in the park. They were not calling his name. Not today.

151

As the light infused their bedroom, he studied the stain on the ceiling. Was it getting darker? Bigger? He'd paid a bloke good money to fix the blasted roof before the summer and then this appeared. Another leak? But there had been no rain and this morning's would have barely wet the roof. Mould? A sinister metaphor. A blot the size of a football. He would have to watch it. Couldn't do otherwise — he woke up to it every morning. Should he paint it over and hope for the best? Just another damned thing to obsess about. That led him to contemplate the step-by-step bullshit of getting things done. Such tedium always tempted him to look for short cuts, which risked getting the sequence wrong.

Or of just forgetting what comes next. That happens.

He gave a long sigh.

"Shush," said the Girl, her voice thick and sleepy.

He slowly turned his head to watch her. Dreams fluttered on her eyelids, her breath regular and deep.

So much for private moments! He swallowed, wondering if they had ever had some sort of verbal exchange in their sleep. Subconscious dialogues? Was it possible? He thought it could be. Perhaps he should try talking into her dreams, telling her that he had merely gone ahead, stepped into another room.

He had not realised how powerful that sort of nonsense was until after Jem died. Then, many times late at night, he stood outside his son's closed room, overwhelmed with the feeling that, in some indefinable but undeniable way, the dead boy was still in there, behind that closed door. A door he dared not open.

He never discussed the haunting with Anna, but he knew she had also sensed it.

Their intimacy did not mean they always spoke their minds. Indeed, in many situations their mutual understanding was the very thing saving them from that bother. When they needed to, they could tell each other fibs with straight faces.

And there were things they forgot to declare.

In his case, the regularly purchased extra lotto tickets.

As was to be expected, and as he had disclosed to Blondie, he had a theory about secrets. His basic conclusion being that we need them for our sense of being. They give a body room, psychic breathing space; they get you around that feeling of being hemmed in. And as a wise old paederast once wrote, "A mixture of a lie doth ever add pleasure". Like God, if secrets do not exist, they have to be created. His thinking on this subject had more tendrils than a baroque vine, but theory and practice locked together on the simple truth that the measure of a secret is whether one is willing to lie to protect it — and there was no doubt he was quite brave enough to skate out onto the thin ice of barefaced deviousness. Yes, Ladies and Gentlemen, when he needed to, he could tell a lie, a whopper, taking pleasure in cutting a dashing pirouette while he was at it. Like all liars, he was susceptible to the belief that his falsehoods were primarily for the benefit and protection of others.

White lies.

Besides, as a crafty old Polish Lutheran has pointed out, the Ten Commandments don't actually prohibit lying *per se*. All you have in The Book is no false witnessing agin the neighbours — which is fair enough, but it leaves a lot of open country for personal use. See what I mean about pirouettes?

No sweat.

So what to do, what to say about Blondie?

Well, actually, there wasn't a lot to say. Between them, Carol and Anna had arranged everything while he was off at Woolworths appraising the broccoli and carrots. Anna took the call and they got to talking. As women

153

do. Ted being unavailable and all, Carol had asked to borrow Anna's husband for a daytrip to New Norcia. She told Anna she wished to discuss with Oldie "some new information and a proposal". She would pick him up, do all the driving, buy him lunch and pay him a consultant's fee for his day. She had invited Anna to accompany them, trying to persuade her to take a sickie, but the Girl told her that was not possible.

Carol also let Anna know that she would like to do "a bit of a shoot" of Oldie for her portfolio. That made him nervous. It was the beard. She was going to define him by his beard. What part would she assign him: bushie, bikie or Santa?

Paid work. Anna accepted on his behalf. All he had to do was call back and confirm the date. "She sounds very nice," she told him. "Sensible."

Sensible. Nice. This was starting to sound a bit tricky.

It was nice his wife trusted him to go for a drive in the country with another woman. Not that she thought there was any chance of the fat old bastard scoring with the honey-pot — although he wasn't that much older than debonair Ted. But you had to ask, was it sensible that she should trust him not to make a clown of himself? He wondered whether he should let on that he already felt a certain intimacy was in place between them, that they had commenced what he thought of as "a conversation"? But then, that must be apparent. After all, Blondie had taken the initiative in asking him to make the outing. Very nice.

"New information and a proposal?"

"That's what she said. You need to talk to her about that."

"To be honest," he said, not quite sure whether or not what he was about to say was strictly true, "she's a bit of a mystery to me. I'm not sure what's straightforward in all this any more. She knew Paulo. Apart from the fact that she has lived in Montreal, Toronto and London — Chicago, perhaps — and that she used to do a bit of modeling, I know practically nothing about her. Nothing other than what she's told me. I know she likes Molten Moments. All I can find on Google is just the last few years in Perth. Before that — a blank. Perhaps she used another name when she was modelling. Above all, I'm not sure what she and Ted want from me for their money."

"She likes ... what did you say?"

"You know those biscuits ... Melting Moments."

"You said Molten Moments."

He laughed and, tilting towards the fact that Anna scorned tattoos as self-inflicted graffiti, quickly told her, "She has a Russian tatt. In Cyrillic. It says Blondie. You know, as in Debbie Harry's group."

Anna regarded him a moment before flicking her eyebrows. "Hitler's dog was called Blondi."

"Ooouu ..."

"Well, it's a job," she said, "and it'll do you good to get out of the house for a day. All your social life is on the phone. Get out into the real world and meet some real people! Mister Male Model!"

"Hmm."

"What did the Lone Ranger say to his sidekick when he wanted to get to Canada in a hurry?"

He knew that one. "On to Toronto pronto, Tonto!"

She gave him a pantomime, conspiratorial wink.

"I dunno," he said, "I just never learnt the script."

"No? What script is that?"

"The one where I perform like a trained seal."

Later, before he rang Blondie to accept her offer, he asked the Girl what else they had discussed.

"Don't worry," she said, "I let her know you were

a good researcher and have worked on television documentaries before."

"Thirty-five years ago!"

"Doesn't matter. You need to promote yourself. She was interested. Impressed."

"Christ! I hope you didn't overdo it."

"I didn't. Actually, we mostly talked about learning disabilities. She said she's thinking about documentary possibilities but I think there's a fairly strong personal interest. She has a stepson with problems and she said she had her own difficulties at school."

"Really? Her mother is a university lecturer."

"Was. Her mother is dead."

"Oh? You did have a proper heart-to heart, didn't you? Did she say anything about her father?"

"Not mentioned."

Some new information. And a proposal.

"Did she say anything about her time in London? Where she met Ted? Why she came to Perth? That sort of thing?"

"Nope. You know I don't pry."

Sometimes understanding comes from an unexpected direction. Stones fall into different parts of the pond, the ripples cross and interact, and come at you in ways that could not have been anticipated. He understood that Blondie also had her necessary secrets and haunted voids.

As for that morning's rain, the Bureau of Metrology registered it as "a trace". Most people slept through it. By the time they woke and ventured forth, everything was bone dry and the sky was a hard, staring blue. As usual.

Two days after arranging to accompany Blondie to New Norcia, and five days before their planned outing, Oldie received an email from Steve Lyons. He asked about

Oldie's general wellbeing and inquired as to whether Roger's missing book had surfaced. Registering a mental Uh-oh!, Oldie nevertheless replied that "nothing of note" had happened. He did not consider this a lie as he could say, truthfully, that the book had not been found and he had not heard from any members of Roger's family, or their representatives.

Presenting it as his own idea, he suggested to Lyons that Roger's family may already have his book and were now merely trying to ensure there were no other copies floating around. The businessman responded with a noncommittal "Perhaps".

He did not mention Carol Dubois and Ted Connell because, he reasoned, his primary obligation of professional confidentiality now lay with them and their company, SeeHear Films, which was, apparently, going to employ him. Besides, there really wasn't anything to tell — in his brief follow-up phone conversation with Blondie, she had declined to discuss her "new information" until she saw him.

A few hours later there was a follow-up email from Steve. He told Oldie he had recently been appointed to the South-Eastern Australia Fishing Industry Council (SEAFIC) and wanted to know if he would be interested in cleaning up the punctuation and grammar of their more formal reports and submissions to government. Such documents, once buried in parliamentary libraries with little more than the executive summary ever read, now have a publication afterlife on the internet. It has dawned on some of those who produce said reports that they are a permanent and very accessible record of sloppy work — not a good look. Steve Lyons invited Oldie to give him a call, should he be interested.

Definitely a classic Ugh-oh! moment.

He could hear a clomping and tromping about in the

bushes. He wondered whether Steve Lyons was acting alone, looking after his own interests — or someone else's. Whoever was behind the Nibbelup project, presumably.

But he didn't wonder too hard or very long. The fishing industry's money would be handy, to put it mildly. So he would do the work, providing he could play it with a straight bat and whatever informal strings that were attached did not become too binding.

It was all very intriguing. In-*tree*-ging!

Or it should have been. Oldie just couldn't bring himself to take it seriously. It was, somehow, mundane.

And he had another reason to inwardly groan. Although Lyons saw his offer as a favour, a handout with which he thought he would secure Oldie's gratitude and keep him close, hard experience taught that the business of rendering the garrulous shambles of committee waffle into English was always a far more tedious slog than those paying for the job could ever imagine.

Dot the eyes and cross the tees. How many times had he heard that crap?

But it was that very desirable thing — paid work.

Twice in one week. In-*tree*-ging! In-*tree*-ging!

Perhaps he would allow himself a small celebratory drink. The Girl would be pleased about the work, even though she would say they should not pop corks until the money was in hand. One of them had to be sensible. And he did have to ration his drinks. Even the good old *moloko* was too much of a good thing for Old Alex, or so he was told. Tap water in Perth being so foul, he drank that carbonated stuff supermarkets sell as mineral water. On such a regime, a real drink is occasionally required.

Going through the motions, observing the form, he emailed Lyons for further details of the work on offer and asked for a few days to consider the matter.

158

Yes, he would slip in a celebratory drink as part of a celebratory meal.

Once you have the knack, the making of a good risotto is not difficult. Get the heat and timing right and the thing comes together more or less of its own accord. People muck it up when they introduce too many extraneous ingredients. If you want to substitute leeks or celery for the onions — fine, but use all three and you end up with a sloppy vegetable stew.

Oldie had learnt to keep it simple, to limit himself to a few basic combinations: crispy bacon with peas or, in season, skun broad beans; crab meat or cray tails (cubed) with chives; grilled and shredded chicken thighs with asparagus; and so on. Some people favored Carnaroli or some other variety of rice, but he was happy with supermarket Arborio. He invariably infused a sachet of saffron in the stock. Any commercial stock was acceptable, but for the cheese he used nothing other than genuine Parmesan, which he grated himself. He used a lot of cheese and, when the Girl wasn't looking, added a dollop of double cream (a glass and a half of full cream *moloko* right there). He had experimented with other wines, cider and even spirits, but his standard was a good Pinot grigio — a quarter of the bottle in the pan and the rest, close to freezing, served with the meal.

Wine. Cream. Cheese. Even when the chicken is free range (whatever that means) and the asparagus organic, the meal is not the recommended diet for an overweight man with a gall stone and a compromised liver. But, shit a brick, people have their reasons. There are times when it is necessary to pretend that things are normal, even when one risks injury to do so. It may be irrational and it may seem stupid, but there it is. White lies. As that stern Russian remarked, you cannot expect a man who is warm to understand a man who is cold.

The Girl had the sense and the courtesy to indulge him, to not prick his flimsy delusion, and he had the nous not to give her too big a serve.

Steve Lyons was on the phone from Adelaide bright and early the next morning. The powers that be continued to hide in the bushes, but they had sent their man out to have a chat, to deliver a message. Oldie wrinkled his nose at the phone and immediately remembered Peggy's admonishment not to pull faces. "You never know," she said, "the wind may change and you'll be stuck with that ugly face."

After a perfunctory run through of what the fishing lobbyists' work involved (essentially, the money was good) Steve cut to the chase. He told Oldie that after their conversation at Roger's funeral he had "thought it best" to make a few inquiries. Steve said he had learned that for a year or so the Environmental Protection Agency had been undertaking additional tests on water and soil samples from in and around Nibbelup. He had also heard that Roger had been asking about this, pestering some official he had discovered was working on the testing program. Despite assurances the tests had revealed nothing outside acceptable limits, Roger had persisted in the matter, being particularly interested as to why additional tests had been conducted at all. The answer to that, Steve quickly went on, was that after a newsworthy incident in Victoria, it was deemed prudent to increase monitoring of "potentially problematic sites" elsewhere.

"An incident in Victoria", Oldie cut in, "means Brookland Greens?"

"Ah … yes, that could have been, yes, I believe that was the name of the place."

"The one publicly described as a botched landfill and

a fiasco? Big court case. How much was the damages bill, the payout to residents? Up around twenty-five million, last time I looked."

There was a pause before Lyons spoke again. "Sounds like you discussed this with Roger."

"Not at all! It was in the news and I followed it on the internet. You know, I'm interested in current events."

"I suppose I should keep myself better informed," Steve said. "What was it called again? Brooklyn Green?"

"Brook*land* — L-A-N-D — Greens, plural. Also known as the Stevensons Road landfill."

"Hmm. Thanks for that. But as far as Nibbelup goes, I'm assured by someone in a position to know that there is absolutely no problem there."

Someone.

No point, Oldie told himself, in asking who that would be.

"No problems, as yet."

Steve did not immediately respond and a couple of thousand kilometres of the Great Australian Emptiness yawned through the phone as he considered what to say. Finally, he pronounced with measured deliberation, "As I said, Nibbelup has been carefully monitored and given a clean bill of health. Until there is evidence to the contrary, it is surely, ah, irresponsible to suggest there *could* be a problem. We have to keep a proper perspective on this. We need to wait and see what the ongoing testing shows. Take a longer view. Don't you agree?"

Steve's tone, coming on the back of his clumsy pretence that he had only vaguely heard of Brookland Greens, irritated Oldie.

"A longer view!" he snorted. "That's easy. The longer view is that we die and are soon forgotten. And to cite the case of Roger Kidd — forgotten pretty damned soon at that! Swept under the carpet, as they say in political circles."

"Yes, of course, but ..."

"Steve! You know what? The longer view is that everything falls to pieces. Everything! The longer view! Ha ha haar. Seriously, mate, when you get down to it, where do you think this oh so tidy longer view actually gets us?"

"Well," Steve reverted to avuncular affability, "perhaps we don't have to take *such* a long view and not be *that* pessimistic. It's all relative, you know, a matter of perspective."

"You got that much right," Oldie muttered.

"And, as I was saying, we need to wait and see if there is actually a problem at all. There's no sense in pessimistic speculation. You know, Roger may have been a bit alarmist. I'm told he was talking to someone in the media. Did he mention anything about that to you?"

"Media? What are you saying?"

"Alex, I'm just telling you what I was told when I asked about this. Which, if I might say, I did as much on your behalf as mine. I was told, and this is as much as I know, that Roger had been talking to a journalist who now works as a ministerial advisor."

Oldie heard the faint swish of a door shutting behind him.

"Oh," he said quickly, "that'd be Ted Connell. He was at Roger's funeral. A *former* journalist, to be strictly accurate. He was on the box for a while, but he's not in the media now. You'd probably have had dealings with him, at some stage, wouldn't you?"

"I know who he is, but I can't quite put a face on him. It's been a while since I was based in Perth. So Roger mentioned him?"

"He did, in passing. But he didn't say what it was about. I guess that's one of the things we would have talked about had he kept our appointment at Hillarys."

'So, you haven't spoken to Connell?"

"No, I haven't spoken to Connell. I know him by sight, but I've never actually met or spoken to him." Oldie let a note of tetchiness enter his voice. "You're starting to sound a bit interrogative here Steve."

"No, no, no. Don't be so paranoid, dear boy." Lyons did his amiable bemusement routine. "Not at all, dear chap, not at all! But listen, just to round this off, I should tell you my source gave a strong hint that Connell has a bit of an agenda in all this. He's trying to dig up shit on someone. It's all a bit political, apparently. Connell works for Jack Knight, Minister for Planning, doesn't he?"

"I believe so."

"You know," Steve said, "his nickname used to be Silent Knight."

"Why's that?"

"No comment. When he first got elected, even as a back-bencher, that was all he ever said to the press: No Comment. But he soon learnt the art of obfuscating waffle and now he's a Minister of the Crown."

"So, who or what is Mr Knight after?"

"Good Heavens, I wasn't told that sort of thing. I was stretching a friendship to find out what I've told you. All I'm saying is — be careful in your dealings with Connell. Things may not be quite what they seem with him. Believe me, if he's working for Jack Knight, he'd need a PhD in deviousness. "

Keeping his voice relaxed and casual, Oldie thanked Lyons for the advice and, moving away, asked him whether his source was in government or the private sector.

The businessman quietly chuckled with genuine amusement. "Oh well, these days, that's a question that can't always be answered with any certainty. The answer depends upon who's asking the question. Even former Premiers and Ministers of the Crown ... ah, make the transition, as they say. And people do go the other way. All the time. Ted Connell, for example. On the government payroll, but still has an interest in a PR consultancy." Lyons paused to let that sink in. "But, to answer your question," he went on, "let's just say that, officially — for tax purposes — my man is still in the public sector. At the same time, and I really have to stress this, his dealings with me are private. Deniably so. You understand?"

"I do."

As soon as he hung up Oldie knew Lyons was aware that he and Blondie had been in contact, and that his failure to admit this when given the opportunity would be seen as a lie more grey than white.

Well, so be it. It couldn't be helped. Steve no doubt thought Oldie was besotted with Blondie and made some allowance for such understandable human weakness.

Beauty and the Beast. Yes, that would work.

The house across the street had been rented to a recently divorced bloke in his mid-thirties. For the first few months his two kids stayed with him on weekends, but their visits became irregular and then the day came when Anna remarked that she had not seen them for a while. As civility required, Oldie and Anna waved and nodded to their neighbour, but they kept their distance. Some contact was nevertheless unavoidable and so one morning when Oldie was checking his mailbox, the fellow came across for a chat.

He told Oldie he had quit his job as a carpet-layer, that the bastards did not respect him, were just using him and he didn't have to put up with that and he was going to set himself up in his own business and show them bastards a thing or two and so on. He was positively babbling, glassy-eyed and clearly dosed up on some kind of rocket fuel.

And, the Old Man guessed, other not so legal substances. Raver's garage was so filled with gym equipment that he had to park his car on the driveway. Oldie thought it was a good bet the bloke's body building program was being pushed along by him downing anabolic steroids at the same rate as Popeye gulped spinach.

Soon after his kids disappeared from the scene the fellow acquired a staffie-cross, apparently from someone who saw an opportunity to offload an unspayed bitch in heat. He told Oldie he reckoned he and Deputy Dawg made a rather neat team. The Old Man looked down at the bow-legged, thick-necked creature sitting behind its new master and, wondering if it was also on steroids, murmured something that would pass for vague agreement.

As the property had no front fence, and as the door of the walk-through garage was usually up, the wretched animal, as addled as its owner, could come and go as it pleased. And it delighted in rushing out to bark and snarl at anyone passing in the street. The fellow would then saunter out, calling the dog back and offering a casual apology — Oldie conceded it was a novel method of meeting people. He dubbed the pair Raver and Rover. Anna objected that "Rover" was a boy dog name, but it stuck.

Despite (or because of) Raver's avowals that the delinquent dog "meant no harm" in charging out to bark at evening strollers, it was only a matter of time before the mongrel was reported to the ranger. Oldie would have made the call himself had he not known the pair would soon be leaving, evicted. He was a little worried about Max's safety, but was pretty sure that particular black cat would stand his ground, arch his back and

165

issue a hiss of such freezing malevolence that silly Rover would be stopped in her tracks.

Rover's one saving grace was that she did not bark ceaselessly or, by her rationale, needlessly. There had to be someone entering or approaching the property. Rover's notion of a boundary was probably skewed by the fact that Raver had taken to patrolling the street at night — if the cigarette butts Oldie had started finding on his verge were anything to go by. Whatever: Rover didn't bark without cause.

So when Oldie heard Rover going off her head inside the garage at four in the morning, he knew someone other than Raver was on the street outside.

He was only just slipping back toward sleep after having been woken a half hour earlier by the bedroom air-con icing up. He'd reached over the side of the bed, found the remote and turned the clattering thing off. He thought they needed a bigger unit to cope with the humid nights of February; she thought it iced up because, you know what, he set the thermostat too low and the condenser had to work too hard. He had been drift thinking that maybe she was right when Rover's racket commenced.

What the hell is it *now*?!

He rolled off the bed and pulled on his dark shorts and a black T-shirt. The Girl stirred and he told her he was going out the back and around the side to make sure kids weren't putting graffiti on anyone's fence or garage door. The Girl was used to Oldie's nocturnal outside Commando routine — usually to check on the location of a party that was going on too long for his liking — and she knew to wait in the bedroom for his tap on the window as he passed outside. At that signal she would go into the hall and switch on the front security lights, lighting up the driveway and most of their garden.

By then, hidden in the shadows of the overhanging plumbago, he would be peering through the slats of the securely bolted side gate.

Rover was still barking when the Old Man reached the gate. The instant the lights went on a car parked on his side of the road revved to life and accelerated down the street to the corner, where its lights came on as it turned out of sight. Raver's front light went on a second after Oldie's and the man himself jogged out in his underpants, urgently shushing Rover. It was too late for Raver to see the departing vehicle, but he stood in the road and listened intently as it sped away in the pre-dawn stillness. Partly obscured by the trees and bushes in front of his house, the only description of the fleeing car Oldie could have offered was that it was a dark colored sedan. Even from his covered position, however, he was fairly certain it had taken a turn in the nearby streets that indicated it was probably heading for the freeway.

Fully lit by the streetlight, Raver stood in the middle of the road, hands on hips. He, too, had tracked the direction taken by the car. Taking his time, he looked up and down the street, walked over to and around his car before turning to contemplate Oldie's two blazing security lights. He would know they had been turned on rather than been triggered automatically. His glance shifted and lingered on the side gate.

Oldie stood stock still, confident he would not be seen unless he moved. He held his nerve and breath and waited until Raver turned to walk back towards his place. Only then did he notice his neighbour had something in his hand.

It was a phone. As he crossed his front lawn, Raver tapped in a number and raised the phone to his ear as he entered his house, letting the door bang like a rifle shot up the street.

Oldie slowly stepped back from his gate and crept away down the side of the house.

"We live in a jittery neighbourhood," he told Anna as he switched off the security lights and shepherded her back towards their bed. The visitors, he assured her, had been for the Raver.

It was easy to believe. They had heard the gossip for weeks: the bloke owed money all over the place and had an eviction notice on him. From their own observations they knew there were drugs in the mix. "Don't worry about it," he told her, "he and his blasted dog will be soon gone. Come on, let's go back to sleep."

"Easier said than done."

"Really, there's nothing to worry about. Raver's got the problem, not us."

"I was talking about your snoring."

"Oh."

He offered to get up and read until she was asleep, but she turned on her side to face him, laid her hand on his shoulder and told him to stay where he was. "You'll only start clacking around in the kitchen, making yourself some little treat you don't need."

Denial was pointless. He stayed where he was.

The night had finally cooled enough for them to cuddle into their sleep. He nudged her and made one of their private murmurs. She turned over, presenting him the pillow of her bum. In one smooth motion he lifted his balls free of his thighs and aligned his limp dick to press its length between her buttocks. His hand continued up over her hip, across her tummy and came to rest on her sternum, his thumb between her breasts. With the slightest pressure he pulled her against him, pressing what she called her Off Button. Her breathing settled into a deeper rhythm.

He lay awake.

IX

Daniel rang from Texas Sunday evening, Perth time. He and his travelling companions, a German named Rudi and a Dane named Ella, were still at Lake Tawakoni. The free accommodation (Oldie couldn't get it clear who had offered them the place) and cooking for themselves meant they had no big expenses, so they were content to mark time for a few weeks — reading, walking and, in Dan's case, doing a spot of fishing.

Dan had the cabin to himself for a few days, Rudi and Ella having taken off in Rudi's van for Houston and then down to Galveston and the Gulf coast. Anna took the call and it didn't take her long to get to the point and ask her son whether Rudi and Ella were a couple. He must have been ready for her because later, when Oldie asked her, she told him the reply had been "Not especially."

Anna told Daniel about their proposed trip to Melbourne to visit his grandmother. Raising the subject not only kept it on the table between her and Oldie (if she wanted to obtain her long service leave, she needed to apply for it soon), it also gave her a lead to ask her son about his travel plans, and thereby managed to obtain from him the information that after Florida and some time in New York he would probably be heading back to Australia later in the year.

"But I dunno, it all depends," he added.

She knew better than to quiz him further. Later, after they compared notes on their non-committal son, Oldie quietly remarked upon the fact that he had said Australia rather than Perth.

When Oldie had his turn he asked about the fishing and was told all about catching crappie. Dan had bought himself a license, quizzed the locals about the best spots and, with borrowed gear, gone out early on overcast days. It was cold work, but he pronounced his catch as good eating and worth the effort. As for his reading, he had just finished Roberto Bolano's *The Savage Detectives* and recommended it to his Old Man, who wondered whether Dan knew Bolano died of hep C.

Their conversation was easy-going and apparently candid, but Oldie said nothing about the upcoming results of his latest set of blood tests. When they greeted each other Daniel casually asked his father how he was doing and Oldie replied with matching airiness that he was "fine".

Which, in fact, was true enough. In the circumstances.

The closest they came to discussing viruses was when Oldie asked how he would know his computer was being hacked. He was told his service provider and anti-virus software should block most intruders, but if someone with the resources and know-how was really targeting him then, to put it bluntly, he would never know he had been hit until it was too late.

Oldie asked whether "should block" amounted to "would block". Daniel told him not to be paranoid and asked, on a breath of a laugh, what his father had that would be interesting enough to attract such attention.

"Oh, I dunno," Oldie replied. "Just wondering."

"..."

Then Daniel said that if his father was convinced something was amiss he could give him the name of a former colleague who, if necessary, could go through and clean Oldie's computer. "But just bear in mind, he'd need to look at everything ... all your programs, internet history, everything."

"I don't mind the scrutiny from someone bound by professional confidence," Oldie shot back, perhaps a little too quickly.

"OK, let me see how he's placed and I'll ask him to get in touch with you."

"Sounds good. Thanks. Now tell me, is it quiet where you are?"

"Deathly. The cabins either side are vacant."

"Sounds like my kind of heaven," the Old Man said with feeling. He allowed himself some acid remarks about living in Yoberia, explaining that the nice quiet people on the corner had moved and been replaced by a little prick possessed of (or maybe it was more accurate to say possessed *by*) a concert strength sub-woofer and that the Council seemed to have neither the muscle nor the will to do anything about it other than to politely advise the swine to turn it down. Advice which, it hadn't taken said swine long to discover, he was more or less free to ignore. Oldie asked Dan if he could look into buying a flamethrower in the States, breaking it down into parts and shipping them as separate, individual parcels to him and a few of his friends. A small mortar or a RPG launcher would be better, but he appreciated that obtaining the ammo might be tricky.

Daniel joined in the fun by suggesting Oldie could get one of his shady mates to organise a firebombing while he was away in Melbourne.

They laughed, but Daniel knew his father was a disturbed man.

It had been another warm, uncomfortably humid night and the forecast was for the temperature to reach the high 30s. He reckoned it would be getting hot in earnest, nudging 40 at New Norcia and had half expected Carol to postpone their excursion. But she didn't call and he put a plastic bottle of fizzy water in the freezer. A large notebook and a spare T-shirt went into his bag, chiefly to give him an excuse to take the bag in which he carried his secret first-aid kit.

Soon after Anna left for work, he heard on the radio the first reports of Christchurch having been struck by a major earthquake.

The second big quake in six months shook through already weakened buildings, hurling brick facades and glass into the streets and onto the lunchbreak crowds. It was immediately clear the city had suffered serious damage and that there would be casualties. Oldie tried to ring Mike, but the phones were out.

When Carol arrived he was listening to the News station. For once radio reports were not lagging behind internet postings. He opened the door, waved her in and she followed him into the kitchen. She had not heard the news. Her eyes widened and her hand went to her mouth as she took in what was being reported.

He told her he had been trying to get through to his best friend. He picked up his phone, hit the redial and handed it to her so she could hear the Interrupted Service message.

She said she would understand if he wanted to give their trip a miss.

"But you have an appointment with the curator."

"I have, and ... but I can go on my own."

"No, no," he said quickly. "No, I'll be fine. I'll take my phone and try during the day. I'm sure Mike will be OK. He's a survivor. The outing will do me good. I've been looking forward to it. This is just so," he waved one hand vaguely at the window, "... sudden."

So they put on their sunglasses, he grabbed his old black, broad-brimmed cowboy hat, his bag and the bottle of icy water, made sure Max was out and they set out in her big, new four-wheel drive with its arctic blast air-con turned right up. Her attire (linen shirt, knee length cotton pants and sensible gym shoes) was what you'd expect for a woman who probably went to a Catholic school and was visiting a monk to ask a favour on a hot day. As always when going bush, he wore jeans and his boots.

He noticed her tatt was well out of sight; and she definitely noticed that, having forgotten to wear his dental plate, he was missing a fang.

On the road he told her about his and Anna's time in New Zealand and how in all his years there he had only ever experienced one minor tremor. She asked questions about all sorts of things, including his work on television documentaries.

"Freelance," he said, "that was what we called ourselves back then. It was all 16mm film. I know nothing about video, let alone digital. All that sort of stuff was yet to come, still on the distant horizon."

"But the basics of telling a story on screen remain the same."

"The basic principles do, but techniques — especially editing — are a lot slicker. At least, when the job is done well. I don't watch television much anymore. But the docos I've seen lately have been derivative, badly executed — no flair. Especially the ones purporting to be about history. They rely too much on re-enactments, costume dramas. You know, dress someone up and make them declaim. And the actors are all fresh-faced wanna-be soapie stars — which, you know, creates a really *authentic* look."

She laughed, but had nothing to say on the subject.

Pretty soon they had crossed the suburban plain,

passed the remnant vineyards of the upper Swan and were turning onto Great Northern Highway. He asked why they were not travelling in the silver coupe and she explained that they were on company business and therefore in the company vehicle. She added that she thought he would be more comfortable in it. "Besides," she drawled, "I wouldn't want to bump into a roo with Ted's pride and joy."

He was on the verge of asking about Ted, but decided he was a topic of conversation best left for the return journey. If all went well.

Eventually, she asked him why, at a time when everyone else was rushing off to London, he had gone to live in New Zealand.

"Funny you should ask. It was a French Canadian, a bloke from Quebec who put it into my head. I met him in Darwin, in 1969. Gee whizz, so long ago! I've forgotten his name. Something double-barrelled. Jean-Paul, or Paul-something. But I can still see him. Tall, lean rather than thin, hair down over his shoulders, hawkish nose, steady grey eyes, quietly spoken. A hippy! The real thing! We all were," he snorted. "Hippies!"

He didn't look at her, but sensed a fleeting smile as she flicked him a sidelong glance.

"Oh yes. Oh yes indeed. Let me proclaim with great orotundity, because I'm afraid it is all too sadly true and cannot be denied, I WAS A GOD-DAMN HIPPY!" He turned and positively leered at her with his best gap-toothed grin.

"Or, at any rate," he went on, reverting to a sensible voice, "that's what we were labelled by the rest of the world. We didn't care what they called us, so long as they didn't beat us up. Some of the Darwin locals were pretty hostile. Anyway, that particular fellow traveller was passing through Darwin to hit the overland trail.

174

Heading for Kathmandu, I expect. I didn't really know him that well. I seem to remember there was a girlfriend. What I do remember is one night sitting down and talking with him. It was good to meet someone who had read a bit and he ... I don't know, he chose his words carefully, spoke with deliberation. Anyway, he'd been in Europe, travelled through the USA, Mexico and so on. But the thing was, he had lived in Auckland the previous year and was quite emphatic that New Zealand was the best place he had ever been. He liked the welfare state — which, back then, was still taken for granted and working well — he liked the geography, the people ... he liked everything about the place. And he was absolutely smitten with Auckland. He strongly recommended I take Anna there and that we live there for a year or so. I took his advice, shared his judgment of the place, and we stayed there for ten years."

"I'm glad to hear my countryman gave you good advice."

"Well, yes, he did on that matter. But I have to say, the other thing he said to me with absolute certainty was that Quebec would be an independent, sovereign nation within five years. That was over forty years ago. He said it with total conviction. Five years, at most, he said."

The "Piff!" she blew was just audible.

"I guess it seemed inevitable at the time. But in Australia — we knew nothing about such things. Still don't! We don't care about what happens elsewhere. Not our concern."

"Cuts both ways. Most Canadians couldn't tell you much about Australia. I didn't realise how little I knew until I got here. And I'd hung out with Australians in London. But going back to what you were saying ... my father was Québécois. He was involved. As many were. It will come again. It's still an issue, a little sorer than

175

Western Australia's mild secessionist itch. I wonder how your friend feels about it today?"

"Who knows. When you're young and on the move people come and people go. One day he got on a plane to Singapore. Or perhaps Dili. I never saw him again."

"And you don't remember his name?"

"Interesting, isn't it, how a passing stranger, whose name has been forgotten, could have such a profound effect on one's life? I was thinking about this sort of thing the other day." He almost said something about the girl in the woodshed, but checked himself.

She kept her gaze on the traffic ahead and her thoughts to herself. He took out his phone and tapped the redial. Same message.

They had the green light at the Brand Highway turnoff and, without slowing, went through the intersection to catch and pass a semi-trailer still working up through its gears. A long, clear stretch of highway opened up before them. The land either side had been cleared, with only an occasional low bush beside the road. On such a stretch he would have put his foot down. Perhaps she would have done the same had she been alone, but she just took it up to the speed limit and cruised. A sign said it was 77 K to New Norcia. Time to ask.

"So ... new information?"

"Ted heard that ..."

"Steve Lyons," Oldie cut in, "has been asking questions about him."

"Yes," she replied, taking his statement as a question. "He's been asking people about Ted."

"I know," Oldie said. "He asked me about him. Asked if I'd spoken to him. I told him I hadn't. Which is true. Sort of. He didn't mention you and because he didn't ask I didn't volunteer anything. He offered me work — routine stuff to do with his fishing business — but nothing has happened about it yet. I guess it's what might be called a carrot. To what end, I'm not sure, other than to see Roger's manuscript should it turn up. I'm a bit suspicious of Mr Lyons. I asked my son how I'd know if my computer was being hacked."

"And what did he say?"

"He told me not to be paranoid. But listen, I better tell you, Lyons did warn me about getting involved with Ted. Said he had an *agenda* — his word; said Ted was trying to dig up shit on someone, that he was not quite what he seemed, whatever that means."

The sounds of the tyres on the road, the diesel engine and the air-con filled the cabin. She sat very still, leaning back into her seat, her left arm rigidly extended for her to grip the wheel while she tilted her head against the side window. He looked at her, noted her pursed lips and kept quiet.

"When did you speak to him?"

"Last Friday."

"But Ted only heard about this on Sunday. From a friend at the yacht club."

A calm folded around Oldie's thoughts as he stared at the dry, bleached country whizzing by.

"So ..." he finally said, "when you talked to Anna last week you didn't know about Lyons?"

"No. Not then, I didn't."

"I see. So that wasn't what you meant by new information?"

"No. What I was going to say was that Ted found out something about Reginald Pascoe. Reg the Racketeer, as you called him."

"Now," he said slowly, "why am I not surprised to hear that maggot's name?"

"Ted says he worked for a gentleman named Frank

Sarno," she said, leaning forward to tap on the radio just as the hourly news bulletin commenced.

They immediately heard that the spire of Christchurch cathedral had fallen. They heard of buses crushed under fallen buildings, of smoke rising from a collapsed office block in the city, of power lines down while dazed and injured people roamed the streets. Deaths were to be expected. The airport was closed, the army was being called in and the phone companies were asking people to send text messages rather than make calls. And there were reports of ground liquefaction, that strange phenomenon Oldie first heard of after the previous September's quake.

"I've been up that cathedral's spire," he said, for something to say.

She turned off the radio and, on a small rise, pulled over onto the road's shoulder. Lowering her sunglasses so he could see her eyes, she looked him in the face and asked what he wanted to do.

"Drive on Blondie," he said without hesitation, returning her gaze. "I think we have a lot to talk about."

She let the name pass, but he sensed he had better tread carefully. Then, as she pushed her glasses back up her nose, her eyes shifted over his shoulder and she nodded at the view behind him. "Where do they get the water for all that?"

Through a gap in the roadside bushes they could see a vineyard, stretching away along the rise for about a kilometre. In the bright sun the rows of trellised vines were almost as black as their shadows on the dirty white sand.

"Bore water," he told her. "Where else could they get it?"

"Wouldn't it just drain away in this sandy soil? And evaporate in this heat?"

"Drain away. I suppose. But how quickly? I dunno. There are a lot of old swampy patches on the coastal plain. As for the heat, grape vines are pretty resilient. Depends on the variety. But, still, I reckon this lot might be struggling. I doubt the people who planted these had a prolonged drought as part of their business plan."

She suddenly banged the vehicle into Drive, tramped the accelerator and, throwing up dust, they shot forward onto the highway's tarmac. He glanced in his side mirror to see the semi they had passed at the Brand turnoff rapidly approaching.

"And it's not in my business plan," she said, "to be stuck behind a long-haul truck."

"Well, I didn't notice the Sarno logo on it. At least it's not one of theirs."

"That would make it interesting, wouldn't it? Pursued by the Sarno family! The plot thickens!" Her raucous Game On! laugh gave no hint of nervousness.

"So then! Tell me! What does Ted think Reg Pascoe did for Papa Sarno?"

"Sales Manager and Frank Sarno's Mr Fix-it. For about two years in the late fifties. He was on the Sarno payroll right up until he went into Parliament. Officially, that is; unofficially ... who knows and who would tell? There was a rumour Mrs Reg had some stake in Sarno Holdings. I guess that in those days the notion of Disclosure barely existed. Anyway, the key news is that one of Sarno's activities back then was clearing land for suburban development. Bulldozing the bush, burning it and levelling the land — that sort of thing. But sometimes, as part of that work, they carted in stuff to fill old swamps. And if they had awkward, particularly dirty stuff to get rid of, well then, they had access to a few unofficial sites further out in the bush. People used to joke about bodies being disposed of in Sarno's unofficial landfill sites. Nibbelup was probably one of those sites."

"And can we prove any of this?"

"That's one of the things we'd like you to look at. But, of course, not the only thing."

"There may be no records. If anything was written down in the first place, it's almost certainly been rubbed out since. I can but look. You never know until you look."

"How much of State Archives is online?"

"Not nearly as much as they claim. It seems like a fair bit until you see what's in their warehouse. Also, bear in mind there are problems with their cataloguing and, a further complication, some sensitive files and material are still held by the responsible agencies and their successors, such as Environmental Protection."

"Have you been to the EPA before?"

"Yes. The deal was I could go there, read the file and make notes but could not photograph or copy it in any way. Had to surrender my phone. Cone of Silence and all that."

"Did you find anything?"

"Nope! I did not. And I have to admit, I never knew Reggie Boy worked for Sarno. You know, he later became Transport Minister. That would have been handy."

"Very. According to Ted. That's when Sarno Transport really, as he puts it, got wheels."

"When did Frank Sarno die?"

"Sometime in the late nineties. By then the business was run by Frank Junior and Aldo. Siblings running a business together ... sometimes it doesn't work out, but the Sarno boys complement each other and run a tight outfit. They're well into their fifties and both are still very much involved in the daily doings of the business. Basically, Frank's the front man and Aldo does the books — he's a qualified accountant, got the diploma on his wall. Trucking is still their main business, but they have other investments, together and separately. We don't know what specific property developments they have been in ... there's a maze of family trusts. Aldo is very good at hiding a bundle of money and anything else that needs to be hidden. And, oh yes, one last thing — it's no secret Frank Senior taught his boys how to grease more wheels than just those on their rigs."

"And Ted's absolutely sure Reg Pascoe worked for old Frank Sarno right up until he went into politics?"

"He is. In fact, he was told that Frank Junior and Aldo still call him Uncle Reg."

"You're joking!"

"God's truth."

"Well," he said after a while, "let me ask you this: Where did the Lone Ranger take his rubbish?"

"What!?" She gave him a look of bewildered incredulity.

To the tune of the old TV show's theme music (pinched from Rossini), he sang, "To the dump, to da dump, tarda dump, taarda daarmp, tada *dump*!"

She shook her head. "Sorry, I don't get it."

"Yes," he sighed, "I forget, way before your time. Either that, or you're an intellectual."

She frowned, perplexity drifting towards annoyance.

Although it was a bit lame to explain the ancient joke, he did so anyway, adding that Billy Connolly had once defined an intellectual as someone who can listen to the William Tell Overture without thinking of the Lone Ranger. It crossed his mind that he might salvage something by telling her the Onto Toronto Pronto Tonto one, but immediately understood it would be better for him to just cut his losses.

"I'm one of those people who can never remember jokes," she told him, mollified. "Can't tell them either.

Someone once told me the ability to tell a joke is the mark of a natural actor."

"You're interested in acting?"

"Oh yes. I had my heart set on it. But, you know, youthful aspirations ... I realise now that I wasn't focussed enough. And, to be honest, didn't have the talent. Modelling was where I ended up. Just stand around looking moody. And the highlight of that career *was*? Yes, you guessed it — Ta Daah! — Stamina batteries! In the end, for all sorts of reasons, I found I'm happier behind the camera than in front of it. Of course, the experience of being in front teaches you a lot you can use behind it."

"Do you have tapes or copies of the ads?"

"Somewhere. Packed away. *Deeply* packed away."

"Yeah, well," he said slowly, deliberately, "I'm not that fussed about being photographed myself. You never know where the image will end up."

He waited, but she made no comment. They listened to the noise of the road as they passed a bedraggled, dusty pine plantation on their left, a dull contrast to the natural open savannah dotted with spreading marris on her side of the road. Many of the marris were in full bloom, covered with their distinctive large flowers.

"I knew some flowering gums were white, but these ... they look like clouds!"

"Or giant cauliflowers."

"Oh c'mon! I've got to get this. There! That big one out by itself."

"Wait a bit. This," he waved at the pines, "gives way to the native stuff up ahead. We might see some wandoo in flower as well."

A couple of hundred metres on from where the pine plantation ended she pulled over on the shoulder of a gentle curve. Peering through the small trees and bushes between the road and the fence line they saw a couple of suitably photogenic subjects.

Oldie sized up the old, slack wire fence and saw that he could go through it. There was no way he would risk climbing over a barbed wire fence. As too many others had found out the hard way, ending up astraddle the top strand was no way to impress a young lady.

He was no sooner out of the vehicle than he had to hold his hat as the semi-trailer they had been keeping ahead of flew by, air horn blowing. From his glimpse of the driver, Oldie wasn't sure whether he was giving him a friendly salute or showing him the finger.

The rush of dry wind in the truck's wake intensified the heat.

Watching carefully where he trod in the dry grass, he went up the small embankment to the fence and took a good look at the flowering gums. He took off his hat, wiped his brow and looked up and down the fence line. The glaring, high overcast pressed the heat close to the earth and all that moved upon it. Apart from bush flies, the only living things to be seen abroad were dragonflies, gangs of which hovered on the light breeze downwind from the blossoms.

Later that day, passing the trees on the way home, he had the sudden thought: Where were the bees? But as he stood there by the fence and took in the scene there were other quick, living things on his mind. He called back to Carol to wait by the car.

"What's up?"

He looked down at her holding her camera, eager to join him. His eyes lingered on her bare calves, golden in the sunlight. She hadn't lit a cigarette and he guessed she understood doing so was not an option.

"Not the kind of day you'd want to run into a fire," he said anyway, to be sure.

From a small tree near the fence he twisted and broke off a near dead branch, stepped on it to break off the brittle tips and made for himself what looked like a makeshift walking stick.

"Snakes," he told her, slashing the tip like a scythe through the dead grass. "You know, ya gotta watch out for them god-damn snakes in the god-damn grass."

Carol's photographing of the painting went without a hitch. She was very efficient. Oldie and Dom Kevin (a dead ringer for a middle-aged Kevin Costner with neatly parted jet black hair) stood to one side and made small talk while she set up and took three or four exposures. The men looked at each other with meek surprise when she said "That's it" and started packing her gear back in its case. Oldie had not asked what SeeHear Films paid to use the eighteen-sixties image of Perth, but noted that no money changed hands on the day.

After the monk excused himself, Oldie shunted Blondie around the various indigenous and settler artefact exhibits, the religious paintings, vestments and statues. There were no other visitors and the floors creaked in the hush; an air-conditioner laboured somewhere not quite out of hearing. Although mildly interested in what the collection revealed about the history of the mission, she was not especially impressed by any particular item. She had, she mentioned, once spent a day in the Escorial.

They carried her gear back to the car, then stood in the shade of the largest tree in the near empty car park while she smoked a cigarette and checked the messages on her phone. She made a call and, lowering her head and voice, wandered over to the next patch of shade. She had her back to him but from the tone and cadence of her side of the discussion he guessed she was talking to

Ted. As she wound up her conversation she dropped her almost finished smoke at her feet and forcibly ground it into the yellow, dusty gravel. With the edge of her shoe she pushed some loose earth over the ragged butt and tapped it down. Catching him watching, she said, "Don't worry, Mr Bear. It's out."

She immediately turned and marched off up the slope, heading directly for the hotel, with him taking long strides to catch up with her quick ones. "Ted says Hello," she said over her shoulder. "I need to take a piss."

Mr Bear? As in Smokey? Let it go.

Oldie got through to Christchurch as he and Blondie nursed mid-strength beers, waiting for their lunch in the hotel. Mike said everyone he had been able to reach was safe. When the first quake hit he had been a few miles out of town at a horse sale in a big tin shed. Unlike September, there had been no warning rumble — the thing just hit, sudden and hard. The shed and the people in it had been rattled, but contrary to what one would have thought, the horses showed no signs of panic or distress. He was still there when the first big aftershock came a quarter of an hour later and the geegees met that with the same composure. It was, he said, a bit strange. One of his companions jokingly suggested the animals had been inured by bouncing over country roads in poorly sprung horse floats. Mike made the observation that it was easier to stay upright on four legs than two. He'd just got back to his house to find the ceiling plaster, brought down by the September event (its replacement only a few weeks fresh) was down again. The aftershocks had been almost continuous, with severe jolts mid-afternoon. Power and water were gone, traffic lights were out and the roads were a mess. It was starting to rain but he had found a couple of bottles of good wine intact and was going to check on his neighbours. Then the phone dropped out.

After leaving a brief message on Anna's phone, he was telling Carol what he had just heard when their meal arrived. They contemplated the platters of grilled chorizo, sundried tomatoes, roasted capsicums, artichoke hearts, local olives, cheeses and Turkish bread.

"This looks delicious," he said, keen to show his appreciation of a meal for which, so far, he had done nothing.

"I guess your friends in Christchurch ..."

"... would appreciate this if they could get it tonight!"

She nodded.

"They would," he said. "So it's up to us to do it justice." He picked up a piece of bread in one hand and, with the fork in the other, jabbed a glistening slice of hot, juicy meat. "You're happy with the painting?"

"I am. Very detailed. We can do a nice long pan across it. Match that against the present view. Shows how they've filled in the foreshore."

"And *shows* ... in a genuine documentary manner. No re-enactments necessary."

"It will be interesting to see what emerges from Christchurch on tonight's news. Between CCTV cameras and stuff captured by tourists, there may be some interesting vision of the moment the quake struck. Remember all that incredible footage that came out after the Boxing Day tsunami?"

"Which sort of leads to the question of how an old style documentary competes with all that. What is required for such work to attract funding? To be backed financially?"

"Narrative," she said, emphatically. "Narrative. On message narrative. Which, guess what, is where you come in."

"Narrative and sponsorship."

She took a piece of bread and, holding his gaze, patted it around the edge of her plate, soaking up oil and juices. "To sponsors, who butter our daily bread. Amen."

As they relaxed and settled into their meal, Carol told him her documentary would be primarily about examining the options of a city outgrowing its water supply. Perth's circumstances were attracting increasing international attention. But what happened with waste disposal fifty years back was of interest only in as much as it was a factor in current water management — if the ground water was polluted, for example. She told him plainly, if they broached that subject it would have to be on the basis of hard scientific evidence. If they had to talk about pollution, it would be the fact that it exists, as in dealing with a present problem, rather than an account of how it may have got there. The Sarnos and Reg Pascoe are all very well, she said, but they are essentially a local story, which couldn't be allowed to overshadow and distract from the water story.

He looked at her and thought: So, tell me again, what is it that you want me for?

"I meant what I said about looking into Nibbelup," she said quickly. "Find some photos of the area before all the development began. It could be a useful example of the dangers of pollution — and help create perspective, but Ted and I don't think it's the main story, the story we are asking for funding to tell. And, listen, here's the thing, we don't mind if you quietly let Steve Lyons know that. In fact, Ted thinks it might be a good idea to do so."

Oldie leaned back in his chair and slightly nudged his half-eaten meal away from him. The sing for your supper moment had arrived. "You want me to pass messages?"

She looked away, her shoulders dropped and, flustered, she puffed her cheeks. "You're right, that didn't

187

come out too well. I'm doing it again. Sorry. Let me go back a step. OK?"

"Before you do, let me tell you, I don't mind telling Steve." He shrugged. "Why should I care? If that's your position, that's your position. It's no skin off my nose and I'm sure he'll be pleased to hear that should Perth have a major earthquake, the liquefaction at Nibbelup won't be too toxic. If that's what you want me to say, I can do that. If that's what you want."

"It's what Ted wants," she said, and finally met his eye. "I don't want to put you in an awkward situation."

"I can handle it," he said, with studied airiness, letting his voice crack with mock nervousness.

She gave him her most winning, coquette smile. "OK. But, you know, Ted's right — we can't let a limited local story get in the way of the bigger one. Perth is running out of water. Hard fact. Faster than most people realize or anyone wants to publicly admit. There's something …" she paused to narrow her gaze and weigh her words, "something Biblical about it."

He thought of mentioning that the long-term trend did not rule out the possibility of the river flooding — something pretty damned Biblical about that, too — but he held his tongue.

"At the same time," she went on, "if something on pollution does turn up, we would definitely look at how we could use it. You know, even with the best intentions, things in this business are rarely straightforward. But let's just see how it goes. And to be clear, let me say that Ted and I do not always agree. It'd be a bit odd, unhealthy if we did, wouldn't it?"

He pulled his plate back towards him and stabbed another slice of sausage, which he waved at her as he said, "I do think there's something buried back there, something embarrassing, something nasty, somewhere in the archives, somewhere at Nibbelup or someplace like it. There are just too many people too damned interested in this for it to be clean. There's got to be more than just Frank Sarno and Reg Pascoe maybe doing a bit of illegal dumping. That's just not enough. Not after all this time. No, there's a piece missing. I don't think poor old Roger was just seeing will-o-wisps. He thought — I mean, believe me, I spoke to him and he *really* thought he had something. But even with the stuff you told me this morning, I just don't quite see what it could have been. Did Roger know Pascoe worked for Sarno? Did Ted tell him?"

"Ted didn't tell him. He only found out the other day. But Roger may have found out for himself. He was a local. He knew people and it wasn't exactly a secret at the time."

"One way or the other, whatever Roger wrote up — that, apparently, has gone with him. Disappeared, it has to be said, in circumstances more than a little murky."

"Ted did tell me there's a story going around that Roger had an aggressive cancer. You've not heard that?"

Oldie popped the morsel into his gob and chewed vigorously, thinking. "No," he replied after he swallowed. "News to me. And I reckon it'd have been news to Roger, too. Bloody Hell! Well, all right then, what is it exactly, apart from running messages, that you and Ted want me to do?"

"You're angry."

"No, actually, I'm not. Not angry. I'm more — What's the word? — confused. You know, the ground's shifted in more than one place this morning."

He saw the grimace behind her taut face.

"What Ted and I want you to do? Yes, we would like you to be our channel of communication with Mr Lyons. But primarily, we want you to work with me as co-writer, script editor, sounding board, researcher, consultant — call it whatever you want to be credited as. Your name will be on the project. Apart from anything else, Ted's just too busy. Confidentially, he's now writing most of the Premier's press releases. Anyway, we've checked you out and think you have the right mix of experience, knowledge and ... and, well, let's call it judgment. I guess I kind of need you to hold my hand a bit, if that's all right. Payment will depend upon funding, but you won't be out of pocket. In the meantime, Ted's willing to front up with a couple of thousand, a retainer for you to just take the time to look and listen, to think about what we are trying to do. And, of course, the archival research. That's what we want you to do."

He played hard to get for as long as it took him to down the dregs of his beer.

"Okay. It seems pretty straightforward to me. I liaise with you. So, here's an idea — aerial photography for survey maps started in Perth in the late forties. There should be a useful series of images showing the changing use of Nibbelup. I've been trying to remember what we did about that ... I have a feeling Steve said his client already had them. I'm sure it would have been discussed, but, honestly, I can't recall what happened. If you like, I can ring whatever it is they call the Lands Department these days and check price and availability."

"Excellent," she said, and offered to buy him another beer. He asked for a cup of tea, and then made a show of clearing his throat and asked her if the job description still included her taking photos of him.

"We can do that somewhere here today if you like."

He told her he was one of those people who didn't feel comfortable being photographed. "If it's all the same to you, maybe we could leave it for some other time."

She gave him that smile again, "I can wait."

"Uh huh."

She rose to place the order for their tea at the bar. Stepping past him, she gave his shoulder a reassuring squeeze. "Mr Bear," she purred.

On message narrative. He was in trouble, and he knew it.

That night when he took out the bin he saw the house opposite was in darkness and Raver's car gone.

The car did not return the following day and there was no sign of Rover. Raver and his little mate had done a bunk.

The next day after that, the owner of the house knocked on the Old Man's door to ask if he had seen anything. Oldie told him what he had noticed and the landlord confirmed that his tenant had cleared out. Oldie made sympathetic, understanding noises as the man recited his grievances. Raver owed a month's rent and legal proceedings would be required to obtain it. "He owes money all over the place," he said. "I'm not sure he's worth chasing."

"Do you know where to find him?"

"I know where his brother lives. But he said the family have given up on the bastard. He's on drugs, you know. Frankly, I've had such a gut full of this bullshit. I'm thinking I'll just sell the place and be done with it. It's not a good market, but it's just as likely to get worse or stay flat rather than pick up. Now I'm gunna have to change the fricken locks! The aggravation I've had over this! I tell you, honestly, it's just not worth it."

Oldie thought it best not to mention that it seemed other parties were also interested in Raver's whereabouts. It was obviously one of those messes that would just not end well. The smart move would be to stand clear.

He could not resist, however, taking a swipe at the

young snot on the corner, the immediate neighbor of the house going on the market. He told the owner about the noise problem and suggested he may want to have a word with someone at the Council in case the bass thump put off potential buyers. For good measure he added that Raver and the bass addicted lout had been "as thick as thieves".

Which was true.

That night, apparently unaware Raver had flown the coop, someone put a brick through the vacant house's front window.

"Never a dull moment," Oldie said to the Girl.

"Could've been worse," drawled the young cop who came to ask if he heard anything go *crash* in the night. "Could've been a bullet or a petrol bomb."

He had a point.

"Hope they got the right house," said Sid Wedge, a comment Oldie later repeated as his own in the general conversation when he eventually got around to telling Steve Lyons of his association with Blondie.

X

There was a problem with Max. His domain was being invaded by Sylvester, a younger, bigger cat. Sylvester came up from the neighbour who rooted out his garden in order to install a plunge pool. The lanky black and white puddy tat needed fresh water (Oldie's fish pond) and somewhere to sprawl about in the shade (ditto's overgrown backyard), lying in wait for a honeyeater named Tweety Pie. Sylvester's last straw push into scrambling up the retaining wall and jumping the boundary fence was when his owners got themselves a yapping pup, which (hand on heart, God's Truth) the woman of the house yipped back at. Oldie assumed she thought she was conversing with it. It was not clear what she thought she was saying, but the dog clearly understood her to be encouraging him to yap louder and longer. The poor animal was being trained by the dumb owner to grow up as a nuisance barker. When the woman tired of that, Oldie would take bets on it, she would turn the volume down by having the mutt's vocal chords cut. As people do.

But for now, Max was being crowded. He had to move over in his own territory and he did not like it. Not one little bit.

He started to piss and spray inside the house.

On the dining room carpet. Next to where Oldie and

the Girl ate their evening meal. Near where they seated guests.

They did not know what to do. She scrubbed and shampooed the carpet, sprinkled lemon juice and vinegar, opened wide all the windows. He made sure the malefactor was locked out and started his own irregular patrols of the garden, doing a bit of his own defensive pissing about in places where Sylvester may have liked to loiter.

They agreed, Max would have to be an outside cat — "for a while".

Perhaps it was because he was in the house all day, but Oldie had to get down on hands and knees to sniff the carpet before he could smell the cat's piss. Anna said she could smell it immediately she came home and stepped through the front door. She had another go at scrubbing and deodorising.

Despite the heat, the air-con was turned off and the windows left open all night. As was the back door. With only the flyscreen door on its flimsy snib keeping him out of the house, Max spent half the night rattling it, all the while yowling and yodelling. Oldie consoled himself with the hope that Sylvester's owners were also being kept awake.

The next day the Old Man walked over to the shopping mall, found a place selling incense sticks and got a packet each of sandalwood and patchouli. Using a saucer and jug, he put together a jury-rigged holder on the dining room table and lit a dozen patchouli sticks. Fifteen minutes later the smoke alarm in the passage went off.

That night Max settled fairly quickly on a blanket in a carton on the table at the back of the house. He, along with all others concerned, needed a good night's sleep.

At twenty something past three in the morning the Old Man and the Girl woke suddenly.

They lay still and listened. "What was that?" she whispered.

"Dunno. What'd you hear?"

"Not sure. Did something go bang?"

"Out the back?"

"Maybe. I think so."

"Yeah ... Do you think Maxie has company?"

"Sylvester? Wouldn't they be, you know ... sounding off?"

"Caterwauling."

"Cat Concerto."

"Hmmm."

They listened. The silence was steady. After a while, about a minute, he carefully got off the bed, pulled on his undies and a T-shirt, and crept down the passage towards the kitchen and the back door. He got a whiff of the incense and was a little surprised at how quickly the smell of stale ash had become dominant.

Not a sound. He switched on the outside light and peered through the kitchen window. Max was in his nest, head up, ears pricked, alertly staring at the back door into the laundry. The moment he caught sight of the Old Man he stood and stretched, preparing to get down off the table and take up moaning position by the back door.

"Forget it," Oldie muttered, snapping off the light and turning to shuffle back up the passage.

A few hours later he found his morning shower only tolerably warm. By the time the Girl got in it was entirely cold.

He opened the hot water cupboard in the laundry and looked at the tank. It seemed intact, but there was ... something, something in the air he tasted more than smelt. Out at the switchboard he found the safety switch for the electric hot water system had thrown; and as many times as he reset it, it loudly banged back to OFF.

It dawned on him that this was probably what they heard bump in the night.

God-damn it! That tank was only eighteen months old.

Danny the plumber returned his call soon after nine o'clock that morning. He'd have to send an electrician to check, but he reckoned the tank's element had blown. There had been a lot of them packing it in lately. It was, he said, the water. Perth was relying too heavily on ground water and there was a lot of crap in it. Elements and anodes corroded. The bad news was that although the tank had a three-year warranty, the elements were only guaranteed for a year. So ...

A bit later the electrician Danny had organised rang to say he'd call by that afternoon to have a look at the situation. If the element was the problem, he could install a new one the following morning. That would get the hot water back. Changing the anode could wait, and Danny would come later in the week to do that. The possibility of a new thermostat being required was mentioned.

Element, thermostat, anode, tradies who came promptly — it was going to cost him money. *Dengi.*

It was the water. The god-damn water. And the crap that was in it! It sure as hell wasn't Perrier or Borjomi coming up from the aquifers beneath the coastal plain. No way.

Well, then, we'll just see about that. Danny said a lot of hot water tanks "were packing it in lately" — well then, if that wasn't something worth looking at, he didn't know shit from clay. He would talk to Carol about this. Her documentary should look at this. It definitely should. This was about consequences.

When he told Anna about it she asked him what "the crap" was.

Thinking quickly, he said, "limestone".

Better check with Danny before talking to Carol.

And besides ... What the Devil is an anode?

The next morning, instead of immediately facing the cold shower, he wandered down the passage to stand in the kitchen, eyes half closed against the bright light filtering through the back patio shade cloth, the fernery, the lacy curtains and half drawn blinds. On automatic pilot, he started to set the table for their evening meal. The salt pig and pepper grinder stared back in joint reproof. Wrong flight plan. He returned the indignant seasonings to their place on top of the fridge and poured himself a glass of cold water.

There is always damage to repair.

He'd put the trip to Melbourne out of mind. But as the time approached for Anna to book tickets and apply for time off work — the time when he would have to commit himself to the journey — a dull thud of recognition hazed through his mind. Oldie felt his feet going cold.

You can't go home again, said Mr Wolfe.

He made noises about how his prospective work for Steve Lyons and the Fishing Industry Council, together with his commitment to help Carol with her documentary, meant he was not sure this was the best time for him to be racing off to Melbourne.

And then he had a call from his sister to tell him their mother had taken a tumble. Fell out of bed and bumped her head. She was apparently all right, but an ambulance had been called and the impetus to put the old girl in a home had just gone up by a few notches.

"SEAFIC, SeeHear," Anna said with a particularly bright smile. "Well, here's another one — See you later! If you're not coming, I'll go on my own. May-June, late autumn, early winter — I fancy a bit of cooler weather."

He looked at her and knew she was not joking.

So, that settled that.

Debts. The nature of debts. Who knows what we truly owe to others? Or them to us? How much can you say is owed to you? People say they owe their life to someone else. They usually mean to acknowledge that they would not be alive without the intervention of the other. But do they feel they would give their life if their saviour asked for it. Some people do give their lives for others — but that's usually because of love. A parent's love of a child, for example. But that's not exactly from a sense of debt.

He told himself he could make the trip useful by having a look at the Stevensons Road landfill site; by seeing if he could find a good talking head for the Brookland Greens affair. When things got too grim with his mother, he and the Girl would take a long drive up into New South Wales to find out what the pie shops were like in Deniliquin, Junee and Canowindra.

It had been a while since he had fronted up to the SRO reception desk. A pleasant, efficient young man Oldie had never seen before was on the counter. All the documents he had called for were there, waiting for him. From the desk he looked over the reading room and noted the four lost souls already perched in there — he was on no more than nodding terms with any of them and would be left alone. It was beginning to feel like a lucky day.

Then, from the office area up on the mezzanine, he heard Baba Yaga hectoring one of her colleagues. She had one of those whining, needling, mewling voices that really, really carry.

He was tempted to politely request the young bloke on the desk to ask his colleague upstairs "to keep it down". After all, researchers in the reading room who raised their voices above a whisper were relentlessly cautioned — more often than not, let it be plainly stated, by Baba Yaga.

Just as he was about to say something a tall woman materialized beside him. The young man behind the counter shifted his attention and smiled at her. Oldie held his tongue about Baba Yaga, gathered up the stack of files he had requested and started to move away. He snuck a peek at the woman next to him and, for a startled heartbeat, thought it was Sophie the Owl. But when she looked him in the face and he saw that she had matching green eyes, he knew it was not Sophie. The resemblance was there, however. She could have been Sophie's sister. What witchery was this?

He realized he had stopped and was absent-mindedly staring at the woman. And she, with a bemused smile, was looking back. The look on her face was essentially the question: Well, have you worked it out yet? The SRO fellow was staring at him with the same knowing smile.

The Old Man muttered something meaningless and hurried off to the far side of the reading room. The other researchers had their heads down. There was something suspiciously concerted about the way they seemed to be collectively avoiding any eye contact.

As he placed the files, his notebook and pencils on a table as far from anyone as he could get, he looked up to see Baba Yaga staring down from the mezzanine. That, he thought, was probably why nobody acknowledged him.

He looked back, intending to give Baba Yaga a friendly wave, but she had disappeared.

He heard music. Someone had a radio on up there! Jesus! What next? What was that? Bizet's *Farandole!*

He started to take off his jacket. But his shoulder was somehow caught. The harder he pulled, the tighter the garment became.

The music got louder.

He struggled and heard fabric rip.

There was a bad taste in his mouth.

His right hand gripped the edge of the bed as he freed his left arm from the torn sheet.

The woman on the radio was cheerfully wishing him a Good Morning.

Damn!

He rolled over to tell the Girl about his dream and found she was not there.

The bottom sheet was torn down the middle for most of its length.

Propping himself on an elbow, he listened to the house. She wasn't in the shower. No sound came from the kitchen.

He groaned. He knew where she was, and why. She was sleeping on the couch because his snoring had kept her awake.

Kept her away.

Snoring. A family trait. Old Jim and his father were shockers. Now him.

He swung his feet off the bed and pushed himself upright. He felt shithouse.

When he did present himself at the SRO later that morning he was greeted by a pleasant young man he had never seen before. He showed his ticket and was let into the reading room. All six of the files Oldie had called for were waiting for him. He let out a mirthful grunt and glanced up at the mezzanine — no sign of Baba Yaga. He thanked the attendant and took himself and the files to the back table, where nobody would have any excuse to wander by and look over his shoulder.

There was one other researcher in the reading room, a young woman (PhD student) who didn't look anything like Sophie. Hadn't he intended to call Sophie? Shake her tree? *Whoo! Whoo!* What became of that big, bright idea?

Blink.

Blinkity blink.

It having been decreed that six files were all the archivists should fetch for any member of the public at one time, Oldie had to be content on his first morning's work to examine only half the batch he had cited in the Nibbelup report. The tricky thing would be how it would go when he asked for the file dropped from the online catalogue. That would bring Baba Yaga to the front desk. In the meantime, he'd have a careful look at everything else. See if anything jumped out at him.

Although now under the control of the Department of Environment and Conservation, most of what he had before him had once been classified as "general files relating to metropolitan reservoirs, tanks, bores, sewerage treatment, water purity etc". It was the odds and sods shuffled in under that flat "etc" that could sometimes turn out to be interesting reading. The minutes and "associated material" of various sub-committee meetings, especially, could become very fertile ground (just add water).

Before Nibbelup was Nibbelup it had been Hogan's Road Reserve, and before it was Hogan's Road Reserve it had been Chinaman's Swamp. That name went back to the eighteen-nineties when Luk Kee and family grew vegetables (onions!) there. What that swamp had really been called before it was occupied by Luk Kee and, before him, the Royal Navy officer who had the original land grant from Governor Stirling was anyone's guess. But the guess was given to old Billy Swan and he came up with Nibbleup — which, all things considered, was fair enough.

Anyway, the Luks were gone by the start of World War Two, when the Army took over the place. The military apparently never got around to doing much with the land and by the mid-fifties it was back in municipal hands, gazetted as Hogan's Road Reserve, a rubbish tip. But the official dump site only occupied about a quarter of the reserve. There were a few other, unofficial places in the vicinity, to which the blind eye had been consistently turned.

Oldie could not remember anything of the previous occasion he had gone through the files. It was a blank but, when all was said and done, there was no reason why a couple of routine visits to the archives more than a decade ago should stick in his memory. What did he know about the Sarnos back then? Certainly not that Reg the Racketeer was their boy. To all intents and purposes, he told himself as he opened the first folder, he now returned to the job with fresh eyes.

He was soon drawn into the work. For people of a particular cast of mind there are some very seductive pleasures in the handling of old documents. Oldie warmed to the sense of a writer's proximity that lingers in handwritten documents. Apart from the actuality of the paper one holds having once been held by the writer, handwriting offers an experienced reader subtle but nevertheless tangible clues, if not to a writer's character exactly, then of his or her ... well, let's call it "disposition". You have to be careful not to read too much into it, but those accumulated indications of education, class and disposition can sometimes allow meaning to be discerned in a text that would otherwise be obscure, ambiguous. While practically everyone else tapped away on their laptops, Oldie persisted in writing his notes. Longhand, as he liked to call it. He reasoned the practice kept him attuned to the tempo of the document, that through it he maintained an affinity with the *work* of the document's creation.

That's what he told himself, but he had the sense to not go on about it. He understood such notions were all just a wee bit too mystic to cut much ice with the bright young things sporting their new matt-grey toys.

While it is true that most of the higher level official correspondence from the nineteen-fifties was typed, much of the daily, procedural stuff of the civil service of that decade was still being churned out in a thousand various scrawls. Such material may initially baffle modern type-orientated eyes, but generally, with patience and practice, the substance can be discerned. On the other hand, some of the carbon copies of typed documents are so faint and fuzzy that even patient readers may miss something.

Had he missed something back then? A name? Did Roger come back and spot it?

It took him more than an hour to work through the first two files, checking that each page was consecutively numbered — that none were missing. These were the papers dealing with the process of Chinaman's Swamp being handed over to the local council for use as a rubbish tip. It was all pro forma stuff, creating the appropriate legal and administrative framework for an existing state of affairs. Nothing was said directly beyond occasional references to "unauthorized tipping" when the land had been under military control; and, implying it was not just the local citizenry dumping household rubbish and burnt out stolen cars, there was some discussion about the damage done to Hogan's Road by heavy vehicles. No names were attached to any of these activities.

Oldie became aware of a pair of ruddy middle-aged blokes who had come into the reading room a while earlier. They sat at adjoining tables a few rows in front of him and were whispering and tittering away together like school kids. Where was Baba Yaga when you needed her? The PhD student who didn't look anything like Sophie was glancing her irritation, but Tweedledee and Tweedledum were oblivious.

Scattered throughout the files were maps, charts and plans of the designated reserve. Oldie was almost certain he had some of these photographed for Steve Lyons, but if so he had not kept copies with his own notes — you can't keep everything and it just wasn't interesting enough at the time. He knew the SRO's computer retained a record of what he copied and he didn't want to make it easy for anyone tracking him, but unique maps had to be copied precisely so he now stuck his USB thumb into the SRO camera and did what he had to do.

His hope was that accurate identification of authorised refuse sites, set against the aerial photographs he had ordered from Landgate, would show where and roughly when that unauthorized tipping had occurred. Steve Lyons's client and perhaps Lyons himself must have made that comparison a decade ago.

It was with a private sigh that Oldie accepted he could no longer avoid the task of identifying that damned property developer, a half remembered set of corporate initials. He knew in his weary bones he'd find at least one Sarno in the mix.

Seek and ye shall find! Hey Presto!

Attached to the fourth page inside the third file was a small Post-it note. Pencilled on the yellow slip was the brief message: The principal shareholders of AITF Holdings were Rosemary Elizabeth Sarno and Antonia Lucia Sarno.

Yes. AITF Holdings. That was it. He recognised it. For the empty space in Oldie's memory there was a piece that fitted it.

He sat and stared. Blinked and stared some more. Maybe he saw something he remembered in the handwriting but ... yes, that was Roger's note all right. Crafty little fucker! Christ! Sticking adhesive material on archival material! Cheeky little fucker.

Oldie was ready to bet London to a brick that he was looking at the names of the wives of Aldo and Frank Sarno Junior. You'd have to be mentally defective to think otherwise.

He glanced up at the mezzanine balcony, made sure nobody was eyeballing him and deftly transferred the sticky note to a blank page at the back of his notebook. Ha! Try that with a laptop! Flipping back to where he had been working at the front of his notebook, and marking the entry with a small but clear asterisk, he set about summarizing the document Roger had stickered.

It was a page of a 1991 submission the Environmental Protection Authority made to the State Planning Commission.

An investigation of the contamination caused by liquid waste disposal at and near the Hogan's Road Reserve found that although there was "no inventory of the types or volumes of liquid waste" dumped there, it was known "to include brewery effluent, septic sludge and night oil, oils and other industrial wastes". There were "significant levels of some heavy metals and petroleum hydrocarbons" in the soil; and the ground water was contaminated by "ammonia-nitrogen, oily substances and substances (probably of an organic nature) emitting odourous gases".

"Night oil" was surely a typo on "night soil". But if that was the real shit, then what kind of shit was that "of an organic nature"?

A few pages into the submission there was a map of

the proposed urban zone. Yes, the official landfill site was now occupied by playing fields and a park with an ornamental lake sign-posted as Rehabilitated Wetlands. But where were the unofficial dumping sites on the old reserve? And how many of them were beneath the present housing?

Those aerial survey images might be very interesting indeed.

The next sticker was on the last page of the EPA submission. It read: Reg Pascoe was an Army weapons instructor. Based in Perth from mid '45.

So ... Reggie had been in the Army and Chinaman's Swamp had been Army land. You don't need a lot of imagination to make something out of that.

Once again the Old Man looked about before smoothly detaching the sticker and palming it onto his notebook. He eyed the three remaining unexamined files on his table. Where else had Roger left his droppings? How many more of his notes were there to be found?

Then a darker question emerged: Why would Roger Kidd have set up this paper chase?

Really, there were obviously much better ways than this to get the story out.

Perhaps it was insurance, a sort of backup in case ... a manuscript went missing.

On the other hand, there was no doubt the fellow had a mischievous streak. He really did. Accusatory notes scattered about the place for anyone to find was pure mischief — just the sort of thing Roger would do for the sheer fun of it. Or, perhaps, to settle a score. Someone trying to clean that mess up could never be sure they'd chased every rabbit down every hole. It occurred to Oldie that he should put the notes back where he found them.

Then again, maybe not.

If he found repeats, he'd note their location and leave

them in place.

He opened the thickest remaining file and quickly leaved through. No yellow stickers. He was reaching for the second last folder when, suddenly, there was an excited rustling of papers, shifting of seats and huffing and puffing on the Tweedle front. One of them half rose from his seat and actually said "Cor!" The PhD student who didn't look like anybody other than herself was now positively glaring, looking about for someone in authority to deal with the miscreants.

"Cor lummy! That's the original signal box!" one ruddy chap declared to the other ruddy chap.

Railway buffs!

Oldie could not help but smile. The looking glass would focus on them. And sure enough, just then flew down a monstrous crow, which (didn't) frighten both the heroes so.

"Gentlemen," Baba Yaga pronounced, and paused for effect. "I must ask you to not disturb the other researchers. Please keep your voices down. We can even hear you upstairs." SRO veteran that he was, the Old Man was once more amused at the way Baba Yaga's head wobbled in time to her sing-song voice. Apparently a wind change could also catch you out with a silly voice.

One of the Tweedles stood up to report, "We found the plans for the Clevedon signal box!"

"It burned down in 1931," his mate (bless him!) added, helpfully.

Baba Yaga stiffened slightly as her cloudy eyes studied the men. She folded her hands together beneath her bosom and smiled. Och oh, thought Oldie.

"I'm pleased for you," she said sweet and even. "If you want those plans copied, speak to Michael on the desk. He will give you the rates and waiting times. But in the meantime, please keep the noise down."

She waited for the naughty boys to say they were sorry but they, confused, just looked at each other and shrugged.

"We would not like," she went on gaily, her eyes widening to stare them down, "to have to ask you to leave. Would we?"

At the first contrite murmur Baba Yaga turned and strutted towards the front desk. Young Michael would now be told something about how she should not have had to come down from her roost to deal with the disturbance. The doctoral candidate kept her head down, eyes averted, busy. Oldie leaned back and, grinning like the Cheshire Cat, waved at Baba Yaga. He did arm movements like a railway signal. She ignored his idiotic antics.

Well, she would, wouldn't she?

He stood, stretched and walked around the reading room, making something of a show of rolling his shoulders and slowing turning his head side to side to exercise his neck. Normally, he would have gone outside for a saunter around the plaza, or maybe a stroll over by the museum to take the air beneath the avenue of plane trees. But from the window he saw the leaves turning and flashing against the wind-polished sky. The north-westerly was blowing hard and it was becoming uncomfortably warm out there. Better inside than out. And with Baba Yaga pecking about, he did not want to leave his work exposed.

At some stage, sooner rather than later, he would need to go out for a piss. And he wanted to ring Carol to tell her of his discoveries. He told himself it was good business to keep the client interested. Maybe she was in town ... nearby.

He hoped Baba Yaga would bugger off before he lodged his call slips for the afternoon retrieval. With a little time to spare, he returned to his table to look for more sticky notes in the two unexamined files from the morning retrieval.

There was another one. Much the same as the first, it stated that Rosemary and Antonia Sarno were the principal shareholders of AITF Holdings. Like the one about Reg Pascoe, the second item about AITF Holdings seemed to have been stuck in more or less at random. Making a note of where he found it, Oldie left Roger's message *in situ*. He also recorded that a page appeared to be missing from the numbered sequence of documents in the file where he found the sticker.

Baba Yaga was gone and the Tweedles were busying themselves to make arrangements about copying their very important discovery. No doubt they'd want to discuss the matter in detail at the desk.

Oldie quickly gathered up his notes and folders, returned the files to the front desk, lodged his call slips, retrieved his bag from the locker and headed for the Library's *pissyaar*.

By the time he had relieved himself and washed his hands he had decided it might be better not to call Carol just yet. Best thing would be to find somewhere quiet and cool to have a think about what was what before he opened his trap.

Best to wait and see. He might find more of Roger's notes that afternoon and who knows what would be in them. He asked himself what the dead man would have wanted him to do with them. Who would keep the originals? He was uneasy about Roger. He suspected the man was sort of messing with his head when he was alive, but now that he was dead Oldie felt there had been some private understanding between them that superseded all other obligations. Handing the notes over to Blondie was all very well and good but that also gave them to Ted Connell, political advisor and all-round backroom boy. He was uneasy and putting Roger's notes in anyone else hands was not a bridge to cross without careful consideration.

Still, if he was to earn her dollar, he had to give Blondie something. A few aerial photos — a series of at least three covering the decades of interest — would be sufficient for the time being. Visual material is self evident, but untidy allegations as to who did what when can always be denied. More to the point, they can lead straight to the courthouse. So there would be the tiresome matter of Oldie having to take the time and make the effort to chase up company records and somehow get hold of Reg Pascoe's service record, documents he suspected may have already been lost or misfiled.

He reminded himself to call the Landgate bloke he'd spoken to about the photos. See where his order was in the fricking queue. He'd do it when he got home.

He was tired, losing the thread ...

Somewhere quiet and cool was at a table under a tree in the courtyard outside the entrance to the old Perth Gaol, a building now incorporated into the museum and housing that institution's cafe. Had Blondie been with him for his salad roll and iced tea, he decided, he would have told her the story of Kenneth Brown. It was just around that corner, by that wall over there that Kenneth, son of a prominent pioneer family, was hanged in the winter of 1876. In a drunken rage, he had shot dead his second wife. They were moving house and, it was said, had an argument over her having thrown out a pair of his old shoes. It took a few goes to get up a proper trial in such a tight-knit community, but Kenneth was finally convicted and delivered to his maker. Rumours later arose that he had been spirited away and lived out his days in America. But that's nonsense. Kenneth Brown, aged 38, was hanged. Ask his ghost.

One reason historians remember Kenneth is because one of his orphaned children, a daughter of his first marriage, was a fifteen-year-old girl named Edith. Edith went on to marry a man named Cowan and by that name is remembered as the first woman elected to an Australian Parliament. A university is named after her and, for many years, her face has graced the Australian fifty dollar note. Edith did well. Oldie, however, was more interested in another daughter, Edith's half-sister, Rose. Born in 1875, Rose was literally a babe-in-arms when her mother was murdered by her father. She died in 1950, and had therefore lived into Oldie's lifetime. She was more than a decade older than his Peggy, but in their middle and later years the women would have been seen as contemporaries. There were people living in Perth who had known Rose Brown. She was, as the phrase has it, within living memory.

It was a hanging that broke his childhood pact with Peggy.

In early 1967 he was once again living at Cameron Street, boarding with Peggy (and Jim and Bobby) while he worked during the summer holidays before commencing university. The big news that summer was the controversial decision to hang Ronald Ryan, found guilty of shooting dead a warder as Ryan and another man escaped from Pentridge Prison, barely a mile up Sydney Road from Peggy's place. People held strong opinions and argued the matter with passion. Young Alex and Old Peggy were of different opinions. He thought he could change her mind. And then, one shining morning as he was leaving the house, she turned on him with withering anger and told him to "grow up".

He was eighteen, cocky and already had the gift of the gab but he had no answer for that. She stopped him in his tracks.

That evening she buttered him up, as only she could, but he had grown up enough to no longer take a couple of things for granted.

At eight o'clock the following Friday morning the packed green and gold tram he was riding to work stopped in Lygon Street while Melbourne observed a silence as Ronald Ryan went to Pentridge's gallows, protesting his innocence to the last.

He gazed at the shadows of the plane tree flickering on the facade of the old Perth Gaol and remembered the morning heat of that summer day all those years ago and a continent away. He must have been standing near the front door of the tram because he remembered glancing at the back of the driver's head as he sat motionless in his cab. Cars were not permitted to pass stationary trams, so stopping the trams effectively stopped the city. Oldie remembered how quiet it suddenly became. Nobody spoke. They all sat still and avoided one another's eyes.

And then someone sighed, the driver put his hand on the throttle, the ticking of the tram's electric motor increased to a whirr, the wheels rumbled beneath the floor and life rolled on.

As though nothing had happened.

Blondie's photographs from the New Norcia trip arrived by courier mid-morning. Four 8x10s. Three images of the flowering marris and one of him. There was no accompanying note, but her business card was taped to the cardboard sleeve stiffening the envelope.

She had captured his image when they stopped and he stood at that barbed wire fence, preoccupied in checking that it was safe for her to come up the bank to join him. His back was square to her, but he had turned his head as he removed the hat and in doing so brought his face almost into profile in the crook of his extended arm. It looked as though he was doffing his hat in salute to the parched country before him. She had washed out the background colors until the sky was the palest blue and he, in his dark clothes, stood in silhouette against the blond grass and the cloud-like trees. He had to admit, with his gut hidden and his face in sharp focus, it was a flattering image.

The images of the flowering gums arrayed across the paddock were three versions of the one photograph. The first was printed with deep, saturated colors and closest to a record of what they had seen on the day. In the next version she had toned everything back to the light pastel shades backgrounding his portrait. Lastly, there was a lovely black and white, full-cream thing ranging across the entire greyscale.

He dithered, picking up the phone several times and even commencing to dial, but each time refrained from making the call. At midday he carefully composed and sent an "in haste" email expressing his thanks, praising her work and promising to phone her as soon as he had something to report. He signed off with "All the Best".

He had resisted the impulse to tell her about the notes Roger left in the archives. Roger's unquiet ghost and its bucket of coiling worms made him nervous. Tell Blondie and he would have to tell Steve; because if she knew, Ted knew. Then, as sure as God made little green apples, the Big Fisherman would hear a whisper — he had ears to the ground all over — and if Steve knew Ted knew, he would be obliged to report to the Sarnos. That could have consequences.

Yes, better to keep the lid on those snaking worms until he had a better idea of what else was in the bucket.

Besides, as he once again felt the need to remind himself, Blondie had made it plain enough she did not see past skulduggery as the primary concern of her project. "A limited local story," she had said. "A separate program," she had added.

He looked out the window and saw the exiled Max drowsing in the shade of the hedge. "When you see a god-damn snake in the god-damn grass," he shouted to the disconcerted cat, "you have to decide pretty damned quick which end is the head."

He presumed his neighbours also heard the advice and sincerely hoped they would ponder it.

XI

He plunged into the fishing reports and found "Sustainable" (always qualifying "Development") and "Sustainability" (mostly "Managed") morosely clogging the opening sentence of every SEAFIC document he looked at. It was part of his job to re-enforce this conceptual objective by deploying tangential synonyms; he was there to lard the reports with as many quotable sound bites as all concerned could then cast about like berley upon the waters of public discourse. The consulting marine biologists and their secretaries who had banged out the initial drafts went no further than what their computers' programmed Synonym functions threw up, which had not got them much beyond "Maintain" as a variant. So he hunted out his high school *Roget's Thesaurus*. Its soft pages had yellowed around the edges yet the dear old thing still had its two tone red covers. The price sticker was still attached, eight shillings and sixpence. Gone are the days.

His moving finger wavered down the list: Continue, Strengthen, Perform, Support, Preserve, Aid and Endure. Hmm. Preserve and Endure might do, providing they weren't done to death in imbecilic slogans. Yes, judiciously scattered about, they would earn their keep by leavening the loaf.

Other than initially being a little disconcerted by the

technical complexity of algal research for feed and bio-fuels, Oldie soon had the gist of what the Fishing Council and the businesses it represented were after. They were about facilitating a very rapid and a very large expansion of aquaculture — the fishing industry's Sustainable Future.

Algae? Really?

Well, as a matter of fact, yes.

The problem was that on its own algae was not a good look; not attractive and hard to promote, even as bio-blah-blah-sustainable feed for what or whoever. Chooks and pigs? Yes. Body builders?

So ...

Yes, just so.

Fortunately, more conventional produce — oysters, mussels and other shellfish — were proven ventures and all goody-goody to go. Tuna, too, could be declared a steady success story, just so long as it was understood that there could be nary a word uttered about such small fry tribulations as pilchards and their attendant viruses. Then, looking towards the glam end of the market, he was hardly surprised at how strongly yellowtail kingfish and mulloway (species with established market profiles) were being pushed for commercial cultivation. With its firm, white flesh so suited to sashimi, kingfish demonstrated especially promising potential.

He guessed Mr Lyons had his particular pile of money on the showcase flash of the kingies rather than the algal sludge. But of course, as is often remarked, there's money in muck. Oldie had no doubt Steve Lyons would always be prepared to reach deep into the shit to get his hands on a gold coin. But then, given the opportunity, most people would. No sense in kidding ourselves otherwise. It always amused him how people make a retrospective virtue out of missed opportunities, kidding themselves but nobody else that they had deliberately stepped back from the tainted chance.

As if!

Patience, Peggy had said as she catered to his every whim, is a virtue.

Oldie's father had been a fisherman. What would he have made of kingfish being bred in captivity?

It was the legendary fight in a kingfish that kept his father standing alone on a windy beach for half of many a night. Wading out in the wild darkness to cast sinkers and bait into the deeper water beyond the breaking surf. Standing shoulder to the wind as the tide came in, Tilley lamp hissing, finger on the pulse of the taut line; time after time, six or more hours of wet and cold, waiting for the strike that rarely came. Some nights a gummy shark or a snapper was taken to put a feed on the table and pay for the bait and lost gear, not to mention the two hour drive each weekend to the beach house. Oldie had never possessed his father's steadfast patience. He scarcely understood it. Many times the luck went no further than a stingray and as many nights again there wasn't even a bite. But his father kept going back and always let it be known he was after that big kingie. He caught a few over the years but it was his lot that there was only ever the one big one — a beauty, more than thirty pounds in the old weight.

And yet it has come to pass that such beauty can now be bought and sold with the same ease as were the souls of men in the markets of Babylon.

He understood that while most would be indifferent, some (those who would joke about the appropriateness of it being a shitty liver that saw him off) would derive smug satisfaction from his impending demise. People have always been blamed for their own deaths. Once upon a time it was Fate or Divine Retribution, nowadays it will probably have something to do with the notion that they didn't exercise enough and ate the wrong foods. It truly is a righteous comfort to write off such slackers with an unspoken "Serves 'em right!" He also saw that there were those who, while in no way malevolent, would nevertheless secretly welcome his death. It was hard to put a finger on it, exactly. People do not always react as you would expect and you have to leave room for surprises, but even so, he reckoned he discerned something in a couple of those he had already told. They were the ones who had somehow stepped away, who had already written him off. He would spare himself the embarrassment of contacting them.

Other than Anna and Daniel, he had told only five people in Perth. Perhaps because those five were all unknown to one another, that many, at first, didn't seem a lot to confide in. But it turned out to have been at least two too many. They were the two who had drifted away. He was fairly sure one of them had since betrayed his confidence to a mutual acquaintance, a fellow who seemed to be asking just too many questions and wafting into those pseudo intimate moments intended to facilitate the sharing of confidences.

It served him right for not thinking the thing through. You either shut up completely or you accept that the cat will get out of the bag. He knew who he'd told, but had no idea of how many others they had then told. Despite being asked not to, people talk. They just do. They can't help themselves. They'll give away someone else's life secret to relieve their own boredom, to divert and amuse themselves.

People! Who needs 'em!?

To cut to the chase: he and scores of other patients were sitting in the reception and waiting lounge, suffering the usual televised crap as they waited their turn at the hepatology clinic. Scores of others trooped past on their way to other clinics. He was there for all the world to see — waiting, patiently. Attending twice a year, it was only a matter of time before someone recognized him. Perhaps it would be some Kafoops he didn't know very well, or maybe didn't even recognize, but that intrepid Kafoops would go out into the wider world and somewhere down the track blow in someone else's ear, "By the way, you know that old bloke ..."

And so it goes, as a beleaguered young Kurt said one fearsome winter's day back in Dresden.

Yes ... people.

Along with the patients there was a solid contingent of Significant Others. Having someone to get you home should the news be bad was all very well, but the down side was the increased risk of recognition. He had persuaded Anna not to take the sickie, assuring her that he was fairly confident the test results would be more of the same. She didn't argue.

Then, along with the other patients and their mates, there were all the attending staff and, elsewhere in the system, those who had access to the medical records. Come to think of it, he was pretty sure a school friend of Dan's worked in the hospital's IT dept. People are curious. They just can't help themselves.

Cover stories of gall bladder trouble would only go so far. At a certain stage those who know a thing or two see that something is not so hunky-dory and — click! — they step up to the plate and make that educated guess. He'd done it himself.

Weighing it all up, he felt there was more dignity in not broadcasting his situation. Anna told him it was his call but he, as they say on the radio, was conflicted. On the one hand, with hepatitis C's association with illicit

219

drug use giving it a reputation as heavy as AIDS, public knowledge of his infection could be unpleasant for Anna at work. Legally, it shouldn't cause problems, but fear and ignorance make their own rules.

There were times when he thought it would be a relief to just tell everyone and let the chips fall where they may, even if some people then disappointed him. Except that, explaining it would be a problem. People did not always understand "incurable"; didn't want to understand it. And ... should his mother hear of it she would make his life hell.

"And, believe me, I *really* don't have time for that!" he told Anna, with just a little too much hissy heat.

He had never quite settled on a clear answer to the question of what he sought in telling others of his situation. Secrets and trust may entail intimacy (in his heart of hearts he wanted to tell Blondie), but that wasn't even part of it for most of those he had told. A certain regard, in the sense of consideration, perhaps. All right, OK, he understood — everybody has their own cross to bear and all that — but he could not help wishing they would just cut him a bit of god-damn slack, that they would make a conscious effort to spare him at least some of the petty bothers of daily life. Was that small charity too much to expect?

The phrase kept coming to him: "I don't have *time* for this!" It was aggressive, coming *at* him as much as to him.

It may have been the exasperated truth, but it still sounded trite. And even if it were a natural enough thing for him to think, it was quite another to be saying it.

"I don't have *time* for this!"

He might get away with saying such an eye-roller to Anna (although not too often), but for those who did not know of or suspect his illness, it was meaningless. It came out as a petty pomposity. It had, however, seemed comfortably appropriate the night he cut Sid Wedge off as he was launching into one of his more offensive theories. As many a philosopher has noticed, morality is often invoked for grubby purposes.

The nurse called him over to the scales, recorded his weight without comment or interest, and directed him to take the seat in the corridor outside Mayakovsky's consulting room. Pole position. The session was running only forty minutes late and he was next. With luck, he'd beat the worst of the peak-hour traffic home.

His luck was holding. Associate Professor Mayakovsky ran his large hand over his large shaved head, grinned and almost laughed as he told Oldie his results were much the same as they had been six months earlier.

One day. But not this one.

Oldie clapped his hands. "OK," he said, "then I may yet get my hands on an old age pension?"

"I sincerely hope so!" declared Vladimir Vladimirovich, with all the benevolence it was his to bestow.

"So, let me just ask," Oldie was suddenly very serious, "just out of curiosity, for the purposes of private research: Would it be possible to be infected by kissing better a small but bloody scratch on the arm of a two-year-old, the daughter of a woman who had the virus when her baby was born?"

Mayakovsky hadn't expected that one. Not even from Oldie. He puffed his rosy cheeks and bulged his dark brown eyes as he put his hands behind his head and tilted back in his chair. He gave Oldie a moment of the penetrating, inquiring look before exhaling. "Possible, but very unlikely ..."

"Possible?"

Mayakovsky leaned forward, rested his forearms on the desk, clasped his hands together in his most

221

professional manner and asked his patient why he was inquiring about this particular possibility.

"Oh, nothing to do with me," Oldie laughed. "I saw it in a novel, that's all. The father of the kid, the husband of the infected woman, took offence over something and sought vengeance by infecting the offending party through the blood of the innocent child. I was just curious as to whether such an assassination was medically possible."

"I've never heard of such a case. There'd been surer ways to do it. But, if the plot requires it ... Are you saying the father deliberately scratched the child to draw the blood?"

"Could have. But it may have just been opportunistic."

"What was the offence?"

"Slighted the wife."

"Oh, well ... fair enough!"

They pondered this before exchanging further banter of the same existential tenor. Mayakovsky told Oldie to get the sugar out of his diet — fruit juice and lo-fat yoghurt is full of it. Oldie said he'd look into it and told Mayakovsky the old "pass me the sugar, Honey" joke. They laughed together, too loudly, shook hands and agreed to meet again in six months.

After the moment of immortality, life rolls on.

Next!

He picked his moment. The day after he passed the first tidied up SEAFIC document back to Steve Lyons, Oldie rang to tell him he had been approached by Carol Dubois to work on her documentary.

Talking the talk about the forward-looking, sustainability focus of Carol's project, and emphasising how Ted Connell was going out of his way to avoid any real or perceived conflict of interest, and (above all) insisting that he treated each client's work with the strictest confidentiality, Oldie said he would understand if Steve nevertheless thought there was a problem and wanted to withdraw his offer of the Fishing Industry Council's editorial work.

Oldie hadn't drawn a breath, but good old Steve didn't miss a god-damn beat. He assured Oldie that his masterly work would be essential to the success of further fishing reports — "I'll have a lot of explaining to do if you back out now," he said — and smoothly added that, really, just so long as they kept each other "reasonably informed", he could see no reason why a conflict of interest should ever arise for two alert gentlemen such as their good selves.

"*Glasnost*," Steve declared. "That was the word, wasn't it? Mr Gorbachev's word, back in the day. Openness! As long as we have that, we can have an understanding. Right? Comrade! Hmm, yes, understanding. Openness and understanding. So be sure you let the delightful Miss Dubois know you've spoken to me. Absolutely! I mean, if I am reading this the right way up, she has assured us Ted Connell really is keeping his hands off this one. Clean noses all round. Let her know that's my understanding. You haven't met Teddy Boy yet?"

"No. He's pretty busy. At the beck and call of the Premier, I'm told. But Perth's still a small town and I guess there may be some occasion when we could bump into one another. As it happens, he walked right past us while you and I were talking at Roger's funeral."

"Is that so? Well, there you go. I never noticed."

"Have you heard the rumour that Roger had cancer?"

"Is that so?! Well, I guess that may explain things ..."

"Ted Connell is putting that story about. Carol told me."

223

"Is that so?! Well, well. What do you think?"

"I don't know."

"Look, Alex, it would be odd if there weren't occasions when you and Ted weren't in contact, directly or otherwise. So look, let me just say I trust your judgment. And if Ted does re-enter the game ... well, then, I'm sure he would only do so for what he saw as a good reason. And if we were to know what that reason was ..."

"It would tell us what's sensitive."

"Yes, that, you get my drift. But it could also give us an opportunity to make ourselves useful. Doesn't hurt. All part of keeping an eye open and an ear to the ground. Just remember, though, what we said about separate agendas. Now, as we speak, thanks to the wonder of internet banking, at the press of this button ... payment of your invoice is going through."

Oldie politely thanked Steve and dutifully spoke for a few more minutes about some aspects of the work he had done.

He later rationalised his decision to drop the conflict of interest situation in Steve's lap as intuitive, that he had instinctively veered towards something that simply had to be confronted if he wanted to get from A to B. But where he went after that was more to do with up-ing some unspoken ante. Whatever the impulse, he did not think about it, something just slipped loose inside him and he asked the question. He asked as though he was only making conversation, more or less as though it was merely for something to say. He asked Lyons if he knew Reg Pascoe used to work for Frank Sarno.

"Sounds like," Steve quietly laughed, "forgive me for saying, but it sounds like you've really got into the business of being the Private Eye."

"People tell me things," Oldie shot back.

"Ah, yes, of course," Steve sighed, "you're right, people do talk. They do. And do I have to guess who it was that told you about Frank Sarno?"

"Carol told me. And, yeah, she probably got it from Ted. But she did say she was more interested in the present water crisis than ... well, the history."

"She said that?"

"Words to that effect."

"Hmm. Well, I guess I did hear about Reg somewhere along the way. But, really," he gave an abrupt, edgy laugh, "at one time or another, haven't we all worked for the Sarnos? You must've worked that out by now."

"You mean AITF Holdings?"

"You have got a good memory! Or have you been digging?"

"Bit of both."

"Yes, AITF. That'd be the one. Archie Bunker's company."

Oldie kept quiet.

"All in the Family," Steve explained.

"Oh."

"I agree. But, hey, it could have been TIF Holdings — *Tutto in Famiglia*. That really would have been rather blatant, aye? I reckon Aldo would have put his foot down on that one. I'm surprised he let AITF through. But there you go — life is full of surprises. In business, of course, the less surprises the better. But seriously, I'm relying on your judgment to find the right balance of *glasnost* and confidentiality. You have to be careful. My dear old Mum used to tell me: Don't talk to strangers. You understand what I'm saying?"

"I do. And for what it's worth, my dentist told me I've got very tight lips. So there, that's official — I'm tight-lipped."

"Ah ..."

"But tell me," Oldie rushed on, "in the spirit of the *glasnost* side of things and all, there's one thing I'm still not clear about. I hear your message about all of us having taken the Sarno dollar at some stage of our careers. But what I need to know — and I mean cards on the table need-to-know — is whether we are in any way still working for the Sarnos."

Steve was back on his feet. "Do you want to be?"

The Old Man cleared his throat but said nothing.

Steve let a few seconds pass. "Well, to answer your question, we are certainly not on their payroll at this stage."

"Straight up?"

"Absolutely! It has been a while since I had any substantial business dealings with either Frank or Aldo. But, you know, we know where to find each other. I usually dealt with Aldo. I get on all right with him, too. I never met Frank Senior, by the way, only ever dealt with the boys. Matter of fact, now that I think of it, the last time I spoke to one of them was when I bumped into Aldo at Sydney airport, two or three months ago. Just before Christmas. He had people with him so ... we shook hands, exchanged a few pleasantries and went our separate ways. It's like that."

"So how do you think they're going to take it should there be a problem with Nibbelup?"

"Depends upon the nature and size of the problem. My guess is they'd take most things in their stride. I doubt they'd think too much about it. Why should they? These are people who have lawyers, supernumeraries and various wizards to sort out those sorts of things."

"Wizards! And what would such wizards do?"

"Well, all right," Steve displayed a moment of uncharacteristic impatience, "bad choice of words. My point is that people like the Sarnos have people around just to solve their problems. They have people to deal with awkward things at a remove, people to pay others to pay others to make things go away. I suppose, if they wanted it, or the necessity arose, they'd even have someone to wipe their arses."

"What kind of necessity?"

"Oh look ... let's just say that nursing homes are full of people who need their arses wiped. It sounds like old Reg Pascoe's got to the stage when he needs his arse wiped. For Christ's sake!" Steve caught himself and gave a chuckle. "I don't quite follow you here. What are you on about?"

"I'm just curious, on the hypothetical off chance I discovered a problem about Nibbelup, would you report that to the Sarnos? Or one of their supernumeraries?"

"Hypothetical?"

"Of course."

"Well, like I said, it would depend on what you're talking about. I would not want to be involved, but I guess if it were something serious ..."

"You would talk to them?"

"I could. I suppose I'd have to. But listen ... complex things are better discussed face to face. I'll be in Perth late next week. Let me take you to lunch."

Oldie sensed Steve wanted to get off the phone, so he told him about the brick through Raver's window, finishing off with, "I hope they got the right house."

"Oh, my dear chap, dear boy! Of course they got the right house! Perhaps it was just kids. You know what the little shits are like these days. Wrecking things is their main entertainment. Some little bastard sprayed his damned tag on our front wall a few months ago. We cleaned it up, put a security camera on the front gate and he came back and did it all again. First thing he did was climb up and do the camera. I don't know what to do.

Get a bloody big dog. Seriously, I was thinking of asking about Tyson — you know, Roger's dog. Heard he was in a kennel while the family decide what to do. I don't suppose you know?"

The mention of Tyson took Oldie by surprise. He hesitated and Steve swept over the silence by quickly saying that he had encountered Tyson when Roger lived in Queensland.

Oldie told him he had no idea what had happened to the dog and that Steve would have to ask the family.

"Yes, I'll do that. I'll give Brenda a call. I believe that animal has a good pedigree. Yes, I'll do that. And, listen, let's make that lunch on Wednesday, when I get in. That'll be the ninth of March. OK? Discuss some fishy business of one sort or another. Perhaps at my hotel?"

"Of course."

"I'll send you the details. And listen, just a little something for you to consider ... a word to the wise on the question of Perth's water supply. The real, long-term issue is how the de-sal plants are to be powered. Think about it."

"Nuclear?"

"They wouldn't put him down, would they?"

"What?"

"Tyson! They wouldn't put him down, would they? I mean, that's a pedigree animal."

"Why would they have him put down? He wasn't responsible for what happened ..."

"Of course not, but it's just that, you know, he may be ... some sort of a reminder. Know what I mean?'

"Yeah, I guess. But that doesn't mean they'd kill him. They'd find him another home. Give him away or maybe sell him."

"You're right! I'd better get onto that before I miss the chance."

After Steve rang off Oldie felt something itching at the back of his memory. He closed his eyes and focussed on the darkness. Breathed deeply and exhaled.

March ninth. Yuri Gagarin's birthday. He would have been seventy-seven. A little old man.

Maxie's pissing problem had been sorted out, sort of.

Several people advised Oldie and Anna that their animal was most probably stressed over Sylvester and, if that were the case, the way to deal with it was to spray feline facial pheromones — kitty crack, as his sister called it. The spiel was that this made the cat "comfortable" and the pissing would then cease. So, they bought a small but expensive aerosol from the vet and did their own pre-emptive spraying.

It worked.

But then they wondered how long they would need to put the stuff around the place and what would happen when they stopped. Oldie speculated that his cat's stress may not have been entirely because of Sylvester, that Maxie may also have been picking up on his or Anna's anxieties. Again, he thought about asking Dr Lou for some happy pills.

If nothing else, he reckoned he'd need them to handle the visit to see his mother.

And how would Max handle cat boarding school?

Silly question.

He'd hate it. If he wasn't neurotic going in he would be coming out. Oldie reminded himself that, as a responsible pet owner, he had a duty of care; and just by thinking about how responsible he was his brow glowed with a perceptibly more noble aspect.

But then, wouldn't you know it, his brow clouded as a somewhat more cynical truth seeped into his thoughts. There was no way of disguising it — call him a sentimental fool, but he was mourning the fall of Christchurch more than that of his own mother. He was fascinated by an interactive map on the web showing the quake and its aftershocks. Each event was a shockwave disc that burst on the map, the size and color of the disc indicating the strength and depth of the event. Running the clock through the afternoon and evening of 22 February was like watching aerial footage of a bombing run. He watched it over and over again.

The truth was he resented having to go to Melbourne. He resented doing something so pointless and which he was sure would only generate further misery. He resented the waste of time and money he and Anna didn't have — wasted on something essentially being done for nothing other than form's sake. But the Girl countered with the notion that some things should be done for form's sake; that doing things for form's sake usually headed off more headaches than those which may be created by not making the effort.

Well ... maybe. He told her she had never really understood the savage dynamic of a large family competing for their father's attention and their mother's affection. Someone always got left behind, missed out.

"Move on," she replied. "Get over it."

Hmm.

"Sit up straight!"

Yes dear.

At the end of the week he received in the post from Landgate a disc carrying hi-res files of three aerial photographs used in mapping the area around Hogan's Road Reserve. Not much had happened between 1946 and 1957, but from then until 1963 the refuse dump expanded at least fourfold. Growth, as investment advisors say, was exponential. When matched up with maps, recent satellite imagery and location footage, the aerials would give Blondie's documentary strong visual evidence of potential ground water pollution. Tie it all together with some of that computer-generated imagery stuff and — Hey Presto!

No big prize for guessing what all that could do for property prices in Nibbelup.

The chips would fall where they always did. A government agency would take the blame because the property developers could show they had complied with all legal requirements. Rats may be smelt, but they wouldn't be seen. The usual story.

But should that contingency so transpire, Oldie told and convinced himself, it would be Blondie and Ted Connell's worry. His job was to find what further dollops of cream Roger Kidd had used to garnish the historical record.

XII

Oldie wasn't feeling too flash after his morning shit and he thought twice about making the trip into town. The persistent tickle in his throat threatened to explode into a coughing fit that would leave him breathless and sore. He'd had a few such attacks lately. Bad enough to see swirls of yellow stars. Nobody seemed to know or be willing to tell him what might be going on.

Asthma and allergies had been mentioned. It had been suggested he keep Ventolin handy and that he see a specialist.

Another one.

But in the meantime, there was the business of going to town. He would rather not have to put himself to the wretched botheration. The kilometre walk in the heat to the bus stop would just about exhaust him before he even got out of Yoberia. And then there was the prospect of the further tribulation of suffering through the same dreary walk when he returned, done in, in the afternoon.

But he had to go, even though necessity was, for him, the mother of boredom.

So he made the effort and was rewarded to find the SRO front desk attended by the nice, helpful young man (Let's call him Tom!) and all six of the files he had ordered awaiting him. Furthermore, the *strashno* Baba

Yaga was nowhere in sight. Apparently nowhere within earshot either. Small mercies.

The only other researcher in the reading room was the young woman who'd been there on his previous visit. She glanced up and gave him a brief nod as he passed her table. He recognized an old Education Department letterhead on the document before her, something from the late nineteen-forties or early fifties.

So, another thesis on Baby Boomer education. Harmless enough — but those files would never say anything about having to learn your multiplication tables by rote and getting the cuts if you didn't. Time may heal many wounds, and too many of his contemporaries claim (a little too quickly) that such treatment had done them no harm, but Oldie knew he learned more in one year from a gentle old Irish woman than in all the years of beltings from the brutal dolts who staffed many a post-war Australian school. At least he never had the misfortune of being fiddled with.

He took himself to the privacy of the back table, laid out his 2B pencils, eraser and best sharpener beside his modest stack of files, and scanned the shadowless mezzanine balcony. Not a soul in sight.

So far, so good.

He then opened his main notebook, the one he called Old Sneaky — a tatty, half-filled 192-page A4 spiral-bound job that opened flat and offered several ways to quickly conceal stray papers. For this day's work he had the bright idea of dressing up Old Sneaky with half a dozen yellow 75 x 80 mm sticky notes posing as place markers. They looked the part and he was pleased with himself. Finally, to create a bit of clutter, he opened and laid face down a cheap school exercise book, on the cover of which he had printed "REFS etc".

So far ... so good.

He shuffled through the letters and reports of the first folder. He was keen to get to the meat of Roger's notes, but he forced himself to read some of the stuff — after all, he reminded himself, there was always the outside chance of discovering something useful he or Roger had missed. He kept one eye on the mezzanine and wielded his pencil in a little show of jotting down a few notes. But nobody was watching and after half an hour or so he was drowsy and bored. It was all routine and there were no surprises, no more notes. The bile of his impatience was rising. He caught himself flicking with audible haste through the pages of a 1968 report on the Transportation and Spillage Management of Toxic Chemicals.

And then — Bingo!

Without missing a beat he quickly turned a few more pages before stopping to scrutinize with mild interest at whatever it was before him. As surreptitiously as Maxwell Smart on a good day he peered up from beneath his lowered brow and checked who was where. The coast was clear; which was fortunate, because had anyone been watching there was no escaping the fact that at that moment Oldie looked thoroughly devious. Even more so than usual.

He stood, stretched and did his neck exercises, turning his head side to side. Young Tom was undertaking a bit of polite crowd control with a pair of talkative senior citizens. Nobody on the mezzanine. Still standing, swaying his hips, Oldie turned back to the page with the note attached and quickly covered it with Old Sneaky's front cover. As he did so he saw the message was one word. In Cyrillic.

He quietly sat himself back down and carefully wrote in his notebook the name of the file and the number of the page to which the sticker was affixed. After another glance at the mezzanine, he took a peek.

Диджериду.

He wasn't aware of it, but his lips were moving as he spelt out the word.

Did-zhe-ri-doo.

He went very still.

Oh me oh my oh.

Did-ge-ri-doo! Didgeridoo!

Oh me oh my oh you
Whatever shall I do …
Does your chewing gum lose its flavor
On the bedpost overnight.

He breathed in and then, calmly and smoothly extracted his phone from his trouser pocket, flipped it open and photographed the note stuck to the file. He closed his phone and slipped it back in his pocket. He exhaled. The deed was done in four seconds flat. Without looking up, he straightaway opened his notebook to a page near the back, slid it to one side as he covered the bright yellow note with his left hand, palmed it across and onto his notebook, which he then turned back to the place where he had been writing his notes.

Didgeridoo.

Here was Roger plucking at Oldie's sleeve. Oldie's sleeve — no one else's. It couldn't have been more explicit. What was it he wanted him to look at?

He flipped back to the note. It still said *Did-zhe-ri-doo.* He turned it over. Nothing on the back. *Nichevo.* A blank.

Oldie went back to the page in the file where Roger had placed the sticker. It was the cover sheet of a general review from a sub-committee within the Transport Department, a set of recommendations concerning a proposed revision of procedures and protocols for the safe handling of toxic materials during road and rail transportation. The headline recommendation was for the introduction of what was rather tastelessly termed a Cradle-to-the-Grave manifest system, which would supposedly curtail unauthorized dumping. Other than that it was basically one of those What-to-do-*if* documents. Call the cops and the fire brigade, basically. Lots of equipment specs — *blah, blah, blah* — but nowhere in its 35 pages was there a mention (let alone a list) of organizations making submissions; nor was there any mention of any incident that may have caused the authorities to conduct such a review. There were no cited examples of what could go wrong, no previous history. Nothing had ever happened. *Nichevo, nichevo ...*

No need to ask who had been Minister for Transport and Railways back then. Roger hadn't been one to waste time by pointing at the bleeding obvious. He must have had something else in mind.

But fair shake of the sav, Oldie impatiently wiped his hand across his mouth as he sucked in air, just give me a fucking clue here Mate!

From the back of his notebook he took out a photocopy of the two stickers souvenired during his previous visit. The Cyrillic had been laboriously printed by someone unfamiliar with the script, so it was useless to compare it with the other notes, but the fine calibre of the blue lines (he reckoned 0.5 mm) indicated all were written with the same pen.

Remember what Blondie had said about Roger being a sphinx without a secret. It is true, there are people with a secretive disposition who don't actually have much to hide. But the Roger he knew wasn't like that.

He looked at the three names on the Transport Department sub-committee. Plain, old-fashioned Anglo surnames. He wrote them down anyway. You never know.

And, apparently, those three little ducks had no need to acknowledge the benefit of advice from any of the parties that may have been responsible for administering their recommendations. Even if Huey, Dewey and Louie had never had a quiet beer with mates who just happened to be representatives of private transport companies, they must surely have found time — you'd have thought — to chat with a few of their colleagues at the State Government Railways and the Fire and Emergency Services. Where else had they obtained all those technical specifications they gave for tanks and other containment vessels?

Some of which were quite detailed ...

... back to the pages dealing with road transport.

Again ... comprehensive specs for hoses, pressure valves, seals, load centres of gravity, truck suspension, axle loads: everything.

Everything.

Tall order. Very tall ...

Perhaps that was it. Whoever was getting into or intending to stay in the sludge business would need a new fleet of trucks within a year. Here was an economy of scale to shut out all but the biggest player, the up-front cost of establishing a virtual monopoly. And all done in the name of public safety — a public safety compromised in large part by the very people who now offered the expensive fix. It wouldn't have been the first time such a procedure had been used, but it was rather proficiently done — not bad, not too bad at all.

No need to ask which company had cornered the waste transportation business back then. London to a pinch of desiccated shit the Department's specs were written by old Frank Sarno himself, copying them in his neatest hand directly from brochures for the equipment he was about to order. Talk about writing your own ticket.

There was plenty of smoke, but Oldie was well aware he was yet to eyeball the live and burning flame of your actual *incriminating* fire. He would have to keep looking.

He leaned back in his seat and once again checked out the scene. No new researchers had arrived and the Baby Boomer woman was as diligent as ever. At some stage the pleasant young man at the front desk had been replaced by a beaming young woman Oldie had not previously seen about the place. No sign of that old thunder-clap, Baba Yaga. He wasn't sure what worried him more, knowing where she was or not knowing.

He did find one other note that day, a repeat of the one naming Rosemary Elizabeth Sarno and Antonia Lucia Sarno as the principal shareholders of AITF Holdings. He photographed it but — Plan B — left it where he found it. It would keep.

But while it was all very well for Roger to be building redundancy into his exposé system, Oldie wanted to advance things with something new. He needed an Exhibit A. There had to be some meat somewhere in the sandwich.

Only on the train ride home, after he finally got a seat at Stirling, did he realize that in the rush of the chase he had yet again flitted past the dicey question of why Roger had gone to all this trouble, of why he had felt the need to take such precautions. It was hard to see it as anything other than Roger's attempt to ensure the story would not die with him.

Oldie didn't want to think about the implications of that. He looked out the window at the northbound traffic on the Mitchell freeway. The light glittered and shimmered on and over the crawling vehicles. He could see the immense, ruthless heat pressing on the land. If the city's power failed, he thought, if all the packed trains and their air-cons stopped …

Only that evening, after showing her the material and discussing the matter with Anna, was he casually shown the possibility of Roger having planted that Cyrillic note to suggest — ah ha! — Oldie was the culprit, that he was the one responsible for the whole series of mischievous memos.

But Oldie didn't believe that idea held water, and said so in a tone that could, to some ears, have carried an element of bluster.

Hmmm. Tricky.

So ...

"So," the Girl asked, "why did the drunken Mexican stab his wife?"

He shook his head.

"Te-kill-er!"

He told her that was not very funny.

She shrugged. "Was when I heard it."

"OK, then I dare you to tell it to a Mexican."

"Don't know any Mexicans, but it sounds like it's a good thing I didn't marry one."

Fifty-two minutes after Blondie sat him down in the large comfortable chair in her large comfortable home office and gave him a *beeeg* glass of near freezing, busily sparkling *acqua minerale*, Oldie confided that he had an incurable illness, and confidently stated it was most likely to run its course and reach its lamentable culmination sooner rather than later.

So it goes.

With her, the script had always been at risk of taking the deep and meaningful turn. Modern manners allow very little room for men and women of their respective temperaments and ages to play it any other way. There has to be some display of intimacy, some revelation of vulnerability. That's just the way it is. Roles are cast and the players, comfortably or not, step up to their parts oozing the confidence of seasoned soap opera performers. He knew this in his bones, felt it in his waters, and what he would and would not tell her was all there in that morning's horoscope.

But first, he cleared business matters away. After the refreshment of sissing water (and him accepting a top up), he presented her with the Landgate disc and together they pored over the old aerial photographs of Hogan's Road Reserve. In the course of their conversation he reported that he had not found anything of significance in his archival search. He said he would like to keep looking, but wondered whether it was cost effective.

"It's a bit like scrounging through one of these old rubbish tips," he said, "you can never know what prize thing lies beneath that pile of mouldy garbage until you look. You hope for something ... but there is the distinct possibility that all you will find under the garbage is more garbage. As we discussed at New Norcia, there are other priorities."

Watching him closely, she quickly nodded her agreement.

He took that in and went on to tell her what he had been reading and hearing about Christchurch, where the water supply and sewerage infrastructure had been seriously damaged, and suggested they consider how that example of compromised systems could illustrate their Perth story. He mentioned, as an aside, that he thought they should try to make their case scientifically, as a presentation of evidence without recourse to any apocalyptic "cities of the plains" rhetoric. She shrugged and said she thought they could probably get away with at least one Biblical reference in order to, you know, "intensify focus". She handed him a disc and printouts of her draft script and the accompanying spiel for potential backers — documents for him to take home to examine and edit at his leisure. They worked in smooth and agreeable harmony. She offered to pay him for the days he had already worked, but he told her not to worry about that just yet as his accountant preferred him to bill people on a regular, monthly basis. It was all very professional.

And so, forty-four minutes after she sat him down in that large comfortable chair, they moved on to perfectly brewed coffee, proper biscotti and matters of a more personal nature. That's just the way it goes. Sitting by the open French doors, she lit her first cigarette since he arrived. She asked whether he had ever smoked (he had) and their chat drifted onto health, well-being, life choices and related baloney.

He told her about his disease quite deliberately. The Dying Swan role is brilliant because it tolerates no competition, ontologically speaking; it fixed him in a position where there was no need to puff himself up by mentioning Roger's secret notes.

She heard him out but her few questions indicated she knew more than most people about hepatitis C, genotype one. She offered no pat expressions of sympathy. Contemplating her small garden, she let the smoke from the tip of her cigarette rise with the grace of a prayer through the still air and into the sunlight. When she did turn to look into his eyes she asked about Anna.

"She's OK. It needs that, you know, direct blood to blood connection to pass. Even so, considering how many years I had it without knowing, she's been lucky. In that regard, very lucky."

"Yes. In that regard ..."

"And I've been lucky. I mean, I don't know how I'd cope with having passed it on to her. To anyone ... I have the virus, so I am responsible for its containment. There is no cure, so I must be vigilant for ... the sake of others."

242

"No cure, *yet*. But it will come."

"Maybe ... and then later rather than sooner."

"Miracles do happen," she offered.

She was not to know that, for many reasons, "miracle" was one of those words, one of those ideas with which he was especially impatient — really shitty impatient. She could not have missed the scrape of knife edge on steel as he said, "Oh, really, do they?"

"Believe me," she bounced in with her just-a-little-too-ready wry smile, "I'm not into mumbo-jumbo. Not at all. But I did have a Catholic upbringing. Can't get away from that. It shapes you. Even we lapsed souls still see the world in a certain way. I still think it is true that to have faith you've got to have a vision every so often. Some ..." her hands conjured and shaped invisible objects in the air, "some show, some *manifestation*. The Church understands the importance of the occasional miracle. They bring hope. Notice how often visions and miracles are bestowed on the poorest, the lowest — like, Saint Bernadette of Lourdes. We may think it's mostly hocus-pocus, but somewhere in the mix we also know that the reassurance, the hope of a miracle should never be underestimated."

"Visions! Miracles!" he started forward in the big chair. "You mean your actual divine intervention type miracles?"

"Well, yes ... healings, mostly."

"Yes! Healings! OK then, so correct me if I'm wrong, but didn't your Blessed Bernadette — you know, she of Lourdes that they all go to pray to so they can throw away their crutches and all that — didn't she actually die of TB? I dunno, but I'd have thought that was a bit of an own goal!"

"Yes, but faith healings are ..."

"Yes, I know. Attested. Witnessed. I know. But by

miracles you mean *manifestations*." He, too, sculpted the air. "Like Lazarus. Raising the dead, now *that*, that's the ultimate healing, isn't it? Eternal life! Whacko! You can't top that one! And didn't Christ do a couple of other resurrections? Not to mention his own Third Day command performance."

"Yes," she straightened her back. "Resurrection. That is the Christian promise — renewed and everlasting life ... the promise and the *hope* of everlasting life. But specifically, a miracle is an intercession, any clear, unmistakable divine intervention. It's a sign of God's attention."

The clarity of her sincerity almost disarmed him, but he had long ago understood that Christian love and its sentimental derivatives are poor substitutes for human warmth.

"Attention?" he said slowly, considering the word with a show of care. "You mean as in sending down the Flood or dishing it out to Sodom and Gomorrah? That was pretty clear and unmistakable attention. Does this divine policy cover what happened in Christchurch? You know they had a bloke over there posing as a wizard. He's been a tourist attraction in Cathedral Square for decades. How pagan is that? A wizard! A jealous god may not have been entirely happy about that. Wizards, ah ... yes, someone else was on about wizards. Anyway, miracles, divine interventions, do you mean something more friendly? Walking on water, turning water into wine — that sort of thing?"

"Yes, I think it's understood a miracle is something benevolent. As I said, healings."

"Miracles are also," he raised his index finger, "and here I give to you a major argument for your case, miracles are interventions in the natural order, events outside the clockwork of the natural order. Earthquakes, tsunamis and so on are natural events, even though they are traditionally described as Acts of God. The miracle is when the waters are parted, not when they come rolling in. So, yes, benevolent."

"I'm glad to hear you can argue both sides of a case."

"Well, sometimes one has to be God's advocate! No problem. Bring it on. But as for turning water into wine!" he sniffed. "Excuse me, but really ... Big Deal! Try it the other way — wine into water when you've got a fucked liver and no hope of a transplant. Divine intervention! I have to say, I am rather old school on these things and would definitely see it as an act of benevolence should God send down a bolt of lightning to deal with my noisy neighbours. You know, God on your side, out there smiting the pagan bastards on your behalf!" He smacked the arm of the chair with glee. "Imagine that! Just imagine that!"

"That's not quite Christian healing and forgiveness," she murmured, smiling.

"Well, I'll tell you, I can assure you it'd go a good way towards healing me! Believe me, I'd have no problem describing such an event as marvellous. A marvel to behold! But listen, just going back to that matter of the Christian promise of everlasting life and so on ... How'd we get onto this ... this stuff?"

"Old habits ..." she shrugged. "All I am trying to say is that in your situation you should never give up hope. We were always taught that hope deferred is not hope denied."

He looked away. He could not tell her just how exhausting the burden of hope deferred could be.

"If nothing else," she added, "you should make a show of it for the sake of others."

"You're right," he muttered. "But, you know, it's complicated. Particularly complicated."

"How so?"

"I need to ... hmmm." He stared at the floor.

"I hope you aren't saying that you may not be able to continue working with me."

"Of course not! Although they do talk about mental fog, confusion and irritability as possible symptoms. My memory is definitely not what it used to be and I seem to have trouble planning ahead. More trouble than I used to, if I recall correctly."

He half laughed at his own half joke but she did not respond.

"Anyway," he went on, "it's just that I think it's fair to let you know who you are dealing with. You said something just then about doing things for the sake of others. Well, I have to make the best of things for Anna's sake."

She frowned and made a small movement to sit a little more erect.

"No, no," he said hastily, "I'm not chasing you and Ted for more money. Not at all. You have been more than generous. And your sources of funding are your business. But I think I see an opportunity," he paused to hold their eye contact, "for me to use the whole Reg Pascoe thing in another way. Let me put it this way, I could do some archival research on another account. When we were up at New Norcia you said something along the lines of a limited local story getting in the way of the bigger one. Well, I agree, Ted's right, all that suspected corruption is maybe another subject, a side issue. So, how would you feel if I were to put it aside for now? I mean, if something usable turns up — like those aerial photos — well and good. But the nitty gritty of who, when and so on ..."

He waited as she stubbed her cigarette. She looked away, staring at something in her garden.

"Another account?"

"Nothing to interfere with your work. I promise you. Nothing has been discussed elsewhere and if you feel uncomfortable about this ..."

She waved her hand at him with mild impatience. "Don't be so silly," she said quietly, continuing to gaze out the window. "I know someone else with hep C," her voice so low he barely caught what she said. "In your situation, you have an absolute right to get the best deal for yourself. I understand, you have to look after your long term interests."

He waited, but she did not continue.

"Nothing has been settled," he said after a while. "Nobody else is involved."

"Except Steve Lyons?"

"Well, not even him yet."

"Yet?"

He shrugged.

"I presume you'll want to discuss this with Ted. I'm sorry I can't give you more to tell him. But I think you get the general idea."

"There's no need to tell Ted any of this. Not at this stage. He's busy with plenty of stuff he does not discuss with me."

"I haven't discussed this with Anna."

"No?"

"No."

"Will you?"

"Not unless I have to." Then, after a moment, added, "Not at this stage, as you put it."

She half smiled and wagged a mocking finger at him as she reached for her cigarette case. She lit up and they settled into a companionable silence.

"Jennifer Jones," he said, finally.

"Who!?" She was startled. "What?"

"Jennifer Jones. I've been trying to think who had the title role in *The Song of Bernadette*. It was Jennifer Jones."

"Oh," she glanced at him, catching up. "Yes, you're right. I'd forgotten."

"Jennifer Jones. Did the nuns show you that movie at your school?"

"They did," she conceded with mock gravity. "You bet they did. But how is it you remember that old film?"

"Oooff! Jennifer Jones was a big star and I guess *Bernadette* had a few re-runs on TV. Some things stick and you never really figure out why. Perhaps in my raw and gullible adolescence I was susceptible to a bit of the good old mumbo-jumbo. You know, before critical faculties matured and I was handed some of my quota of salutary life lessons. Or perhaps ..."

Blondie clapped her hands with delight. "Or perhaps you carried a flame for Jennifer Jones!"

"Oh no, no, no," he muttered with smouldering intensity. "Not at all. Mine were fairly conventional schoolyard tastes. I only had eyes for and was rather preoccupied by Jayne Mansfield and Brigitte Bardot."

"And Marilyn Monroe, surely?"

"Yes, of course. But there was something about Brigitte Bardot. With Monroe it was by and large about her figure, her breasts, but Bardot had that pouty mouth and those dark eyes ... her face drew you in."

"But what was it about Jayne Mansfield? I thought her persona was even more about her tits than Marilyn Monroe's."

"Oh no, any boy of my vintage will tell you that there was something in Jayne's look, I mean in her eye, her glance ... hmm, yes, well." He smiled and shook his head. "I know it's an overused word, but in a very real sense Marilyn's face was iconic. Warhol didn't make it so, he just recognised the removed reality of it. But Jayne, like

Brigitte, had what my mother called a knowing look. She had some knowledge, some *carnal* knowledge — which she was willing to share."

"Share?"

"Hmm. Or so it seemed. But bear in mind, the way we saw these goddesses — and they were goddesses — was by stills in magazines or on movie posters. We never got to see them on the screen. Especially Bardot. I know her films got to our country town cinema, but they were definitely NOT SUITABLE FOR CHILDREN. That, of course, added considerably to the allure. Forbidden fruit and all that. The blue flowers. But tell me, who did the young girls of your generation fixate upon?"

"Johnny Depp," she shot back without hesitation.

He threw up his hands and rolled his eyes. "Of course!"

"Of course 'of course'! And we didn't have to worry about any of that NOT SUITABLE nonsense. We regularly got to see him toss his head, flick back his locks and melt us with those wonderful dark eyes — every week on television."

"Melt?!"

"Totally fucking hot shameless," she chimed. He observed her cheeks take a freshening trace of color and heard her voice heading for the more breathless realms of husky.

When he left twenty minutes later she squeezed his hand with an agreeable intimacy that left no doubt as to their mutual trust and esteem. Back in his car he took a few deep breaths to slow the thump of his heart and compose himself before he started Betty's motor.

It was a rush, but he managed a short detour to the organic greengrocer to buy the makings of their dinner before collecting the Girl from her school. Amenable as ever, she said she had not minded the short wait. She had used the time to have a nice chat with another teacher.

That evening he poached free-range chicken breasts and leeks in dry cider, blitzed the softened leeks with his bar-mix and added a tablespoon of yoghurt to the boiled down sauce before serving it with buttered petite parsnips, steamed baby carrots and broccoli florets. Over the meal he finally got around to telling her — more or less — most of what he had discussed that day with Blondie. He allowed that although she was a charmer and he would enjoy working on the proposed documentary, he had to say, after having skimmed through her script, that he thought she was a little out of her depth.

"But that's good! Isn't that why they hired you?"

"Giving advice is one thing, but I'm in the middle here and I just know where the whatsits — the chips — are going to fall. I assume that *in extremis* her interests would be Ted's interests and that she would protect them. My problem," he concluded, "is that I don't really know how much leeway I have here." As an afterthought he muttered, "And it seems the winds are changeable."

She did not reply and they sat together listening to the dinning bass from Dickhead on the Corner and the brazen shrieking at a poolside barbeque in the next street — the all too ordinary sounds of a summer evening in Yoberia. You couldn't even blame it on the moon; it was just new and wouldn't wax full for another couple of weeks. "We gotta get out of this place," he droned.

"If it's the last thing we ever do ..." she sang lightly. "We are going to Melbourne," she said. "It'll be a good break."

"Ah, but will that be a better life for me and you?"

She sighed and gave him the look.

"Yes," he said quickly, "it is time to bite that

250

particular bullet. But, you know, I'm sort of serious about getting out of here, permanently I mean."

"For a better life?"

"There must be!"

"But where to go?"

"Somewhere colder than here, somewhere where people don't sit around half the night in their backyards making a damned racket. Somewhere where the climate, the fucking environment is more benign. Apart from the endless summer, this place has one of the worst allergy rates in the world."

"I do get so tired these days," she murmured.

He looked at her. Shoulders drooping, gazing down at her empty plate, she looked tired. "The heat," he said. "Back to school."

She reached over for his plate, placing it on hers. "No fun getting old. It'll be the same wherever we go. And getting there and setting up will require lots and lots of money so until we have a bag of cash — that somewhere is somewhere over the rainbow. So you better hurry up and win Lotto," she said without a smile as she got up and turned towards the kitchen and the task of washing up.

While she was busy he went to his computer and surreptitiously checked the mid-week Lotto numbers he took on the sly. One useless number. Bugger all. *Nichevo*. Again.

Going on for midnight he drafted an email to Steve Lyons telling him he had found "several items of interest" in various archival files to do with Hogan's Road. After some consideration he added that he thought the material may be the work of "a former colleague".

He read it through, inserted the word "suspicious", played a couple of hands of Spider Solitaire and then

251

loitered over the BBC News page — oh look, fancy that, another two-headed snake hatched in Florida! He emailed the link to Daniel then returned to his message to Steve and removed the reference to "a former colleague". Then, just as he was about to press Send, he got up and crept down the passage to the kitchen to make himself toast and Vegemite. Spreading the butter on thick and watching it start to soften and melt on the hot toast, he decided his message to Steve could wait until morning. Sleep on it, he thought.

The scent of the butter brought Max, mewling and scratching, to the back door. The Old Man let him in and treated him to a dollop. It was appreciated.

A couple of minutes later, with the warm butter and Vegemite having gone to his own head, Oldie put back the reference to "a former colleague" and sent his message to Steve Lyons.

"Fuck it," he explained to the black cat at midnight, "the fat's gotta go in the fire sooner or later."

Not for the first time, Maxie wondered at the very human flaw of letting premonitions flower into wishes. Mostly, he had observed, this was fuelled by nothing more than a pursuit of the glib but dangerous satisfaction of being able to say, "I was right!"

Quietly confident the Old Man had forgotten he had let him into the house, the cat snuck off to the lounge room and his favourite corner of the couch.

Steve Lyons had not returned an acknowledgement by the time Oldie left — *Arise, and go into the city* — for another session in the State Records Office. It wasn't until he was off the train and hurrying past the Art Gallery, the SRO in sight across the plaza, that he received a call from the Big Fisherman — *and it shall be told thee what thou must do.* Although as jovial as ever, Steve did sound a little more businesslike than usual. The busy man confirmed their meeting the following Wednesday and also asked would Oldie mind keeping the Friday morning free in case they needed "a follow-up of some kind". In the meantime, he said, there was no need to email or discuss anything about "these extra matters".

"Until we get a proper handle on this," Steve said, and Oldie heard a distinct shifting of gears, "I think we should keep it to ourselves. Secret men's business. OK?"

"Don't talk to strangers," Oldie shot back, panting but with pitch perfect flippancy.

He heard an exhalation that could have been a suppressed laugh.

"Always a prudent policy," Steve replied levelly. There was a moment's silence before he quickly added, just before ending the call, "Keeps the Devil at bay."

As Oldie snapped his phone shut and slipped it into his bag, a sudden gust of wind picked up sandy dust and swirled like a swift dervish across the plaza. He lowered his head and closed his eyes against its hot, cursed breath. After it passed on by and hissed through the dried leaves of the plane trees over by the old courthouse, he looked up at the pallid, dry sky.

Don't talk to ... who? Anyone! Nobody! Was that an injunction or a request?

Look at the wind, Nicodemus, look at the wind.

XIII

Oldie worked up a sweat wielding the hedge-trimmer to clear the plumbago from the door of the small, overgrown garden shed. With a large screwdriver and a deft blow of a heavy hammer he disposed of the piddling padlock. The shed had not been opened since they moved into the house seven years ago and the bottom hinge had rusted rigid. There was some play in it, but to force it risked breaking off the door or bending its frame. Either way, the door would not then close. Not even a drenching of WD-40 and a few careful taps of the hammer could free it.

So, all-righty, he'd take a shower and a nap, leaving the lubricant a couple of hours to do its work. But first, he forced his bulk into the gap of the narrowly ajar door and, holding his breath, sprayed the better part of a can of insecticide into the interior.

Two hours later the hinge remained obstinate but he found the spiders accounted for, dangling and twisting on their last unspooled gossamer threads. He thrust a broom through the doorway, twirling and waving its brush about to gather and clear the pale grey web shrouds. He gave the hinge another dousing, but it looked as though he would just have to maneuver himself and the hefty cartons of Jem's stuff through the proverbial tight spot.

By the time he had lugged three of the weighty cartons along the side and around the back of the house to dump them on the patio's solid old table, he was breathing with hoarse difficulty. His throat felt like it had a swarm of bees in it. He was sweating so profusely his hands were slipping on the black plastic wrapping that sealed the boxes.

It looked like there were a dozen of the buggers in the shed. They'd gone in there unopened after six years storage in the garage of the previous house. Three out on the table was going to be as good a start as he could muster. Getting the thick, grimy plastic off and folded to go in the wheelie bin left him in need of another shower. But the three freshly disrobed cardboard boxes seemed to be clean and in good shape. No apparent water damage. No signs of silverfish.

The bright tip of the box-cutter ran a razor slit along the dry, fragile packaging tape and ...

N° 1: Comics. Each one pristine and secure in its own plastic sleeve. Some "Collectors Edition" Batman sets, but many other sets of quality art work imports — Super Heroes Oldie remembered only vaguely. Presumably, they were worth something. He remembered how fastidious Jem was in handling them. Didn't he have gloves? Cotton archive gloves? Where were they?

N° 2: Comics, ditto. All in mint condition in their plastic sleeves. More than a few rather lascivious, large breasted, gun-toting women on some of these covers. Yes, collectors' items.

After Jem's death, because Daniel had asked, Oldie promised him the collection. But although the matter had been once or twice tentatively raised, Daniel had shown no inclination to discuss it further. In the shed they stayed and the shed stayed shut.

N° 3: More comics ... and personal effects.

He put down the blade and looked about.

He was being watched. Resting atop the low limestone wall in the shade of the woolly bush with his paws stretched out before him, Max stared at him in a credible impersonation of the unblinking Sphinx.

Oldie stared back, blinked, and returned his attention to the thorny task at hand.

What was he doing opening this stuff? It was a riddle. Had he really thought it through?

Of course not.

And yet, he must have known what he'd find. How could he say he had forgotten? He was the one who had packed it all away. Out of sight, but never quite out of mind.

He took a deep breath that came out as a long sigh of inconsolable exhaustion. There are different ways of forgetting; or, to be more precise, of not quite remembering.

He told himself it was about checking that Jem's things — the comic collection mainly — were safe and sound. As executor of his son's estate it was his duty to ensure Jem's worldly goods were passed on in good order. It could also be said that seeing what, exactly, was in those sealed cartons was an essential task in putting his own affairs in order.

Well, then, that being the case — here it is. Take a good look. Take it all in.

He remembered that well-worn baseball cap with the jester on the visor. The boy lived in it, only ever taking it off for his morning shower. And there were jokes about that.

The emptied wallet (cloth with Velcro fastener). The motorcycle gloves. A Spirex sketch book (don't look). School report (don't look). Battered Star Wars figure (Han Solo?). The Phantom watch. The deck of marked playing cards the boy used to practice magic tricks — "Pick a card, any card." These things had been interred for little more than a dozen years, but they all looked so dated, from another time entirely. How quickly the world has turned. And then turned yet again.

He reached out for the cap but immediately thought better of it. No, not a good idea.

Time to get a bit of focus. At this rate the Girl would be home and looking over his shoulder before he could see what was what. That hadn't been his plan. Definitely not. He moved things around so that only the comics were visible on top and closed the box.

This was a job for later. There were other things of Jem's to be found in that shed. There was nothing else for it than to make an early start tomorrow after the Girl left for work.

People have so much stuff these days. Personal stuff. Stuff stuffed away under beds, in cupboards, garages and garden sheds; in storage units. And when they die someone else has to unpack all that stuff and sift through it and then either give it away or flog it off.

Or pack it away again. To be dealt with later by someone else.

That's what he was going to have to do with this lot. Repack it in those giant lunch box style plastic storage bins, run a bit of gaffer tape around to make sure everything was air-tight and crawlie-proof, and bung it all back in the shed. Even if he could persuade Anna to go through it, there was no way she would agree to throw any of it away. These were things to which memory clung like flesh to bone. It is one thing to bury your dead, quite another to abandon them.

God knows what she'd do about all his stuff. There were cupboards, bookcases, desk-drawers and piles of cartons bulging with … with … Good God! Where do you start? He had recently had a go at tidying his room, but it was like shoveling an immense pile of sand. He did just enough to know that in fairness to Anna he really should start some serious culling. But then he had given up. And felt guilty about doing so. The least he could do would be to pull out and put aside the few letters and other documents that may have some value. But mainly, he should make the effort to get rid of the trash and the potentially embarrassing. Not to mention the incriminating. What vain madness possessed him to keep such things?

But then, really, he decided, what did it matter? Why go to the trouble? Might as well leave it for fate to decide. After all, he was pretty sure there would be the inevitable day when Daniel would just dump the lot holus-bolus, unread, in the nearest bin.

Thus it goes.

After a couple of relatively cooler days Anna suggested they should do their beach walk. They arrived with the afternoon sun still an hour or so above a clear horizon, and the new moon's pale rind floating down an hour and a half higher in the sky. The breeze was steady and cool from the south-west and a swarm of kite surfers were getting in one another's way in the light chop off Pinnaroo Point. The genteel couple turned north — the sea to their left, their long shadows swaying and darting at the low scrubby dunes to their right. Apart from half a dozen stray joggers and strollers, they had a good mile of open solitude all the way to Mullaloo.

When they first moved out to the northern suburbs they used to make the short drive down to the sea practically every afternoon. It was quite the tonic, the major compensation for having been flung out to Yoberia. For the first couple of years they had sometimes gone swimming, but after a couple of shark attacks down the coast their twilight water contact had been limited to getting their feet wet by spent waves fizzing and foaming up the broad shore. The novelty had worn off in other ways, too, and they tended to go to the beach more in the cooler months, when they would likely have the place to themselves. They had not, in fact, taken the air at water's edge since last winter. And here it was, already early March.

The walk had been Anna's idea, but because Oldie wanted to talk to her, he thought it was his idea. "There is something I want to run by you," he announced, with the wind pressing on his back.

"Something important?" she inquired, holding her fine hair so that it did not blow across her face.

"I believe so."

"Well then," she took his arm and they fell into pace, "you better go first."

He hesitated to glance at her.

"Come on. You go first," she insisted, tugging at his arm, urging him on. "Giddy up."

"Giddy up a ding dong?"

"That'd be the one."

"OK," he said, and forward they tramped. "The crux of it is this — I think I'm going to be made an offer I can't refuse."

"From Steve Lyons?"

"Yes. On behalf of Interested Parties, as they say in the literature, the legal literature. But, listen, when I say I can't refuse, it's because it'll be a very generous offer for work that I've already done — more or less. If I'm hearing right, we should finalise the details tomorrow."

"And Carol?"

"A separate deal. She and Ted are not really all that interested in what Steve and his people are concerned about. I discussed it with her. We talked. It's not a problem."

"Does she know who Lyons and you are dealing with?"

"Not from me. But, I don't know ... Ted Connell seems to be generally well informed. He seems to have been ahead of the game so far."

They walked on a way in their silent shell of sea and wind.

"There is," he said, "one other thing."

"We are going to visit your mother," she shot back without losing a step.

"Yes, yes. I know. Don't worry, I get it. I won't make trouble. Don't worry. No, the something else has to do with SeeHear. Blondie and Ted don't care too much about Reg the Racketeer and all that historical stuff. What they are really interested in doing is selling the idea of building more desalination plants. This, the wisdom has it, is the way of the future. This is how this particular city of the plain will survive. And then, you see, the logical thing is to ask how such power-hungry infrastructure would be fuelled. Yes ... fuelled. Most people would probably assume that we'd use some of our ample gas supplies. And that may turn out to be what happens, for a while. But eventually ... eventually. So, anyway, the thing is, I think the funding for Blondie's little project may come from some nuclear power lobby group. Up the tree, in the foliage, securely out of sight ... but yes, I reckon that's where the money comes from. That's what I think. These people are very patient, in for the long haul. They understand it is never too early to start softening up public opinion, preparing the ground. So I ask myself whether I should have an ethical issue with this and my answer is that I don't. Are you with me?"

She shrugged and looked out to sea. "Don't nuclear power stations need a lot of water for cooling?"

"They do."

The ocean murmured agreement but otherwise held its peace.

They walked on in silence for a short time before she said, "There is something I have to tell you."

She explained that since resuming work after the summer break the soreness in her upper arms that had bothered her late last year had returned. Over the past weeks she had taken a few afternoons off work to see Dr Lou and have an ultrasound of her left shoulder. She had hoped a cortisone injection would fix the problem, as it had in the past. But now that the results were back Dr Lou wanted her to see a surgeon.

Rotator cuff surgery. Sick leave, extended sick leave. The whole shebang. Surgery — the word fell like a block of ice into his lower guts.

"And probably sooner rather than later," she concluded her report.

He put his arm around her shoulders and they went on, in step. He felt like bawling but he had nothing to say.

"Gosh," she chirped, "this is just like in the movies."

"And what movie would that be?" he swallowed, rising to the bait.

"Oh, something artistic. Probably French. They do good beach scenes. You know, like the one at the end of *Judex*."

He did know. He may very well have been the only soul in a radius of quite a few thousands of kilometres who knew to what she alluded, but he did know and he got it straightaway. It was that magic moment the quick eye sees is legerdemain but which the quicker mind knows to be a necessary gesture, something to be believed anyway because it is the gesture that is the meaning.

They trudged on a way before he responded. "So, I need to pluck something out of thin air?"

"It doesn't matter where the thing comes from — the rabbit out of the hat, the dove out of a hankie — it's the fact that it is real that counts. Judex's dove actually flies away, up into the sky. Does your bird have wings? Whatever it is that materialises — it can't be ignored, it has to be dealt with. Will your pigeon fly?"

"It seems Steve Lyons thinks so."

"Well, then ..."

Catching sight of a sudden gleam in the upper reaches of the sky he stopped to watch the polished silver belly of a passenger jet heading out over the Indian Ocean. Presently, just like in the movies, they heard the far rumble of a heavy marble rolling down the hollow floor of heaven.

She started them forward again, asking whether anything more had been said about the novel Roger claimed he had been writing.

"That," Oldie said with decided certainty, "has vanished into thin air." Then, throwing his free hand skyward, added, "Just like magic!"

Friday morning, at the agreed time, Oldie met Steve Lyons in King Street's best cafe. With only a few late breakfasters mopping up their eggs Florentine and the mid-morning coffee crowd still an hour away, the place was more than half empty. Even so, in the dim interior Oldie did not immediately see Steve, lurking up the back behind an upraised copy of the Financial Review in a booth Oldie had never noticed before.

Steve seemed more relaxed than he had been during their meeting at his hotel two days earlier. He rose, all smiles, hand extended, guiding, almost pushing Oldie into the seat opposite him. "Listen, one thing ... could you turn off your phone and leave it on the table."

Oldie did as he was told, asking who suggested the venue.

"They did. I think Aldo has some connection here."

When Oldie did not respond Steve leaned forward and asked, solicitously, "All good, Mate?"

He opened his bag, took out a sealed, buff envelope and carefully placed it halfway between himself and Steve. "I went in yesterday and retrieved those items I'd left in place. Found another one, which," he nodded at the envelope, "is also in there."

Eyebrows raised, Steve looked him in the face.

"A reference to a *Sunday Times*, January 1982. There's no page given. I had a quick look on the microfilm yesterday, but I couldn't see what it could be. I'll look again, but if I can't make the connection without hints, perhaps that's the best outcome."

Steve was about to answer when his eyes flicked a little to one side, over Oldie's shoulder. His face stiffened. "They're here," he breathed, picking up the envelope and slipping it into his pocket.

Oldie turned to look.

Well now, if it wasn't Mister Mo standing by the entrance, scanning the room. Gee whizz, isn't it a small world! He gave Oldie an almost imperceptible knowing nod as their eyes met.

A slim man of about thirty, neat as a new pin in collar and tie, rose from a table near the door and approached Mo. Other than a token handshake there was little perceptible interplay between the two men. They were approached by a waitress, who Mo immediately directed towards the booth where Steve and Oldie sat and watched.

There was no mistaking Aldo Sarno. The man shone with a natural, god-given grace. He might have been in his sixties, but he had a full head of hair and walked briskly up to the cafe entrance and pushed open the door without losing his stride. He was inside the place before Mo or the other man could spring to his attention. The casual dignity of the light-grey summer suit, the immaculate grooming, the shoes, the sunglasses — all confirmed Aldo Sarno's spotless reputation as a man of impeccable taste.

He knew the value of appearances.

He went to Church. As did all of his family. Regular as clockwork. His wife and two daughters had pearl and coral rosaries blessed by the Pope. His manners were faultless and he did good works. Such things were noted and those in the know said next year's Australia Day Honours list would deliver him a major gong —probably the big one. It was, they said with the seriousness such matters call for, long overdue.

While Aldo exchanged pleasantries with the attendant fellow, who Oldie guessed to be the establishment's managing part-owner, Mister Mo wandered off a few paces to do a chin-rubbing inspection of the cake display. The pretty waitress slowed to look at him over her shoulder, but continued towards Oldie and Steve.

Oldie took his cue from Steve, who said he did not want anything to eat. Oldie did, however, ask if he could have a cool drink before his coffee. The girl suggested a citron pressé and he was rewarded by a smile from her when he told her that was the smartest idea he'd heard all morning.

Mo was suddenly close beside her with his own version of a winning smile. He ordered a double espresso for "the gentleman talking to your boss" and a cappuccino with a slice of cherry pie and cream for himself. He handed her a fifty and, waving at the surrounding tables, said something about the need for a little privacy.

The girl took the note, murmured her thanks and left.

Rocking a little on his heels, something like a boxer readying himself, Mo positioned himself at the end of Steve and Oldie's table. He looked at Steve, who, without being asked, produced his own phone, turned it off and placed it next to Oldie's. Both devices went into the pockets of Mo's jacket.

"Did you sort out something about the dog?" he asked Steve, casually, matter-of-factly.

Lyons started, glanced at Oldie and replied that he had, that it was being flown to Adelaide next week.

Murmuring his satisfaction that a good animal was going to a good home, Mister Mo turned his attention to Oldie. He was about to say something when the Old Man, eyes agog, blurted out, "I've got a cat!" Then, by way of explication, immediately added, "And he can talk!"

He had wobbled. No question about it.

There was a fraction of a second when they caught their collective breath, then the three men were laughing — loud, off the leash hilarity. The few other patrons turned to look, but nobody noticed the barely perceptible shadow of a frown pass across Aldo Sarno's face.

Oldie had wobbled, but it was the others who had been thrown off balance. Mo recovered first. Leaning toward Oldie, he patted his shoulder in the most comradely way. "Clever man owns clever cat," he said quietly, looking him in the eye. "Maybe I get to meet this clever cat one day? Or does he only talk to you and your lovely wife?"

Before Oldie could think of let alone deliver a reply, Mo stood straight and stepped away to sit at the table across from the booth. Steve rose to shake Aldo's hand and Oldie followed suit. Motioning Steve to move over, Aldo slipped in next to him.

He openly studied Oldie's face. "I'm glad everybody is so happy," he said, lightly, with the smile on his lips rather than in his eyes.

"Alex made a joke ..." Steve began, but let it go.

"That's good. We're all friends. Friends can share jokes. But," he addressed Oldie, "I will not be such a bore as to ask you to repeat it because, of course, jokes are a thing of the moment. You have to be there. Is that not so?"

"Well, yes," Oldie said soberly, "you have to hear the joke in the right ... ah, context."

"Exactly!" Aldo tapped the table with the nail of his index finger. "Context. You have the very word there. I see why words are your business. Context. You are right. It is the key to everything. Everything! Nothing is understood without context." His hands flew up to shape something — a small ball? a universe? — out of the air before him. "Context shapes understanding. This is such a simple but fundamental proposition."

He paused to allow the profundity and significance of his pronouncement to sink in. But the moment was punctured, the context altered, by the arrival of the waitress, assisted by another pretty girl, with the coffees, Oldie's cool drink and Mister Mo's Triple X slice of cherry pie topped by a quivering thunderhead of whipped cream.

Spreading his thumb and index finger across his upper lip, and giving a slight nod at Mo and his cream pile, Aldo whispered, "This could be interesting."

Pushing his coffee aside, he leaned forward to quietly say, "Steve tells me you've done a good job cleaning up his fishing reports."

Oldie looked down, modesty personified.

"So, today, we meet in a public place to discuss — just informally, between friends — how some of my family's concerns may benefit from the sort of work you do for Steve. Perfectly normal business meeting. If anyone asks."

"Is anyone likely to? Officially?"

"Officially?"

"As in a situation in which I could not legally invoke business confidentially."

Aldo pulled a puzzled, pained face and shrugged. "So tell the truth! We met here today to discuss how my family's companies may benefit from ... from whatever it is you do. That's the honest truth. There's nothing secret, but — really — nobody else's business. OK? Listen, if everybody does their job ... then, what questions?!"

Oldie nodded agreement and returned the hard, flat gaze.

"Good," said Aldo, as he reached for his coffee. He drank the intense, dark brew off in one swift gulp, licked his lips and smoothly returned the cup to its saucer. "Steve told me you had balls," he chuckled with hearty animation, enjoying himself. "You got the balls? Tell me you got the balls." He lightly slapped the table in playful emphasis. "This is how they do it in the movies, right? Tell me! I need to know."

"Yes, yes," Oldie laughed right back at him. "I've got the balls."

"Okay!"

"Okay."

"That's good. See, I have to be a hundred percent sure I can rely on you. I have to come here, look you in the face, watch you close, listen to you, weigh it all up." He leaned closer and nosily inhaled through his nose, "I have to sniff you. You know, like dogs do. I have to be sure we understand each other. So ..."

With his eyes still on Oldie, Aldo raised his left hand and extended it, palm upwards toward Mo. He immediately stood, took the step that put him next to his boss and, with his broad back to the rest of the room, from somewhere inside his jacket (the sleeve?) produced a taped up envelope twice as thick as a pack of cards. Oldie hardly had time to see the packet of cash touch the table in front of Aldo before Steve covered it with his newspaper. It was all so nimbly done you could be forgiven for thinking Steve and Mister Mo had performed the same move on other occasions.

Mo resumed his seat, his narrow grey eyes also locked on Oldie's face.

Oldie raised the tall, icy glass of citron pressé and took a deep draft. The fragrance of the cool lemon juice flooded his palate and brought forth the warmth of an early summer day long ago. He and Peggy were in the small park on Merri Creek, near the northern wall of Pentridge. He had no idea why they were up there — Peggy probably had some bill to pay nearby on Sydney Road or Bell Street. They were having a rest, and she must have bought them a drink to share before they caught the tram back down Sydney Road. There was nobody about and they sat in silence, content in each other's company. There was no hanged man between them, no growing up — only their endless trust.

"I read somewhere, a long time ago, something I've always remembered: Power is the giving of a gift for which there is no possible counter offering." He paused to see that Aldo had understood him. "The gift that cannot be reciprocated imposes an obligation."

"Ah, I see," Aldo raised his fine, black eyebrows, "I must make this clear. I think I am obliged to you. Yes, you see, you brought this to us — and you brought it freely. Freely. *That* is the gift I cannot repay. My family, they count on me to get things right. It is my duty to them. You speak of power. Well, to me, family is a debt that can never be repaid. So I come here personally, in front

269

of witnesses, put my family's money on the table. Believe me, I do this in good will, as a token of our debt to you ... as a token of our *private* trust. This is the deal I come here to make. My brother and I would like to close this old business," he said, ever so lightly nudging the newspaper and its cargo towards the middle of the table. "No loose ends. Loose ends ... are the threads that unravel."

"Hard to give absolute guarantees in this situation, but no ... no loose ends that I know of. Steve has what I've found so far. I'll look through everything that could still have something and anything that comes up ... will be weeded out. You have all the original notes I've found so far. There are no copies. No loose ends."

"Silence is golden," said Aldo.

"It is for me!" Oldie declared, a little too suddenly and loudly.

He registered Steve's startled frown and slight movement of discomfort, but Aldo just smiled at the joke as he tapped the item on the table. "If anything else comes up," he said, "let Steve know. You can work out things with him. But we do need to close this, to have some certainty and to move on. You understand?"

Oldie eyed the bulge of the envelope beneath the newspaper and heard the ocean spilling down the far away edges of the world. "Yes," he said, "believe me, I do understand." Then, with feigned weariness, he added, "As for moving on, well, I need to do that, too. According to my wife, we have some travelling to do."

He reached over, put his hand on the fat envelope, and in the blink of an eye slid it across the table and into the dark maw of his leather bag.

Steve leaned back in his seat and let out a slow, relaxed breath, but Aldo's watchful brown eyes just smiled in a beneficent, kindly way. "Done," he said softly, and again tapped the table. "Good man."

Nobody moved until Aldo abruptly stood and extended his hand. He held Oldie's hand and gaze for the private moment that acknowledged their accord. Mister Mo was on his phone to say, "Okay, two minutes."

"Well," Aldo said as he let go and stepped back, "let Steve know if there are any problems. I trust that at some stage down the track we will have other, more straight-forward business together. Company reports, prospectuses, that sort of thing."

Steve Lyons reached behind Aldo's back to pass Mister Mo the sealed envelope the Old Man had given him earlier.

Oldie tilted his head to one side and pulled a long face. "I edit, that is, I try to clean up documents rather than write them."

"Well, that's useful," Aldo brushed something unseen by everyone else from the breast of his coat. "A cake should have icing," he said, giving his shoes a glance. "And some cakes have a cherry on top as well."

They waited while Aldo considered something. After a moment he looked at Oldie and continued, "As it happens, it has been suggested, and I have been thinking about it, that we should do a company-slash-family history. My brother and I, some of the others in the family, people who've worked with and for us — we all put stuff on tape, get it typed up and then someone — you, if you're interested — work it all up into a proper book. Add some photos, do a nice cover, good print job, generally organize whatever needs to be done. What we end up with is something of quality we could present to clients and prospective business partners, show them we are a solid, long-term business. I don't see why it couldn't also generate some stuff for our website. Why not? And because we can write it off as a business expense, we can afford to pay for a good job. What do you think? Would you be interested in that sort of longer term project? Later, when … everything is sorted."

"I do have experience in this area. And it wouldn't be the first time I've been written off, to parrot a phrase, so to speak."

Aldo cocked his head.

"If you like," Oldie went on, "I could have a look at it."

"Excellent," said Aldo as he turned and began to walk away. "I'll be in touch," he said over his shoulder. Mister Mo was already heading for the door, leaving Oldie and Steve's phones next to the crusty remains of his half-eaten slice of pie.

As soon as he was out on the pavement Aldo had his own phone to his ear, saying a few words and then listening patiently. A silver Range Rover pulled up and Mo stepped over to open its door. Still listening to his phone, Aldo got into the vehicle without looking back, Mo gently but firmly pushed the door closed, quickly looked about and got in front beside the driver. And they were gone.

Oldie resolved to leave in the opposite direction.

He and Steve sat together at the table for a minute or so while Steve checked his phone for messages. Oldie didn't bother. Finally, Steve cleared his throat and said, "That went well. I didn't think he was going to mention the company history business today, I thought he'd keep that up his sleeve, but it seems he likes you."

Oldie stared out the window and Steve asked, "You're comfortable with this?"

"Of course," he replied, turning back to examine the empty cups and the residue of his lemon drink.

Steve moved to intercept Oldie's gaze and make eye contact. "That's good. Because, believe me, you did the smart thing."

Oldie's look and a raised finger silenced his companion. "I need the money," he said.

Positively glowing with benevolent satisfaction, Steve kept quiet.

"So," Oldie said at last, "Mister Mo was one of those supernumeraries after all."

"Aldo's man? Don't know much about him. Never has much to say. I believe he goes by the name of Ralph but ... ho ho ho," Steve's laugh was as smooth as warm butter, "I daresay his mama back in the Balkans or wherever it is that he hails from calls him something else."

"And Tyson's going to Adelaide?"

"He is! He is indeed. I saw Brenda and ..."

"No offence, mate," Oldie cut in, "but I've had enough of this caper for today." He stood, hefted his bag, said something about keeping in touch, touched his forehead in salute, turned on his heel and strode away. Too late to reconsider and own up that he had kept Roger's Didgeridoo note. Диджериду: that was a private matter and of no concern to the Sarnos or anyone else.

He hurried along the sunlit street, not looking back until he crossed just before the Murray street corner. He paused there. Steve was still outside the cafe, on the phone, watching. He waved to Oldie.

Rounding the corner, the Old Man pulled his bag and his wad of money up under his arm and, before the wind could change, started to run as fast as his poor old legs would carry him.

But it was only for show and he pretty soon slowed down. One step at a time. Across the street and into the arcade. Slow down and loiter in that good stationery shop to check out the notebooks and the pencils. He didn't want to give himself a heart attack. Not now. Now, he had things to do. This was not the time for a sudden death scenario.

Not now.

Not now.

Epilogue

It was a cool and windy day of passing showers and sudden sunbursts. In the morning he saw a rainbow over the sea and in the afternoon he saw another towards the city and the river.

He and Anna had returned from their three weeks in Melbourne only yesterday evening, and yet their time away was already contracting around certain utterances and scenes. It had been a confronting time with many difficult moments and they arrived home exhausted.

After retrieving a disgruntled Max from the cattery, Oldie went to the local post office to collect the mail. There were not many items and he straightaway noticed the disc mailing envelope. Postmarked at Perth's main sorting centre, it did not carry a return address and could have been anonymously slipped through the slot of any street post-box in the greater metropolitan area. The handwritten printing of his name and address rang no bells.

He opened it immediately. There was no accompanying note and the disc was not labelled or marked in any way.

At home he quickly went to his computer and loaded the disc. There was only one untitled, password protected document on it. Oldie knew with absolute certainty what that password would be. Without opening the file, he hastily ejected the disc and hid it in a large old book in an awkward to reach section of his second biggest bookcase.

He told Anna about seeing the rainbow over Perth but did not mention what had come his way.

The next morning he drove to the Joondalup branch of Office Works, opened the document — didgeridoo — and had it copied onto a newly purchased thumb drive. He also had two copies printed out and spiral bound.

Dark Deeds in a Sunny Land. Cheeky.

When he got home he rang Steve Lyons to ask him if he knew anything about the mysterious disc he had received in the mail and the mysterious document on it that he could not open. Oldie was just about to hint that the item might have something to do with Roger when Lyons got there of his own accord.

"Well ... yes, you could be right," Oldie responded with slick surprise. "I suppose I should find someone who can get around the password. I'm not sure ..."

"Let me have it," Steve said firmly. "I'll get someone who can open it. If it's nothing to do with the Sarnos, I'll get it back to you pronto. If it's some loose end from Roger, then we can close the book on it."

"But who could have sent it to me? His sister?"

"Don't know. Maybe. I could talk to her. But, first, let's see what's there. I'll have a look and, ah ... get back to you."

Oldie couriered the original disc in its addressed envelope to Lyons that afternoon. Then, with more interest than he had anticipated, he settled down to read Roger's manuscript. It had been a while since he had read an Australian novel, a work of fiction, and, if nothing else, it was something to do while he waited for the coming of whatever would happen next.

"He saw the arrow loosed," it began, "but it came at him faster than he could have dreamt."